THE CHASE

EVIE HUNTER

Boldwood

First published in Great Britain in 2022 by Boldwood Books Ltd.

Copyright © Evie Hunter, 2022

Cover Design and Photography by Colin Thomas Photography Ltd

The moral right of Evie Hunter to be identified as the author of this work has been asserted in accordance with the Copyright, Designs and Patents Act 1988.

Every effort has been made to obtain the necessary permissions with reference to copyright material, both illustrative and quoted. We apologise for any omissions in this respect and will be pleased to make the appropriate acknowledgements in any future edition.

A CIP catalogue record for this book is available from the British Library.

Paperback ISBN 978-1-80280-263-4

Large Print ISBN 978-1-80280-262-7

Hardback ISBN 978-1-80280-261-0

Ebook ISBN 978-1-80280-264-1

Kindle ISBN 978-1-80280-265-8

Audio CD ISBN 978-1-80280-256-6

MP3 CD ISBN 978-1-80280-257-3

Digital audio download ISBN 978-1-80280-260-3

Boldwood Books Ltd
23 Bowerdean Street
London SW6 3TN
www.boldwoodbooks.com

For David Keast
Thank you for introducing me to the sport of kings.
I think! x

1

'Don't let the price fall below twenty dollars a share.'

'Sure.' Kristen's silky voice purred down the line, echoing above the engine sounds and impatient hooting of other drivers stuck on the M25 – the infamous London ring road more commonly referred to as a car park. Today it was living up to its reputation and the mood of those stuck on either side of Isaac was becoming increasingly ugly.

'Get Patrick to take the shareholders' meeting,' he added. 'Doesn't look like I'll get there in time.'

'*Soo* frustrating for you,' Kristen said, her voice now oozing sympathy.

'Right, catch you later. Possibly,' he added, glancing dubiously at miles of stalled traffic ahead of him and sighing.

Isaac Fernandez pushed the button on the steering wheel of his Lotus Emira, a gift to himself after completing his latest company takeover, and ended the call. The sapphire-blue speed machine was drawing envious glances from fellow road users who had nothing better to do than drool. He ignored the smiles of a glamorous driver on the inside lane and thought instead about all the things he ought to be doing at that precise moment.

Isaac inched his car forward. It was stop-start for miles, until he reached the turnoff for the M23. On a whim he cut across a lane when a gap appeared and took the slip road. He'd never make the shareholders' meeting but Patrick was more than capable of deputising, and taking all the inevitable flack. Perhaps the traffic stall had done him a favour, he reasoned. For the first time since he couldn't recall when, Isaac had decided to award himself a morning off.

He joined the M23, which was mercifully clear, and put his foot down. The engine responded with a purr that would have made Kristen weep with envy. Isaac felt an adrenalin surge from the sheer explosion of raw power that put him in mind of his racehorses leaving the starting gates.

And that was where he planned to play hooky, he'd already decided. His three horses were with the latest training sensation, Guy Levant, in Newbury. Isaac seldom visited and never without making an appointment; he didn't have the time to waste if the people who mattered weren't available to answer his questions. Besides, he wouldn't thank anyone else for interfering in the day-to-day working of his own company and winced as his mind reverted to his demanding shareholders who were happy to take the profits as they rolled in, but also seemed to think they knew better than he did when it came to the complexities of the money markets. He was required to handle them with kid gloves, a bit like Guy was obliged to soothe the egos of eccentric horse owners.

Only Guy exercised more tact and patience than Isaac customarily managed.

As far as he was concerned, the trainer knew his business and Isaac paid him a king's ransom to get the best out of his horses. It was just a hobby, albeit an expensive one, but Isaac was never off-duty. He saw his status as an owner as a golden opportunity to entertain would-be clients, enticing them to place their trust in his investment company. But he had grown increasingly enthusiastic about the thrill of the chase. Having a winner gave him the same hard-on as identifying an ailing company that would benefit from his expertise in taking it over and making it profitable again did.

There had been one or two disappointing results with his horses lately but Guy had explained that he'd entered them in higher classes where the competition was stronger. It was all part of the game and Isaac accepted that you couldn't win 'em all.

Even so, Isaac didn't like failing at anything he did and wanted to reassure himself that his horses were fit and well. That was the downside of being a control freak, he reasoned. He always needed to be on top of things, to understand them, and he most emphatically didn't understand the complex world of horseracing, where charlatans appeared to lurk around every corner.

'An error of judgement,' he said aloud, taking a wrong turning in the labyrinth of country lanes. Momentarily unsure of his location, he slowed to a crawl and realised that he was on a track that led to the back entrance to Guy's yard.

'The tradesman's entrance,' he said aloud, chuckling.

The gravel track took him directly past all the paddocks, as opposed to the parking area for owners. He felt a surge of optimism as the sun filtered through trees green with new growth and he drove past paddocks in which leggy young horses were enjoying the spring grass. Isaac assumed they weren't in training yet. Those that were had to adhere to strict diet and exercise schedules – vital, apparently, to ensure optimum performance on the track. He'd taken the foreman's word for it.

He halted the car when a familiar horse stuck its head over the post-and-rail fencing. A grey horse with a distinctive dark blaze. He'd know him anywhere. It was one of his.

'What the fuck? he muttered, stopping the car and getting out to stroke Federal Force's muzzle. An inquisitive three-year-old and Isaac's first acquisition, the horse was supposed to be racing the following week so what the hell was he doing out to grass? He was unshod and his coat was dull through lack of grooming. Whenever Isaac had seen him before, during one of his *scheduled* calls, he had been impeccably turned out and glowing with health.

'Hi, fella,' he said, rubbing the horse behind the ears. 'Recognise me, do you?'

It was highly unlikely, given that Isaac had minimal contact with his horses. His busy schedule didn't allow for anything so frivolous. His horses, just like everything else in his life, were a business investment. Besides, emotional attachment always led to disappointment, a lesson learned and never forgotten from his dysfunctional childhood.

Force lost interest when he discovered that Isaac had no mints on offer, turned away, put in a massive buck and chased down the paddock with an impressive turn of speed.

More inquisitive than concerned now – there was bound to be a plausible explanation – Isaac got back in his car and drove through the impressive archway with the horses' barns on either side. He often thought that his horses lived better than a lot of the people he knew. The barns were pristine, not a blade of hay out of place. You could almost eat your dinner off the floors.

He slipped his car into what was obviously the staff car park, given the array of muddy four-by-fours parked there. Isaac's shiny Lotus looked as out of place as Federal Force would in a paddock full of cobs. *Talk about slumming it*, he thought, perfectly at home in such surroundings. He ought to be, given that he'd grown up with few advantages and only bad examples to follow and made something of himself by virtue of his own endeavours.

It could so easily have turned out very differently.

He headed towards the barn where he expected to find his other two horses eating their heads off but paused when he heard voices raised in anger coming from the tack room. There was no one else about. Presumably the grooms were out on the gallops, which was where Guy would be at that time of day, watching his charges being put through their paces. It was probably where Isaac should be, too, so he wouldn't be caught eavesdropping. Not that he cared if he was. He had every right in the world to be here and took a dim view of full-on arguments being conducted so openly in the middle of a working day.

It was unprofessional.

Isaac recognised one of the raised voices as belonging to Dale Drummond, Guy's foreman, mentor and trusted right-hand man. And he was giving the woman he was talking to merry hell.

'I don't give a flying fuck what you think. You're here to do as you're told, not use that pathetic excuse for a brain of yours and stick your oar into situations that you don't understand.'

'You really are a misogynistic bastard,' a quiet voice, laced with seething anger, replied. 'But I know what you're doing. It's not right and I don't intend to keep quiet.'

A brittle silence ensued, broken only by the sound of a soft whinny from a horse in a nearby box. Tension radiated and Isaac remained right where he was, curious to know what the fight was all about. Something and nothing, he suspected.

The only thing that surprised him was that Dale could be so arrogantly aggressive. Times had changed, Isaac knew, but he was old-fashioned and would never speak to a woman so disrespectfully, no matter what the provocation. And, he thought, rolling his eyes when he recalled some of the women he'd dated who didn't seem to understand when an affair had run its course, there wasn't much that anyone could teach him about provocation. Even so, he prided himself upon keeping his temper in check and remaining civil.

'You know sod all, little girl.' Dale's voice was deep, sinister and patronisingly threatening. 'Now get out of here. You've had your last warning. You're fired and don't expect a reference.'

'You can't fire me,' the woman shot back. 'I work for Guy.'

'Wake up, darling.' Dale gave an unpleasant little laugh. 'I run this place, in case you weren't aware, and I decide who's hired and who's fired. Guy won't even notice you're gone. You're less than a speck of dust on his expensive boots. Now get out. You're trespassing.'

'But the horses. My horses...'

There was a wail in the woman's voice now. Clearly, she loved the horses that she looked after and the fight drained out of her when she realised that she'd no longer be caring for them. Her voice was familiar but Isaac couldn't remember where he'd heard it before. Probably here during one of his visits, he decided.

'They aren't *your* horses, sweetheart. They belong to all those rich buggers with more money than sense who don't know a fetlock from a forelock.' Dale's voice had turned scathing. 'Now get out of here and think yourself lucky that I haven't put the word out in the industry that you're disloyal. You'd never work with horses again if I did. You know how incestuous this world is.'

'You won't get away with this.' The fight had returned to the woman's voice.

Dale gave another harsh laugh. 'Get away with what? It's all in your imagination. Still, I'll say it again, if one word of this gets out then you'll rue the day you were born, little girl. Now go. I have work to do.'

The door flew open and Isaac stood back in the shadows, not wanting to be seen and dragged into a dispute that had nothing to do with him. He needn't have worried. The woman strode straight past his hiding place, muttering uncomplimentary comments about Dale, without looking in his direction. A dark ponytail flew out behind her as she headed for the staff car park, her slim hips drawing his attention.

And holding it.

Now Isaac recognised her. She was the lass who looked after his horses. He snapped his fingers as he recalled that her name was Farah something or other. He'd have recognised her attractive profile anywhere, even now when she was frowning as she passed him and her large, expressive green eyes were pooled with tears. She'd led his winners in at various race meetings, beaming as though she had achieved the win in person. But he always had would-be business associates with him at such times, so they'd never exchanged more than a few words of congratulation.

He'd treated her very much like the hired help, he realised with a twang of guilt. Even if that's what she was, ordinarily that wasn't Isaac's way. He prided himself on being on good terms with all his employees, and accessible to them. Watching Farah's distress now, he didn't feel good about himself. He had no idea what it was that she'd faced up to Dale about but did know that he hadn't liked Dale's bully-boy tactics. He wondered if she would be able to find alternative employment or if Dale would make good on his threat and blacken her name in the industry.

Isaac was surprised by the strength of his determination to find out. He didn't have the time to get drawn into someone else's affairs.

But he'd find the time.

'What the hell,' he muttered, thinking back to what he'd just overheard and wondering if Dale considered him to be a rich bugger with more money than sense. He scowled at that very real possibility and that in turn strengthened his resolve. Dale wouldn't be the first to underestimate the boy-made-good from the East End.

He waited a few minutes, then moved away from his hiding place when the clatter of hooves on cobbles heralded the return of the string that had been out on the gallops. He was waiting outside Force's empty box when the horses were led into the barn.

'Isaac.'

Isaac turned at the sound of Dale's voice, now hospitable and full of bonhomie. If Isaac hadn't heard him berating Farah, he never would have believed him capable of being such a Jekyll and Hyde character. There again, he'd had his moments himself when someone had tried to put one over on him. Probably best not to jump to conclusions about what he'd overheard, he decided. Farah was attractive, dedicated to her chosen, poorly paid profession, but he mustn't let her looks sway him. As long as his horses were fit and running well, that was all that counted. His thoughts returned to Force, turned out to grass, and his doubts returned.

'Dale,' Isaac replied, taking the foreman's outstretched hand. 'I was passing so thought I'd drop by.'

'Always welcome,' Dale said, 'although I thought you financial types were glued to your computer screens.'

'Don't believe everything you read. I like to keep a personal eye on my investments. Talking of which,' he added, watching the horses being untacked, rubbed down and returned to their boxes. 'Where's Force?'

'Ah, he's sprained a fetlock, which will put him out of work for a few weeks. He's out in a small paddock. The vet's recommended light exercise.'

That was total twaddle and increased Isaac's mild suspicions. Could Force be the reason why Farah had taken Dale on? She clearly loved his horses and he'd noticed her dedication to them at race meetings.

Isaac, who admittedly hadn't known much about horses when first becoming an owner, now at least knew that much. He never made an investment without doing research and the care and welfare of racehorses had been his chosen bedtime reading for months now, unless he had a date who was willing to distract him. Besides, if the horse was injured, he would have been turned out alone. Isaac recalled Force bucking and the manner in which he'd galloped the length of the paddock without showing the slightest sign of lameness.

Something was definitely off but Isaac knew better than to show his hand before delving deeper and merely nodded – the obedient dupe.

'Come and see your other two.' Dale clapped Isaac's shoulder. 'They're just back from the gallops.'

Isaac duly admired Federal Compliance and Federal Dalliance, both of whom looked fit and full of running. He pretended not to notice that they were being looked after by a lad he'd never seen before and didn't ask after Farah.

'Will you come up to the office?' Dale asked. 'Guy will be back and glad to see you. Besides, the sun's over the yardarm somewhere. I dare say a nip of whisky would slip down as smooth as you like.'

Since it was only eleven in the morning, Isaac could have given the man an argument on that score, but refrained. His florid face and the broken blood vessels decorating his nose were, Isaac guessed, not just a consequence of living the outdoor life. This man enjoyed his whisky, perhaps a little too much, making Isaac wonder why an ambitious trainer of Guy's ilk put so much trust in him.

'Thanks but I need to be somewhere.'

'Sure you do.' Dale laughed easily as he gave Isaac's person, clad in a Savile Row silver-grey suit, a disparaging once-over. 'Money to be made, is my guess.'

'If you want these equines of mine to eat then I guess you're right.' Isaac laughed.

Two could put on an act, he decided, now deeply suspicious of Dale's motives. He took his leave and went back to his car, wondering how to find Farah. He had some questions that he wanted to put to her, to say nothing about feeling responsible for her welfare.

But he didn't even know her surname.

* * *

Farah stumbled towards her beaten-up Suzuki jeep, her vision blurred by the tears pouring down her face. Tears of anger. Tears of regret. She should have kept what she suspected to herself, but hadn't wanted to believe it and felt duty-bound to share those suspicions with Dale.

Dale, who had been a bit like a surrogate uncle to her: always willing to get his hands dirty when they were short-staffed, always friendly. He'd forgotten more about horses than she was ever likely to learn and she had trusted him.

Well, the blinkers had well and truly come off after that little encounter, she decided, dashing at the tears with the back of her hand as she took three attempts to unlock her car. It was so old that it pre-dated key-fob locking and was literally on its last legs. She spared a scathing glance for Isaac Fernandez's flashy Lotus, thinking he must be slumming it to be parked amongst the hoi polloi. She hadn't known he'd planned to visit today and wondered if Dale did, maliciously hoping that the hapless owner would catch Dale out in a lie.

Not that he ever would, she accepted, turning the key and simultaneously pumping the accelerator to encourage the engine to turn over. It did so on the third attempt but the fuel light blinked red at her.

'Shit!'

She thumped the dashboard with her fist, aware that she couldn't afford to fill up and likely wouldn't get home on what was left in the tank. She'd been running on fumes for days. Defiantly, she left the vehicle where it was, got out and resigned herself to a walk to the bus stop. The buses ran infrequently out here in the wilds, hence the need for a car, but one would come eventually and deposit her at the cottage she shared with her disabled aunt. Farah was her carer and depended upon her earnings from the yard to supplement the pittance that Aunt Daisy got from social services.

Now what the hell would she do to make ends meet?

She stopped at the paddock where Force was enjoying the spring grass and getting far too fat to race. She called to the horse and he trotted over to see her, anxious for a treat.

'Why the hell not, eh, boy?' she asked, patting his neck and producing a packet of mints from her pocket.

She loved this horse with every fibre of her being. The other two were decent runners but this one had character, a personality that had gotten to Farah, and fresh tears tumbled down her cheeks when she realised that she would never see him again. She chose to believe that the soft creature would miss their conversations. Well, Force didn't actually contribute to those conversations, she conceded. Farah did all the talking as she groomed him until his coat shone but he was an excellent listener.

She buried her face in his neck and sobbed her heart out. Force, always intuitive to her moods, nudged her with his muzzle and not, Farah chose to believe, because he was after another mint. She eventually fed him another anyway, then gave his neck a final pat and forced herself to walk away. She didn't trust herself to look back without breaking down but knew that the horse would still be at the fence, watching her go.

Another ten minutes took her to the bus stop. She looked at the timetable secured behind Perspex and saw that she'd just missed one. Of course she had! She had the best part of an hour to wait for another to come along, and so she sat down to have a good think about her future.

Not that there was much to think about. Despite what Dale had said, she knew he would start rumours about her, if only to account for her abrupt departure. She was popular with the owners and they were bound to ask why she'd left. Well, popular with the majority of them, she mentally amended, her head full of visions of the admittedly handsome but remote Isaac Fernandez, who was probably unaware of Farah's existence.

There was nothing else for it. She would have to find an office job with regular hours so that she would be free to care for Daisy and her MS. She was getting steadily worse and it was only a matter of time before she would require full-time residential care. Farah's heart sank at that thought. Her cottage would have to be sold to pay for the care in question, which would leave Farah not only jobless, but homeless, too.

That was in the future, though, and hopefully not for another year or more. Farah's concerns, on the other hand, were of the more immediate variety.

'Office work it will just have to be,' she muttered, thinking longingly of the horses she would never get to ride again. Of the fresh air nipping at her cheeks as she rode at a flat-out gallop, with Force's powerful muscles shifting seamlessly beneath her.

She was lulled out of her pity-party by the sound of a car reversing up to the bus stop and the driver sounding his horn. She wanted to tell him to get lost but the words stalled when she recognised Isaac's distinctive penis-compensator of a car.

'Need a lift?' he asked as the passenger side window glided silently down. 'Farah, isn't it?'

She blinked at him. 'Oh, so you know my name.' She regretted the acerbic response the moment it left her lips but wasn't about to apologise for it.

He seemed more amused than offended, as evidenced by his chuckle. God, but he was handsome, she thought, watching the sun dancing off his rugged features. A sweep of thick, dark hair fell across his eyes and he impatiently pushed it aside with the long fingers of one hand. 'Having a bad day?' he asked.

'Trust me,' she replied, 'you have *no* idea.'

'Wanna talk about it? Come on, hop in. I don't bite.'

Did she want to talk about it? And would this Adonis believe her even if she did, given that she had little more than her suspicions and the odd snippets of conversations she had overheard to back up her assertions? She thought of Force, of his lovely soft muzzle and friendly disposition, and it was enough to make her mind up.

'My boots will make the inside of your glossy car all dirty,' she warned.

'That's okay.' His smile was wide and glamorous, sending an infusion of blood to the parts of her anatomy where it was needed the least. She was most definitely off men, they were more trouble than they were worth, and even if that wasn't the case, she and this one moved in totally different circles. She smiled as she wondered when he'd last shopped in a supermarket. He was bound to be above such mundane occupations as doing the weekly shop, on a budget or otherwise, and probably had a ton of minions who catered for his domestic arrangements.

'Okay,' she said, slipping into the passenger seat of the low car with as much elegance as she could muster. 'But don't say you haven't been warned. Mind you, I don't suppose you have to clean up after yourself so why should you care?'

He laughed. 'I wonder why you would think that. It doesn't do to jump to conclusions,' he said. 'You don't know anything about me.'

Oh yes she did. She'd read every word she could find about him online. He ran a successful finance company called Federal Finance. His horses were business expenses to him, hence the prefix of Federal to all their names. He rescued ailing companies and sold off the profitable bits. Oh, and he was constantly being photographed in the newspapers with the latest supermodel on his arm as he attended various red-carpet affairs.

He was Spanish, or half Spanish, as evidenced by his olive complexion and dark good looks, and spoke several languages fluently. He had a degree in business management from Oxford, probably first class she mused, feeling uncharitably inclined towards a man who had everything when she struggled so hard to make ends meet and give Daisy's life as much comfort as possible.

He was supposedly a self-made man but Farah found that hard to believe. He was only in his mid-thirties. That hadn't been enough time for even the sharpest of minds to amass so much wealth if his business hadn't been given a kick-start.

The engine roared back into life as he moved the car away from the bus stop. No doubt it had offended his car's sensibilities to be seen at such a lowly location, Farah assumed, wondering if she was losing her mind given the turn her thoughts had taken.

The sound system was tuned to a classic rock station, the volume down low, and he drove efficiently, without feeling the need to make conversation. Farah had been up since six and had recently undergone the added trauma of being sacked from a job she loved. She was on emotional overload and physically exhausted. The soft purr of the engine lulled her and her eyes fluttered to a close.

They jerked open again when the car came to a halt and she realised she hadn't told him where she lived.

'Where are we?' she asked, blinking.

'At the Fox and Ferret,' he said, nodding through the window to the quaint country pub. 'You looked so peaceful that I didn't want to wake you. Let me buy you lunch, then you can tell me what you were arguing with Dale about.'

2

Isaac, driving slowly for once as he pondered upon how best to find Farah, struck lucky when he noticed a forlorn figure seated at the bus stop.

'Wanna talk about it? Come on, hop in. I don't bite.'

He stopped to offer her a lift, secure in the knowledge that she would accept and that he would get some answers.

Except, she didn't – accept, that is.

'Why would I get in with you?' She sent him a sceptical look through tear-stained eyes that made him feel like something she'd scraped off the bottom of her shoe. 'You're in with them.'

'Come again. Who's "them"?'

She made a sound that could have been anything from a hiccup to a derisive grunt. 'Like you don't know.'

Isaac scratched his head, blocking the narrow road with his car as he tried to think how best to circumvent her anger. He couldn't remember the last time that a woman had declined to do anything he asked of her, and her reaction only served to increase his determination. It would have done so even if he wasn't keen to know what had gone on between her and Dale.

She eventually got into his car, albeit with bad grace, and stared sullenly ahead. He knew better than to try to engage her in conversation and kept silent until the smooth rumble of the engine lulled her to sleep. He sent frequent sideways glances at her, admiring her creamy complexion, her delicate features and her full, sensual mouth. He felt himself reacting in the time-honoured fashion and was glad that her eyes were closed against the obvious evidence. The last thing he wanted her to think was that he intended to jump her bones – even if the possibility possessed unprecedented appeal.

His growing awareness of his feisty companion's character added to Isaac's doubts about the running of Guy's yard. He sensed an abiding conscientiousness in her and knew – hoped, at least – that she wouldn't be a party to any shady business, especially if it threatened the wellbeing of the horses she loved.

Her physical attributes had nothing to do with his willingness to believe her before she'd opened her mouth. Her determination to take on Dale had already swayed him, especially since Isaac knew he'd lied to him about Force's supposed ailments. Something most definitely wasn't right and he could only get to the bottom of that conundrum with Farah's help.

Isaac ground his jaw as he concentrated on driving. If he were being somehow manipulated or his horses maltreated, then he sure as hell wanted to know about it. Despite what Dale seemed to think, he most definitely didn't have more money than sense. That was the thing about being a self-made man. You understood all the wrinkles, had invented half of them yourself on the way up the greasy pole of success and knew how to play dirty if necessary.

'Ever been in such a lowly pub before?' she asked, waking with a jolt when he pulled up outside the Fox and Ferret.

He sent her a curious look. 'Why wouldn't I have been? I go to pubs, just like everyone else.'

'Probably gastro-pubs. This place is spit and sawdust, log fires and low beams.' She sent him a challenging grin. Clearly, dozing for a few minutes had revived her and she was ready to give as good as she got again. 'Don't say you haven't been warned.'

'Warning duly noted. Your local, is it?' he asked, cutting the engine and opening his door.

'I live fairly close, sure,' she replied, climbing elegantly from the low car, 'but I don't go to pubs much. I have to get up early for work.'

Isaac nodded and after locking the car, placed a hand in the small of her back as he guided her towards the door. They must have made an incongruous couple, he thought, him in his Savile Row suit and her in jodhpurs, an old check shirt and body warmer, her feet in the muddy boots she'd warned him about. Isaac simply didn't care. He thought she looked fresh-faced and gorgeous. He couldn't remember when he'd last had dealings with a lady who wasn't caked in make-up and dressed to impress. Or if he ever had been – impressed, that is. This one was angry and upset and clearly didn't trust him but she was ready to fight her corner, despite the disparity in their situations. He liked that about her.

That and a whole lot else.

'What will you have?' he asked, walking up to the bar and ducking his head to avoid one of the low beams she'd warned him to expect. The bar was half full of mostly working men sipping half pints or lager straight from the bottle. They sent Isaac mildly curious looks and he realised how out of place he must appear. This was very much Farah's territory and yet he felt totally at home, liking the ambiance more than the plastic bars and restaurants he spent so much of his working life frequenting. 'Morning, all,' he said, nodding affably. A few men nodded in response. Most didn't.

'Hiya, Farah,' the young barman said, flashing a smile at her and then bestowing a suspicious frown on Isaac. 'How's Daisy?'

'Good and bad days,' Farah said, looking thrown by the question.

'Send her my best.'

'Will do.' She turned to face Isaac. 'I'll have white wine,' she said. 'It's been one of those days. It's almost noon and I've been up since six, so...'

Isaac wondered why she felt the need to explain herself. Presumably, drinking at such an early hour wasn't something she made a habit out of. He ordered the best wine they had on the list and, mindful of the fact that he was driving, a bottle of low-alcohol lager for himself. He collected up both drinks and steered her towards a quiet table close to the window. She sat down and took the glass that he handed to her.

'Thanks,' she said, taking a long sip. 'Cheers,' she added belatedly.

'Cheers.' He saluted her with his bottle. 'I guess you needed that.' When she didn't respond, he tried a question. 'Who's Daisy?' he asked. 'Your friend the barman mentioned her,' he added when she blinked at him in evident confusion.

'My aunt. She has MS.'

'That's tough.'

'Yeah, it is. These things always happen to the good guys, not the old bastards.'

'Like Dale?' he suggested mildly.

Her body jerked forward and Isaac knew he had finally secured her complete attention. 'What do you know about that?' she asked acerbically. 'I *knew* he'd told you to come after me.'

'Easy!' Isaac held up a placating hand, worried that she might actually get up and walk out on him. 'Do I look like the type to take orders from the Dales of this world?'

'Appearances can be deceptive and, excuse me, but you don't

know much about horses so will believe whatever bullshit he feeds you.'

'Like Force being lame,' he said softly into the ensuing silence, reaching a hand inside his collar, unfastening the top button of his shirt and loosening his tie. She watched him and seemed fascinated, but whether by the simple gesture or because he'd doubted the line fed to him about Force he had yet to decide.

'You... you challenged Dale? Well,' she added, not waiting for a response but clearly pondering the situation, 'if he saw you parked out back – and let's face it, no one could possibly miss that car of yours, it's not exactly low profile. But anyway, he will know you drove past Force's paddock.'

'I don't think he saw my car, distinctive or not,' Isaac replied, smiling at her provocative tone and not seeing any need to defend his choice of vehicle, no matter how flashy. He'd damned well earned the right to do as he pleased. 'He left the tack room after your dispute and came straight to the barn, where he fed me the line about Force. I pretended to believe him.'

'Why?' She issued the one word as a challenge, clearly reluctant to get her hopes up.

'Why what?'

She huffed impatiently. 'Don't pretend not to understand me. I'm not one of the airheads you date.' She clamped a hand over her mouth but a brief smile – the first he had seen from her – slipped past her defences. 'Sorry,' she added, not looking or sounding the least bit sorry. 'That was uncalled for.'

'I am flattered that you follow my activities so closely.'

'Don't be. You're all over the tabloids when you so much as sneeze. Copies get left hanging around the tack room, impossible to miss.'

'Well, that's me told.' Isaac chuckled and leaned back in his chair, unable to decide when he had last enjoyed a day quite so much. He must definitely be more spontaneous in future, he decided, thinking he liked what spontaneity could lead to. Being a control freak was overrated. 'Anyway, to answer your question, I knew the moment I saw Force in that paddock that something was seriously wrong. He shouldn't have been out to grass this close to race day *and* he was most definitely not lame.'

Farah nodded. 'You're learning.'

'Patronising responses aside,' he said easily, 'you don't need the intellect of a rocket scientist to tell if a horse is lame. As to the race day procedure, I've been there, done that and know the ropes.'

She bit her lower lip and this time her smile was uncontrived. 'Sorry,' she said, 'but we're used to owners having—'

'More money than sense?'

'Ah, that was Dale speaking, not me.'

'You suspect him of fixing races, don't you?' Isaac replied.

Farah felt totally out of her depth in the company of a glamorous man who had turned every female head in the pub when he'd walked in, and was clearly oblivious to the effect that he had on the clientele. There was more to him than a pretty face, she had already discovered. She told herself that she wouldn't have agreed to enter her local with him and set tongues wagging, had she not fallen asleep and been taken unawares. But part of her also wondered if she was being delusional.

He wasn't quite as ignorant as she'd supposed, although why that should surprise her, she was at a loss to know. He would hardly have made such a mark for himself in the fiercely competitive world of high finance if he wasn't clever. And he was most definitely a hunk, she conceded, taking in the sharp, angular cut to a strong jaw decorated with designer stubble. In spite of herself she'd been powerless not to admire his instinctively commanding stance as they walked into the pub and he oozed machismo, dominating the bar as naturally as if he owned it.

He'd caught her gaping at him when he loosened his collar. She'd seen powerful muscles shifting and flexing in his arms and had been mesmerised by the sight. He certainly hadn't let his busy business life interfere with his physical fitness and she would have had to be nearly blind and a hundred not to appreciate his animal vitality.

But that didn't mean she had to trust him, did it?

Although, there again, why not take the chance? she wondered as she took a healthy slug of her wine, feeling it slip effortlessly down her throat. She ordinarily drank the house plonk rather than a decent Chablis and couldn't pretend that she didn't enjoy the treat.

It wasn't a case of trust, she decided. The worst Dale could do would be to bad-mouth her to the rest of the local yards but since she would need to take an office job anyway, that didn't seem to matter. In the unlikely event that Isaac was Dale's spy, she would send a loud and clear message through him that she had no intention of keeping shtum.

'Force shouldn't have gone up a class in his last race,' she said, leaning forward and lowering her voice, even though there was little chance of their being overheard. 'Dale insisted that he was ready but the rest of us disagreed. Don't forget that we, that's I, used to ride him out and know him better than anyone.' She impatiently brushed aside an errant tear. 'We tried him against the better horses and although he held his own, there was no way he would have overtaken them. I tried to tell Dale but he wasn't having it.'

'He's been in the game a long time. Perhaps he made a mistake.'

'He's forgotten more about horses than I'm ever likely to know,' she admitted, articulating her earlier thoughts about the man. 'Credit where credit's due, even if that's the only good thing I can think of to say about him.'

'Has he always dismissed your opinions?'

'No, that's the thing. Up until a few months ago, he would always take on board what we told him and almost always acted upon our advice. As he himself used to say, better coming from the horse's mouth.' She rolled her eyes. 'His idea of a joke.'

'What changed?' Isaac asked. 'Say, would you like something to eat?'

Farah shook her head but of course he ignored her. He went to the bar, bought her another glass of wine and came back with the menus.

'Why do you ask questions if you don't want to hear the answers?' she asked, irritated and yet pleased that he seemed to want to prolong their time together. *Beware what you wish for!*

'Sure you're not hungry?' he asked, flashing a sexy smile when she glanced at the menu and her stomach gave an embarrassing rumble.

'Since you insist, I'll have the special.'

He chuckled, glanced at the chalkboard and nodded his approval. 'Good choice. I will too.'

He went back to the bar to place his order. Jenny, the buxom barmaid, was now helping out since the bar had filled up with the lunchtime crowd. Farah wasn't surprised when she ignored others waiting ahead of Isaac, and leaned on the bar to give him a full-on view of her impressive cleavage as she took her time placing his order and Isaac turned on the charm. She caught snatches of their conversation, from which it was clear that Jenny was interrogating him quite ruthlessly but Isaac deflected her questions without giving anything away about himself, no doubt having been in this situation many times before.

Jenny glanced at Farah when Isaac turned his back to return to their table and fanned her face with her hand, making Farah smile. Jenny was a good sort, despite being a self-confessed man-eater.

'Like what you see?' Farah could have bitten her tongue off when the question slipped out and she felt herself blushing like a schoolgirl.

'Jealous?'

'Insanely,' she replied with a rueful grin. 'Sorry, but I've had one hell of a day and been fired from a job I love so make allowances. I do like Jenny. But be warned, she takes no prisoners and it looks like she has you on her breakfast menu.'

Isaac laughed, relaxed and apparently unconcerned. 'I'll bear that in mind.'

'I dare say you get that sort of thing a lot,' Farah said, leaning her elbow on the table and her chin on her clenched fist. She had started on her second glass of wine. They were very large glasses and she was feeling increasingly mellow.

'Success breeds its fair share of hangers-on,' he conceded. 'You must know that from the racing game.'

It wasn't his success but more his looks that had prompted the comment but she wasn't about to clarify and allowed the misconception to stand. His disgusting self-confidence didn't need a boost from her.

'I see a lot,' she agreed. 'Too much and have yet to learn to keep my mouth shut. If I could do that then perhaps...' Her words trailed off and she stared morosely into her glass, the convivial mood shattered by recollections of her unemployed status.

'More people in your world should have the courage of their convictions. You have and I admire that about you.'

His words put Farah in mind of her appearance and she experienced a sudden desire to be admired for herself. She shrugged, dismissing the whimsical thought. With her hair hastily tied back and not brushed since first light, in her scruffy, unsophisticated stable clothes and without make-up, there was little chance of anyone giving her a second glance, especially not the Adonis seated across from her. But inexplicably she knew that she had his full attention and that he was in no hurry to be on his way. She wondered about that. He must have a zillion things to do but gave the impression that he had all the time in the world. His phone had rung constantly but he'd merely glanced at the screen each time and not taken the calls.

Odd.

Two steaming plates of coq-au-vin were delivered to their table by Jenny herself. She grinned at Farah, plonked a plate in front of her and fanned her face dramatically again, out of sight of Isaac. Or perhaps not. The man appeared to see everything. She then turned to him and made a big fuss out of serving his meal, which required a great deal of bending over. Farah couldn't help giggling, which brought a smile to Isaac's face and sent Jenny scuttling back to the bar.

'You should laugh more often,' Isaac said. 'It suits you.'

'I haven't had a great deal to laugh about recently.' She cut into her chicken, took a bite and closed her eyes as she savoured the taste. 'Lovely,' she said. 'The new chef here is making quite a name for himself, hence this crowd on a weekday lunchtime in a country pub.'

Isaac tasted his own food. It probably wasn't a scratch on what he would be accustomed to in the fancy restaurants he frequented that charged a month's salary for a lettuce leaf. Even so, horses for courses, as was the saying in her previous line of work. She would be interested to see if his response would be scathing or artificially complimentary.

'The chef's got that dark tang from the red wine exactly right,' he said, nodding in evident approval. 'And the herby aromatic taste is spot on, too.'

'Not too rustic for you?' she asked, wondering why she felt so determined to pick a fight with him.

He flexed a brow, looking lazily amused. 'I take food very seriously and never offer false praise,' he told her.

'Good to know.'

'I did all the cooking in our house growing up. It was either that or starve. Not many people know that.'

'Don't worry, your secret's safe with me. It wouldn't do your playboy image much good if the truth got out.' Even so, the comment was telling and set Farah wondering. He made it sound as though his upbringing had been disadvantaged and she still struggled with that concept. The more she got to know about him the less she understood what made him tick.

'You've got me all wrong,' he replied, waving his fork in the air for emphasis, 'but I guess you believe everything you read in those magazines of yours.'

'Not all,' she said, grinning as she waggled a hand from side to side in a considering gesture. 'Anyway, where were your parents when you were whipping up these culinary masterpieces?'

'Ah, now that's a discussion best kept for when we know one another better.' His expression closed down and Farah knew she had struck a nerve.

'Sorry, didn't mean to pry. I expect you get that a lot, too.'

He didn't immediately respond and instead they both concentrated on their food, soaking up the sauce with fresh, crusty bread.

'Tell me more about your suspicions,' he eventually said, pushing his empty plate aside and leaning back in his chair. 'I assume you think Dale is behind whatever's going on which, if you'll excuse me for saying so, makes your confronting him without actual evidence seem a bit dumb. I assume you don't have any evidence?' She shook her head. 'Thought not, so what made you do it?' He smiled that glamorous smile of his, flashing even white teeth that were probably the product of ruinously expensive dentistry. She admired the way that his eyes crinkled at the corners when he smiled. She admired too damned much about him and adjured herself to stick to the subject under discussion. Concerned about being played for a fool, she could well imagine how badly that would go down with him. 'Come on, no avoiding the question.'

That smile had distracted her and right now she was having trouble recalling her own name. She shook her head. 'Actually, it's our head lad I suspect. I know he's in debt and likes to gamble.'

'You're not allowed to place bets on horses from your own yard, are you?'

She again shook her head, this time at his naïveté. 'That's not to say someone else can't place them on your behalf. It happens all the time.' She held up a hand. 'I never bet, I can't afford to, but a lot of the lads do. Jonah, the head lad, has been with Guy since he set up here and knows everyone of note in the industry.' She allowed a significant pause. 'Including all the bookies and their runners.'

'The runners come up to the gallops and watch the horses in training?'

'Yes, but that isn't enough to get the inside scoop, so to speak. If I've got it right then someone is paying off their gambling debts by talking out of turn.'

'I'd kind of decided it must be something like that,' Isaac said, his earlier smile replaced with a grim expression.

'Someone encouraged Dale to enter Force in a class that was too good for him, over my objections. Jonah insists it wasn't him but... Anyway, a couple of other horses owned by rich entrepreneurs, men likely too busy to take sufficient interest to question the move, received the same treatment.'

'Did they win?'

'One did, but Force and the other got left well behind. But, here's the thing, Force was talked up in the trade press. He'd won his previous outings easily in the lower class so it wasn't difficult to convince the pundits that he would place at the next level.'

Isaac's expression turned increasingly sombre as he slowly nodded his understanding. 'It's easier to fix a race and have the horse lose rather than have it win and risk drug testing.' He paused, his frown deepening the lines across his forehead. 'A bookie takes a big bet on Force but doesn't lay it off because he knows he won't win, thereby cleaning up.'

'There you go.' But Farah didn't smile. 'You've caught on straight away. I went to Dale, thinking it odd that he hadn't realised what was obvious and hoping I was wrong about it. It didn't occur to me in a million years that he might be involved rather than Jonah.' She lifted one shoulder. 'Perhaps they both are. Dale and Guy are really good friends, practically joined at the hip, and I didn't think Dale would risk the reputation of the yard in that way. I also thought his loyalty was beyond corruption.'

'Does Dale gamble?'

'Presumably more heavily than I realised. I can't think of any other reason why he would chance shafting his friend's reputation, other than financial necessity.' She sent Isaac a distracted smile. 'You, of all people, should know that everything comes down to money in the end.'

'Okay, I'm with you so far, but why has Force been withdrawn from his next race given that he isn't actually lame?'

'That's what I would very much like to know.' Farah tapped her fingers against the surface of the table, feeling frustrated. 'It's what first aroused my suspicions. Well, that's not exactly true. I think I always had suspicions but chose to ignore them, until one of my horses got involved. Sorry.' She flapped a hand. 'One of your horses.'

'They're more yours than mine. I barely know them, which perhaps confirms your suspicions and explains why Dale and his cronies chose my horses to pull their scam. I have never called at the stables unannounced before, as well you know, and pretty much leave them to their own devices. I have to say though that Dale didn't show any signs of anxiety when he saw me in the barn. If he's up to something, he's damned good at keeping his nerve.'

'Why did you call in today?'

'Traffic snarl-up on the M25 meant I missed my meetings. I just came on a whim.' He smiled at her. 'And I'm very glad that I did.'

'Well, at least it means I didn't starve,' she said flippantly.

'Are things so very bad?' he asked softly.

'I will have to take an office job,' she said with a sigh. 'Dale will make sure I don't work in this industry again. If he's up to something untoward then he can't take that risk.'

'I can always use good people in my Brighton office.'

She flapped a hand, taken aback by the offer. 'You don't even know what I'm qualified to do.'

'I know you have ethics and the courage of your convictions.'

She huffed. 'Much good that's done me. Anyway thanks, but I have to find something locally. I can't leave Daisy for too long, talking of whom...' She glanced at her watch and made to stand. 'I need to get back.'

'You live with her.'

'Yes, she brought me up. My own parents were killed in a climbing accident when I was still quite small. I barely remember them and so Daisy is the only mother I've ever known. Since she got ill our roles have been reversed and she depends on me.'

'Then let me get you back to her and we'll talk some more. I'll just be a minute.'

She watched Isaac go to the bar and skilfully deflect Jenny's flirting as he settled the bill.

'All set?' he asked, returning to their table.

'Thanks, that was nice and just what I needed,' she said.

'My pleasure. Come on, I'll drive you home.'

'There's no need, I can walk from here.'

'There's every need. We haven't yet decided what we're going to do about Dale in order to get you your job back.'

3

_____

Isaac followed Farah's instructions and less than five minutes later he pulled his car onto the verge outside a rambling old cottage in the middle of nowhere. He briefly compared his surroundings to the hustle and bustle of Brighton, where he lived and worked, and where there never seemed to be absolute quiet, not even in the early hours. The differences gave him pause, which surprised him. He was a city boy through and through, wasn't he? The countryside was all well and good but he lived for the buzz he got from being a high-flyer in the middle of all the action.

Farah sent him an odd look, which made him realise that he'd been sitting there with the engine running and allowing his thoughts to run amok right along with it. He smiled at her, came back to the here and now, cut the engine and watched her climb from the car. She went straight to the railings bordering a field at the side of the property, where a single horse had been turned out. It trotted over to her with a whinny of recognition and nudged her shoulder with its muzzle.

'Yours?' Isaac asked, joining her.

'For the past fifteen years,' Farah replied, patting the bay's neck and producing a mint from her pocket which she fed to the gelding. 'Marius and I are joined at the hip. I broke him myself and we're the best of friends. He's retired now, mostly.'

'Fifteen years ago and you broke a horse.' Isaac nodded. 'I'm impressed. How old were you?'

'What sort of question is that?' She sent him a look of mock outrage. 'Do you ask all the women you mix with how old they are by such nefarious means?'

'God, but you're spiky.' He chuckled. 'I was attempting to pay you a compliment. I'm thinking you wouldn't have been more than nine or ten. I'll be the first to admit that I know next to nothing about horses but I should imagine that breaking one to the saddle is adult work.'

'Why thank you, kind sir.' She glanced over her shoulder at the cottage, with its sloping roofs, climbing shrubs not yet in flower creeping up the walls. Following the direction of her gaze, even from a distance Isaac could see that the windows were in urgent need of a little TLC. Distracted, she flashed a plastic smile. 'I was twelve at the time but I could ride before I could walk. And I did have advice from my uncle, who was a horseman through and through. He made sure I got things exactly right. He's gone now, of course, and I miss him like crazy. Anyway, to save your poor brain from straining itself, I'm now twenty-seven, if that's what you wanted to know.'

Isaac laughed and patted Marius's neck. 'I wouldn't be that rude.'

She sent him an arch look and sighed. 'I think there is very little you wouldn't be. Anyway, come on, since you insist upon hanging around, I'll introduce you to Daisy.'

'Lead the way.'

Farah entered the cottage by a side door that stuck but which she expertly nudged open with her shoulder. 'It's only me,' she called out.

'You're back early,' a voice that sounded slurred replied from deep within the building. 'I'm in the sunroom. I saw you with Marius. And with a hunk of a man. Who brought you home and why?'

'My aunt,' Farah explained unnecessarily, a spontaneous smile lighting up her features. 'Her illness has made her sometimes difficult to understand but there is nothing wrong with her brain. She's still as sharp as a tack. There's nothing wrong with her mischief-making either,' she added, rolling her eyes. 'Don't say you haven't been warned.'

'I look forward to meeting her. She clearly means a great deal to you.'

'She is all I have,' Farah said simply. 'I seldom bring people here so you will be subjected to yet another third-degree, just in case you didn't already get enough of that from Jenny.'

Isaac shrugged. 'I'm a big boy.'

'One who only tells people as much about himself as he wants them to know.'

'I'm shy.'

Farah sent him a look that implied she wanted to give him an argument on that score but refrained from comment and instead led the way from what was obviously a boot room, given that Farah used a scraper to remove her boots and slipped her feet into a pair of pumps.

Isaac followed her down a long, narrow corridor, looking around with interest. The place was probably several hundred years old, as evidenced by the low, sloping ceilings and doorways that required him to duck in order to avoid bashing his head. The cottage was overdue for redecoration. Paper peeled off the walls in places, there were no obvious signs of central heating and he noticed patches of damp on the ceilings. Added to the warped windows with their peeling paint, these indications reinforced his impression that Farah and her aunt were short of funds. But there was also a warmth and comfort about the shabby interior that was spotlessly clean and clearly loved.

Isaac felt instantly and rather disarmingly at home.

He followed Farah into what was obviously a later addition since it was double glazed, south facing and enjoyed the benefits of the spring sunshine. A woman Isaac estimated to be in her sixties sat in a wide armchair with a walking frame parked next to it. Her lap was covered with a rug and a book lay open on it. Her face was remarkably unlined, she had a pair of glasses perched on the end of her nose and her eyes sparkled with speculative interest when she looked up at Isaac. An empty mug sat on a side table, along with a glass of water and several bottles of pills. A small TV sat in the corner and the remote control was also within the lady's reach but Isaac suspected that she preferred the written word to banal daytime television.

'Daisy, this is Isaac Fernandez, one of our owners,' Farah said, bending to kiss the lady's forehead. 'Isaac, my aunt, Daisy Bishop.'

'It's a pleasure,' Isaac said, smiling and offering her his hand.

'You will have to excuse me, Isaac,' Daisy replied in her slurring voice, 'but shaking hands is not easy for me.'

'Of course.' Isaac dropped his own, feeling rather foolish.

'Damned illness,' Daisy muttered. 'Do sit down. I don't often have the pleasure of the company of handsome young men nowadays.'

'Daisy, behave!' Farah chided, sending Isaac an I-told-you-so look and smiling. 'How are you feeling?' She held up a hand. 'No, don't bother. Given your determination to embarrass Isaac, you are obviously having a good day.'

'Well, darling, you know me. I've never been one to waste opportunities.'

Isaac laughed as he lowered himself into the chair opposite Daisy. 'I'm sorry you've been inflicted with this wretched ailment,' he said.

'Why?' Farah demanded to know as she too took a seat. 'It isn't your fault.'

'I have first-hand experience. My gran had it,' he replied, revealing something about his background that he seldom told anyone.

'Oh,' Farah said. 'Sorry.'

He sent her a challenging look. 'It's my turn to ask you why.'

'Stop it, you two!' Daisy's reprimand brought an end to their staring contest and had them both turning in her direction like guilty children. 'Flirt in your own time. Right now, I'm more interested to know why a busy owner such as yourself is here with my niece. And, come to that, why Farah is home in the middle of a working day.'

'Dale fired me, Daisy,' Farah said glumly.

'No! You didn't confront him, did you?' Daisy shook her head. 'Your principles will be the death of you yet. How often have I said so? I despair, really I do.'

'I can't just stand back and watch wrongs without attempting to put them right.' But Farah's protest lacked conviction and Isaac wondered if she now regretted her impulsive actions.

'Tell her, Isaac.' Daisy sighed. 'She needs to have her ducks in a row before she runs her mouth.'

'I have tried,' Isaac replied, 'but at least I happened to be there today, unexpectedly, and I have to say that I think she's on to something.'

'See!' Farah said, bouncing on the edge of her chair like a child high on a sugar rush.

'My Ralph knew Dale when he was starting out in the industry. Thought he had potential and so took him under his wing. I don't like to think that he's gone over to the dark side.'

'Gambling is a curse and has a lot to answer for. The true addicts, just like addicts of any type, lose all control,' Isaac said.

'It's what Farah thinks this is all about and I must say, I tend to agree with her, given the contents of her notes.'

Isaac's head swivelled in Farah's direction. 'You've kept notes?' he asked. 'When were you planning to tell me?'

'Whoops!' Daisy said, covering her mouth with a shaking hand. But Isaac suspected that the revelation had been deliberate. She understood what drove her niece, clearly cared about her and was astute enough to realise that she needed someone with Isaac's clout to help fight her corner.

'I'll make us all some tea,' Farah replied, standing and sweeping from the room.

'That was no mistake, was it?' Isaac said, smiling at Daisy.

'Farah is a fiercely private person.' Daisy sighed. 'I have tried everything I can think of to make her put herself first and leave me to my own devices. I have carers come in during the day but she insists upon being here at night and doing more for me than any person should have to. I have learned to live with the loss of privacy and dignity, but there's no reason for someone of her age to give up everything for my sake. None of this is her fault.' Daisy lifted her arms a little way and then allowed them to fall back in her lap. 'She has no social life and it's a crying shame.'

'I won't disagree with you there. She's lovely.'

'And about the only person who doesn't realise it,' Daisy said with an exasperated sigh, her gaze focused on the spring flowers waving their heads in the breeze in the gardens beyond the windows. 'The fact of the matter is that I will soon have to go into residential care. I'd go now but that will leave Farah heartbroken and homeless, so we soldier on. What other choice do we have?'

'I understand,' Isaac said.

'But now, Farah's determination to right the world's wrongs has seen her thrown out of a job she loved. A job she was born to do. She takes after her uncle in that regard.' Daisy's gaze now focused on a framed picture of a smiling man with a craggy, outdoors face and a head of silver hair blown about by the wind. 'Now what will she do? I know that nothing will persuade her to move away to look for work and there's precious little to be had in this backwater other than with horses.'

'These things have a way of working themselves out, Daisy. I have a vested interest in getting to the bottom of whatever scam's being perpetrated at Guy's yard and I have resources that Dale Drummond can only dream about.'

Daisy chuckled. 'That I can easily believe.' She gave a crooked smile. 'Perhaps things will work out for Farah after all if you've taken up her cause.'

* * *

The kitchen was directly behind the sunroom and if Farah stood close enough to the adjoining wall she could hear every word Isaac and Daisy uttered even above the noise of the boiling kettle. She smiled to herself, thinking that eavesdropping had a lot going for it. But did she completely trust Isaac? That was a question she had yet to find an answer to. Her doubts in that regard would explain why she hadn't told him about her notes. Daisy clearly did trust him but then she was likely influenced by Isaac's pretty face and her desire to see Farah restored to her previous line of work.

Even so, she reasoned, she needed him. Isaac was right, at least about that. What was the worst that could happen if she let him read her notes, other than being obliged to spend more time with him? There were worse ways to endure her unemployed status.

Aware of her scruffy state, she ran upstairs to her room, tugged the band from her hair and brushed it out. She glanced in the mirror and had to admit that her crowning glory, when looked after and let loose, did a lot for her. She was tempted to leave it as it was but that would imply she'd made an effort, just like all his other women. Besides, she really didn't care what Isaac Fernandez thought of her.

Defiantly, she tied her hair up again and made her way back down to the kitchen, just as the kettle came to the boil. She made the tea using old-fashioned leaves and carried it through to the sunroom on a tray bearing three mismatched delicate cups and saucers, a milk jug and bowl of sugar cubes, along with biscuits decanted onto a plate from an out-of-date packet.

'Here we are,' she said, placing the tray down with a loud clatter and using a tea strainer to pour. 'Milk and sugar?' she asked, turning to Isaac.

'Neither, thanks.'

'Ah, sorry, there's no lemon.'

'Not a problem.'

Isaac shook his head when she proffered the plate of biscuits. 'Still full of lunch,' he said.

'We've been to the Fox,' Farah explained, wondering if she was now feeling the full effects of all the wine she'd consumed. It would account for her willingness to confide in Isaac, she supposed. If he moved his horses to another yard, perhaps he would do so on the proviso that she was employed to care for them.

But no, she was getting ahead of herself and anyway, it didn't do to get her hopes up.

'Ah, I see.' Daisy's eyes sparkled, making Farah want to throw a cushion at her. Her speculations were way out of kilter. Isaac's only interest was ensuring that no one played him for a mug and, presumably, to ensure that his horses were not being manipulated in a way that could come back to bite him on his admittedly trim backside.

They chatted about this and that whilst they drank their tea. When Daisy finished hers, she gave an ostentatious yawn. She tired easily and always napped in this room during the afternoon at this time of year.

'I think I'll go to my room,' she said. Farah sent her a disbelieving frown that Daisy pretended not to see. Her aunt was nothing if not transparent. 'If you'll help me, darling.'

'Here, let me.'

Isaac was on his feet in seconds, taking Daisy's arm in a gentle hold and easily helping her to her feet. Then he shocked Farah, and Daisy, too, it seemed, when he swept her from the floor and into his arms, carrying her with effortless ease.

Daisy gave a fluttering laugh. 'Well, this is unexpected,' she said, 'but not unwelcome.'

'I take it your room is down here,' Isaac said.

'Second door on the right,' Farah said, shaking her head and laughing.

She followed Isaac as he carried Daisy in that direction and deposited her gently on her bed.

'Sleep well,' he said, turning for the door and leaving Farah to settle her.

'You've made her day,' Farah said, joining Isaac in the sunroom again a short time later, a spiral notebook in her hand. He was busy texting on his phone, no doubt responding to all the calls he'd ignored earlier. She expected him to continue but he surprised her by pocketing his phone straight away and giving her his full attention.

'I'm glad it gave her some pleasure. It's a cruel disease and she doesn't deserve it.'

'No.' Farah sighed. 'She doesn't.'

'You and she seem very close.'

'We are and I can't bear to think of...' She swiped impatiently at a tear when it trickled down her cheek. She didn't ordinarily cry but today she couldn't seem to stop.

His hand gently touching her shoulder jolted her. 'Daisy is resigned to her fate, I think. My advice, for what it's worth, is to make the most of the time you have left together.'

'I know, but sometimes it's hard,' she said with a sigh, responding to his empathy somewhere deep within her core and looking upon him with a little less suspicion. There was nothing in the rules to say that a handsome and successful man couldn't also be kind and considerate. She just had never met one before. 'Anyway, my notes.' She sat across from him and handed him her book. 'Best you read them and let me know what needs clarification.'

Their fingers touched as he reached out to take the book from her. She felt a jolt of awareness spiral through her bloodstream and widened her eyes at her unexpected reaction. Glancing up at Isaac, she found him watching her, a small, satisfied little smile playing about his lips that she yearned to wipe off by issuing a taut riposte. Annoyingly, nothing appropriate sprang to mind that he wouldn't immediately counter. She ought to know better than to indulge in a battle of that nature with a man of his calibre, she privately conceded.

She had the good sense to realise that he was out of her league. In all respects.

Obviously, the contact hadn't been accidental and he knew precisely how she would react, which infuriated her. She hated being so predictable.

'Are you going to read or keep staring at me?' she asked acerbically.

'Oh, I think I would much prefer to do the latter. I enjoy looking at you.' He flashed a glamorous smile. 'I never know quite what to expect.'

'Which has novelty value, I dare say.'

Isaac tutted and shook his head. 'You really do have a low opinion of yourself.'

'This isn't about me. It's about my suspicions.' She gave a significant nod in the direction of her notebook. He finally took the hint, looked away from her and started to read.

He quickly became absorbed, and Farah took the first real opportunity she'd had to assess him. *How could one man have so much?* she wondered, feeling disgruntled by life's unfairness. Looks, intelligence, wealth, a sense of humour and compassion for Daisy. Daisy, who knew her life would be cut short, who suffered physically and endured the indignity of no longer being able to help herself without ever really complaining.

Farah, who had youth and good health on her side, was getting her knickers twisted because she'd been separated from an underpaid career and the horses she loved but which were not hers. She really needed to get things into better perspective.

'You only started taking notes when Force was entered up a class.'

Isaac's deep voice jolted Farah out of her reverie. 'Yes, I'd noticed the odd thing before then, but it was the Force fiasco that made me decide I needed to do something about it, which is when I started writing down the things I saw or overheard.'

'Why didn't you show Dale your notes?'

'For the same reason that I didn't tell you about them. I assumed he would have drawn the same conclusions as me and be on top of things. I didn't for one moment expect him to react the way he did, but now I don't trust him. Perhaps, on a visceral level, I never really did, which would explain why I didn't show him my notes.'

'You don't trust me?' Isaac pointed a finger at his own chest and wasn't smiling. 'Since you didn't plan to show me your notes until Daisy mentioned them, that's the only conclusion I can draw. Do you really think I need to get involved with grubby scams of this nature?'

She held her hands towards him, palms outward. 'Sorry, that was uncalled for.'

'Yeah, it was.' His angry expression softened but not very much.

'If it's any consolation, I had the book with me and had intended to show Dale. But when he reacted with such hostility, I decided against it. He must have noticed some of the same odd things that I have. Not much gets past him so if he's innocent, he should have given me a chance to explain. When he didn't, well...' She paused to draw breath, aware that the sun had disappeared behind a bank of cloud and a light rain now pattered on the glass roof. 'Anyway, for what it's worth, I know now that you have nothing to do with this. It would be foolhardy to involve owners but I hadn't thought it through before. Your arrival threw me.'

'You name a couple of bookies' stringers.' He glanced up at her. 'Why those particular two?'

'They've both been up on the gallops a lot recently and are always there when I'm exercising Force. And I've seen them both talking to Jonah in out-of-the-way places. I was in the village a while back, picking up Daisy's new prescription and I saw Jonah and Bob Ellis talking in a doorway behind the chemist. I don't think they saw me, in fact, I know they didn't. I asked Jonah the next day if he'd been into the village and he said he hadn't for a while.' She spread her hands. 'Why lie if it was innocent?'

'He could have just been passing on form, or skiving off to meet a woman.'

'He could, and that's what I thought at the time. But in the light of subsequent events...'

'What bookies do these guys work for?'

'Joe Shrimpton is Ellis's right hand and Mark Bright is with Dave Fenton.'

'I've seen both of those on the courses.'

'You would. They're well known and as far as bookies go, well respected.'

Isaac sent her an amused smile. 'That's a bit of an oxymoron.'

She conceded the point with a tilt of her head. 'Bookies generally get a bad press when all they're doing is serving a public need.'

'And lining their own pockets.'

She sent him a challenging look. 'Do you work solely for the good of others?'

'Fair point.' He chuckled. 'Even so, I know a few unhappy punters who will give you an argument about bookies being respectable.' His expression sobered. 'Anyway, leave them to me.'

'What will you do?'

'Have someone delve into their backgrounds and see what comes to light.' He yawned and stretched his arms above his head. 'It's a shame you're not still employed by Guy. You could have—'

'You could get me my job back,' she said, sitting forward and resting her forearms on her knees, a germ of an idea occurring to her. 'Guy will walk on water in return for the kudos that comes with having an owner of your stature. I hate to say this, but you get him good press coverage. Even the newspapers and gossip magazines remember to mention Guy's name eventually.'

'I could, but it's risky. Dale knows you're on to him and I overheard his angry response to your concerns. He sounded defensive, which means he might get physical. He will be putting self-preservation first and can't guarantee that you won't run to Guy with your suspicions. Especially if this is a race-fixing scam. Big money and tough characters will be involved and Dale is probably out of his depth, running scared.'

'Don't go all caveman on me, Isaac.' She airily waved his concerns for her safety aside. 'If Dale knows you're on my side, he'll think twice before he tries anything stupid.'

'And might well abandon the scam.'

'Which means that the bookies pulling the strings will transfer to another yard where the workers are in debt,' she shot back at him.

Isaac inhaled. 'You're not going to give up on this, are you?'

'Not a chance. I enjoy working for Guy and don't like to think that his best friend is shafting him. If there's anything I can do about that then I won't hesitate. Besides, as Daisy mentioned to you earlier, my uncle mentored Dale so I feel like I have a responsibility...' She grinned at him and covered her mouth with her hand as she realised she'd just admitted to listening in to his earlier conversation with Daisy. 'Oh shit!' she said, giggling.

Isaac laughed too. 'Eavesdropping, Miss...?'

'Ash. And I was just making sure that Daisy didn't get carried away,' she replied, looking away from him.

'All right,' he said. 'I'll think about talking to Guy on your behalf but that's the best I can do. I'm due to go to the yard on Saturday.'

'Ah, to Guy's open day when he gets all his well-heeled owners pissed and then tries to sell them another horse.'

'That would be the occasion,' he replied with a grin. 'I will notice your absence and see how Guy reacts but I'm not making any promises.'

'It's not as if I'm asking you to sign a contract and marry me,' she snapped. 'Come on, Isaac, you need me and you know it.'

'Talking of contracts, didn't you have one with Guy?' Isaac raised a brow when she responded with a blank look. 'Don't tell me you were working on a cash-in-hand basis.'

'No, of course not. That sort of thing doesn't happen in Guy's yard, but we don't exactly have a thriving HR department to take our complaints to either.'

'Even so, you can't just be sacked for no reason and even if you are, you deserve severance pay.'

'Wake up, Isaac, in the real world things don't work that way – not with small employers. If I kick up a stink and force Dale to keep me on, you can bet your life that he will make my life uncomfortable in all sorts of ways. I'll get put with the worst horses—'

'Are there such a thing in a thriving racing yard?'

'There are the difficult ones that bite and don't like being handled and I'd get all the shitty jobs, literally.'

'Okay, I get the picture but you still need to ask about severance pay.'

'Or threaten to speak out about what I suspect is going on at the yard.' She plucked absently at her lower lip and a slow smile spread across her face. 'Not a bad idea.'

Isaac rolled his eyes. 'And a good way to get hurt if these high roller bookies are behind the scam. Something tells me that they won't take any prisoners.' He grasped her upper arm in a light hold. 'Promise me you won't do anything quite that reckless.'

'Well, I won't have to if you speak to Guy on my behalf,' she said sweetly.

'Okay, okay.' He threw up his hands. 'Sure I can't give you a job? You're a natural negotiator.'

'Desperate times. That's when a person finds out what she's made of.'

'Right. Ask about severance pay. It will look odd if you don't. That will draw your situation to Guy's attention, just in case Dale tries to spin a yarn about you quitting, and leave the rest to me. You want me to drive you back to pick up your car?' he asked.

Farah felt her cheeks warm. 'It can stay there for now.'

He looked at her for a long time but didn't push it. 'Okay,' he said, making her feel as though he knew why she'd left it there in the first place, which was totally humiliating. 'I'd best be on my way. Give me your number.' She reeled it off and he programmed it into his phone. Hers pinged a moment later. 'There, now you have my direct number,' he said, turning for the door. 'Call me if anything happens or if you feel threatened.'

She thought he would then leave but instead he turned back once more, kissed her cheek and then reached for the door handle. 'Ciao,' he said.

4

Dale leaned his backside against a counter in Guy's well-organised, purpose-built office and tried not to resent the success that his mentee had made of himself. Well, he wasn't exactly self-made, he assuaged his wounded pride by reminding himself. It helped to have a wife whose doting connections had been willing to finance the operation.

Dale had known Guy as a gangly, snotty-nosed kid with a natural aptitude for horses. Dale recognised right from the off something in his determination to literally pick himself up after a tumble, listen to Dale's advice and get straight back in the saddle. Dale had been responsible for encouraging Guy's raw talent and shaping him into what he had become but his contribution had been overlooked and he'd somehow been left behind during the course of Guy's meteoric rise to the top of the pile. The world and his wife now wanted Guy to train their pampered babies, seemingly forgetting that Dale bore the responsibility for making it happen.

It was enough to test anyone's loyalty.

'Everything on track for Saturday's open day?' Guy asked.

'Course.' Dale shrugged, aware there were still a ton of preparations to be made insofar as the horses they intended to auction off on behalf of their disillusioned owners were concerned. But Guy didn't need to know that. Dale was the details man; Guy took all the accolades, occasionally remembering to throw Dale the odd crumb. Was it any wonder that Dale had become resentful? Bitter. The place would fall apart without him at the helm but Dale appeared to be the only person who remembered that rather vital fact.

'Bloody owners.' Guy looked up from the email he was reading with a good-natured smile. 'They trust you to do the training, then tell you how to go about doing it. Fucking Morcombe will never stay the distance over two miles.'

'Welcome to the real world.'

Dale hadn't intended to let his bitterness show but the edge to his voice had Guy staring at him with concern. 'What's up?' he asked.

How long have you got? 'The usual crap,' Dale replied carelessly. 'Nothing for you to worry about. That's what you pay me a pittance for.'

'Whose bed did you get out the wrong side of?'

Guy sent Dale a questioning look, shrugged and returned his attention to his computer screen, causing Dale to wonder when the intimacy between them had evaporated and why he hadn't realised that he and Guy had grown so far apart. Had he been paying closer attention instead of concentrating on his extraneous activities, he might have been able to stop the rot. But Guy now hung out with the high-flyers, brown-nosing it with the rich and influential owners, like fucking Isaac Fernandez.

Part of Dale was jealous, but he was mostly disgusted by the changes in the pretty boy from the local housing estate who'd pulled himself out of the gutter by clinging to Dale's bootlaces. Then leaving him behind.

Dale had more immediate problems than his fragmenting control over his former student. He never should have lost his temper with Farah and definitely shouldn't have given her the sack. Not only was she one of the best, most instinctive lasses he'd ever worked with, but she was also head travelling lass and had a way of keeping the horses calm and focused on the job. The others were asking questions about her sudden disappearance and he knew they wouldn't buy it if he said she'd left of her own accord, or been sacked for inefficiency.

It would have been better if he'd kept her on; that way he could keep a lid on what it was that she thought she knew.

The fucking interfering bitch!

She would put herself, all of them, in danger if she ran her mouth, but he could hardly tell her that without implicating himself in a sordid business that he'd denied all knowledge of and had never expected to involve himself with. *How the fuck had it come to this?* And more to the point, what should he do about it?

'What?' Guy asked.

Dale snapped out of his funk, not realising that Guy had been watching him.

'Woman trouble,' Dale replied, knowing that would satisfy Guy because he had a reputation as a ladies' man.

'Not like you to let their demands get to you,' Guy replied, grinning and returning his attention to his email. 'What the fuck?' He looked up at Dale again, frowning.

'What's wrong now?' Dale asked.

'Farah Ash is claiming unfair dismissal.' Guy's scowl intensified. 'I wasn't aware that she'd been dismissed.'

Damn, Dale thought. He should have realised that she'd run to Guy, telling tales. Just how much *had* she told him? Dale went hot and cold all over as the implications struck home. *Guy wouldn't believe it, but even so...*

'We had a difference of opinion,' Dale said with a casual shrug. 'I won't be talked to like that, lost my rag and told her to get out.'

'Why?' Guy looked perplexed. 'What did she do? I thought you and she were solid and went way back. She's one of our best. The owners like her, the rest of the lads like her, the horses love her. What the fuck, Dale? Why am I only hearing about this now?'

'We had a barney and she got above herself. I told her to clear off but never thought she would. You know what a quick temper she has. It's something and nothing.'

Guy visibly relaxed. 'Then get her back.'

'How can I? I'll lose face and every kid we have will think I've gone soft. You leave the hiring and firing to me, Guy. Don't interfere.'

'I leave it to you because I assume you won't put your own fucking pride ahead of the welfare of the yard.' Guy had gone red in the face. He wasn't one to ordinarily lose his temper; Dale knew he'd pushed him too far. 'Besides, if we don't take her back then another yard will snap her up, and she'll take all our secrets with her.'

Not if I put the word out that she's toxic, they won't. 'I'll talk to her.'

'No, you—' His phone rang. Guy glanced at the display and snatched it up. 'I need to take this. Just sort the Farah situation out and do it quick.'

Dale left Guy's office in a foul temper, wondering if that's how it would be in future. Guy was gaining in confidence and starting to actually believe that he was the boss. Dale was obviously losing his edge and wondered about the wisdom of taking Farah back. Keep your enemies close, and all that. Not that she actually *was* the enemy; he liked her and respected her skill with horses, but she was getting too damned nosy.

What the hell to do? He kicked at a wheelbarrow and bawled a lad out for leaving it in the wrong place, even though he hadn't, as he headed back to his cottage. What the hell was he supposed to do now? Taking her back was the obvious answer, but for the fact that he couldn't trust her to keep her trap shut about what she thought she knew. He couldn't contain this. He would need to tell his paymasters and let them decide; that way, whatever happened wouldn't be on him.

He hesitated, with his hand hovering over the phone in his pocket. *What did she actually know for a fact, or could prove?* Very little, he decided, relaxing slightly. Even so, her knowledge barely scratched the surface of the hole Dale had dug for himself.

He could, he supposed, offer her a generous severance package on condition that she went quietly, claiming personal reasons. That way, his masters needn't know the truth. They were not the sort of people it was wise to get on the wrong side of, Dale knew. He also knew that Farah needed an infusion of cash and needed it badly. She would want to get a job in another local yard so that she could be close to her aunt, Daisy, and he wouldn't put the kibosh on her ambitions if she kept her suspicions to herself. And that's all they were, he tried to convince himself, as he let himself into his cottage and made straight for the sideboard, pouring himself a much-needed large measure of single malt and downing it in one swallow.

She had fuck all evidence to back up her theory and he would make it very clear to her in lots of subtle little ways that it would be within her best interests to keep her suspicions to herself. Dale would protect her as best he could. He felt ashamed of depths he'd fallen to.

Sighing, he extracted his phone and dialled a number from memory. He would have to tell them what had happened, he decided, self-preservation coming to the fore. Farah's departure wasn't something he could keep from them and if they heard of it from anyone other than him then he would lose what little advantage he still had.

He would spin this and make it sound as though Farah had walked out for the aforementioned personal reasons. After all, none of this was his fault. Not really. She'd talked back to him and pushed him too far so it was all on her.

* * *

Isaac took a perverse sort of pleasure from parking his Lotus in the staff car park when he arrived in time for lunch on the open day. He noticed that Farah's mud-splattered Suzuki was still there, but parked in a different place. In the two days since he had seen her, they hadn't spoken and he was unsure what her situation now was. In truth, he'd barely had a moment to draw breath. Despite employing the best of the best, playing hooky for a day had left him with a ton of stuff that only he could deal with.

Even so, he felt bad for having ignored her.

There had been a black-tie do the previous night that had gone on until the early hours, obliging him to hobnob with investors and pay attention to his glamorous yet high-maintenance date. He couldn't help comparing her to Farah, even though there was nothing remotely similar about them. Samantha, he knew, wouldn't be seen dead in muddy muckers, whereas Farah probably felt more at home in that type of footwear and likely didn't own any heels.

Always one to appreciate the effort his dates put into looking their best, he now found himself dwelling upon Farah's fresh-faced look, no make-up necessary.

And preferring it.

Guy greeted him with a surprised look when he approached the gathering outside the barn from the wrong direction.

'Get lost, did you, Isaac?' he asked, hand outstretched. 'Not like you to use the tradesmen's entrance.'

'Oh, I don't know.' Isaac took Guy's hand in a firm grasp and gave an easy shrug. 'It can be surprisingly revealing.'

'What secrets were you hoping to uncover?'

Isaac smiled and accepted a glass of champagne from the tray of a waitress with a nod of thanks. 'I'll let you know when I find them,' he replied.

'Your horses are looking fit, and I have a few more promising ones up for sale if you're looking to increase your holding.'

'Not sure about that.' Isaac paused. 'I understood Force was lame.'

'False alarm. These things happen. I'm afraid the entries for the two furlongs at Newbury are closed now, though.'

'Ah, shame. Still, not to worry,' Isaac said, playing the part of the clueless owner that he knew was expected of him. 'I dare say you know what you're doing. When can he race next? What do you have in mind for him?'

They chatted for a while about the upcoming meetings but when Guy's attention was claimed by another owner, Isaac excused himself and wandered into the barn. He exchanged pleasantries with other owners he recognised as inquisitive equine heads looked over their doors, no doubt wondering what all the commotion was about.

He stopped at the boxes where his own horses lived. Force, he noticed, was back in and groomed to within an inch of his life. No sign of the injury that Guy insisted had been a false alarm. He wondered how that was possible. A horse was either lame or it wasn't and he balked at being forced to accept an explanation that, if the circumstances had been different, he would have challenged.

Force whinnied when Isaac produced a mint from his pocket. He noticed Dale for the first time, watching him from a position further down the barn, where he was talking to another owner. Isaac patted Force's neck and then moved on to his other horses.

He took lunch and chatted about horses with the other owners, listening to them boast about their investments. He himself refrained from so doing. The day job had taught him that the more people boasted, the less they tended to have to boast about. Instead, he watched and listened, aware of Dale moving unobtrusively from group to group, always seeming to keep an eye on Isaac.

There was no sign of the stable lads and lasses. Presumably they were preparing for the parade of horses that were up for auction after lunch, once the owners had imbibed sufficiently to loosen the purse strings.

The parade of horses started and Isaac watched with half an eye as Dale's voice boomed over the microphone, extolling the virtues of each horse as he listed their respective pedigrees and successes on the racetrack to date. Isaac wondered about their failures, which, of course, weren't mentioned, but since he wasn't in the market for another equine, he didn't bother to ask difficult questions.

Biding his time in raising the question of Farah's absence, Isaac was jolted out of his reverie when Dale announced the third horse, a handsome black gelding that pranced at the end of his rope, being led in by Farah herself. Turned out in the yard's distinctive blue and green fleece with Guy's initials emblazoned across the back, pristine white jodhpurs and shiny black hunting boots, her hair pulled back in a neat braid, she looked confident and highly professional. Until her gaze fell upon him and she gave the suggestion of a wicked little smile that affected Isaac in the area of his groin.

What the hell!

How had she got reinstated so quickly and, more to the point, why hadn't she bothered to tell Isaac? He might have been preoccupied but he did pick up his messages regularly and Farah most definitely hadn't left one. He became aware of Dale, despite his MC duties, watching Isaac, his glance going between him and Farah. What on earth had she said to make Dale suspicious of their involvement together? Possibly nothing, he conceded, given that they would have been seen in the local pub on the day of Farah's dismissal, their presence there remarked upon perhaps. Would word have got back to Dale? Was that why he'd reinstated her before Isaac had a chance to raise the issue here today? If so, what the hell had been said to her?

With more questions than answers rattling around inside his head, Isaac got through the rest of the day and took his leave along with the rest of the owners. He didn't see Farah again but called her the moment he got in his car.

'Farah, what the hell...'

'Good afternoon to you, Isaac,' she replied in a whisper. 'I'm still working.'

'Meet me in the pub,' he replied. 'We need to talk.'

Isaac cut the connection and drove to the Fox, thinking that if they'd already been seen there together once, there was little point in hiding their connection. In fact, it would be to Farah's advantage if Dale and his cronies realised that he was on her side.

He glanced in his rear-view mirror, assuming that the 4x4 on his tail, a black Range Rover, was another horse owner leaving Guy's stables and that it would take the next turning for the motorway. When it didn't and continued to follow him, he felt only mildly concerned. He indicated to turn off into the lane that would take him to the pub and the Rover followed.

By then Isaac was starting to get pissed off. And concerned. What were the chances of someone else going the same way as him when he hadn't seen another car since leaving the yard? It couldn't be a coincidence.

He pulled into the pub's car park and continued to watch for the Rover in his wing mirror. It slowed almost to a stop outside the pub, as though the driver wanted to be sure that Isaac had seen him. Isaac pretended to be engrossed with his phone and didn't look up.

The Rover's windows were tinted and he could only vaguely see the outline of a burly individual behind the wheel and another in the passenger seat.

Eventually the Rover pulled away and disappeared from view. Isaac got out of his car, locked it and went into the pub. Today he was dressed casually in jeans and a shirt that hung loose over his waistband but he still felt out of place and probably looked it. He'd eaten and only had a half glass of champagne so felt justified in ordering a bottle of lager. He took it to a quiet table and sat down to wait for Farah, and to have a good think. Something untoward, bigger than Isaac had at first imagined, was going down at Guy's yard and Farah had possibly placed herself directly in the line of fire.

* * *

Farah had felt euphoric when she'd received a call from Dale, asking her to come in and talk about her dismissal.

'I got a bit overheated,' he said, coming as close to an apology as she had ever known him to. 'You know how I can be. Even so, you were out of order, bandying unsubstantiated accusations about.'

'Sorry,' she said meekly. 'Perhaps I got it wrong.'

'There's no "perhaps" about it. Starting rumours like that will be detrimental to the yard's reputation. You do realise that.'

'Sorry,' she forced herself to say, focusing her glance on her feet in a contrite manner, even though he couldn't see her.

'Come in tomorrow then at the usual time, be ready to work and we'll say no more about it.'

Farah cut the call, punched the air and went to tell Daisy the good news. She'd had plenty of time to regret her actions and accept that her job was worth more to her than her principles. Something was off at the yard but if she stuck her nose in again then she would be both jobless and homeless. It simply wasn't worth the risk.

She knew her dismissal had worried her aunt more than she was willing to admit and felt bad for giving the older lady something to worry about. Her first thought was to ring Isaac and tell him the news, too, but something made her hesitate. She'd learned her lesson, would do as Dale advised/threatened when she returned to work and absorb the pep talk, thinly disguised as an apology. She was left in no doubt that her interference in anything that didn't concern her would not be tolerated.

She thought of Daisy and decided that she would, for once, give the impression of doing as she was told. She'd keep her nose clean and mind her own business, at least on the surface. Ergo, she had no reason to involve Isaac.

Even so, she noticed him the moment he arrived for the open day. His tall figure and swarthy Mediterranean complexion a beacon for every female eye in the place. But she kept out of sight, well aware that he was out of her league and she'd be well advised to forget all about him. She was back in charge of his horses and that would have to be enough for her.

She noticed Isaac's reaction when she led the black gelding out, but only because she'd been watching for it. He was good at hiding his responses; she'd give him that much. She knew he would want to talk to her, but how much of what had happened she would be willing to share with him she had yet to decide. He wouldn't be easily fobbed off but her affairs were really none of his business.

Her heart balked at the prospect of not seeing him alone again, but she adjured herself to be sensible. Isaac only cared about the people who were attempting to play him for an idiot. She knew that wouldn't sit comfortably with a man of his stature. She'd seen the pictures of him in that morning's papers, wearing a white tuxedo to some charity do or other, with a gorgeous blonde clinging to his arm. Farah couldn't compete; nor did she have any desire to.

She tidied away Force's day rug, made sure he was snug and warm for the night and kissed his nose. The horse butted her gently and whinnied.

'All right, all right, I missed you too.' She produced a few mints and fed them to him. 'That's all you really want, isn't it?'

With her duties completed, she wished the others goodnight and made her way to her jeep, now mercifully full of fuel. Dale had given her a small cash bonus by way of apology, or bribery, depending upon your point of view. She climbed behind the wheel, checked her appearance in the mirror, defiantly pulled her hair out of its braid and allowed her flowing locks to tumble around her shoulders.

'Take that, bimbos of this world!' she cried aloud, laughing at the same time and wondering if she was cracking up. 'Right, let's face the inquisition,' she told her reflection, squaring her shoulders and turning the key in the ignition.

She drove the short distance slowly, which gave her an opportunity to gather her thoughts. Everything had happened so quickly: being sacked and reinstated and having to pretend to be chastened. What she did know, without a shadow of a doubt, was that Dale, and Jonah, too, were definitely involved in something shady. Now that she knew, she saw something suspicious in everything they did but was determined to ignore their shenanigans. Self-preservation was now her priority.

Afterwards, she assumed she had hit a pothole, puncturing a tyre; there were enough of them in this quiet road. At the time, she struggled to control the vehicle as it veered off into a ditch. She hit her head on the steering wheel as it lurched to a stop and that was the last thing she remembered.

5

Isaac finished his beer and glanced at his watch, mildly concerned because Farah hadn't arrived yet. He'd been one of the last to leave the yard and knew that the evening stable duties had almost been completed at that point. He tried her mobile but it went straight to voicemail. A cold shiver travelled down his spine. Something wasn't right. Could it be that she'd simply decided she didn't need his help? Had he been stood up? Isaac chuckled, unsure of the answer to that one since it had never happened to him before.

'How the mighty have fallen,' he muttered aloud, drawing curious glances from a couple of old guys at an adjoining table, who probably thought that by talking aloud to himself he was losing his marbles. *Who's to say they weren't right,* he wondered. The smart thing to do would be to cut his losses and clear off back to Brighton, where there were plenty of things to distract his mind from the feisty stable girl, whose concerns were really none of his affair.

Even so, he lingered in the warm and inviting pub, where loud laughter and constant bantering emerged from a gaggle of locals congregated around the bar. He tried not to keep glancing at his watch, considered another beer but decided against it.

Isaac wasn't sure if he was more concerned or offended when she failed to show. The least she could do was answer her phone, or send a message, he decided, his mild concerns giving way to irritation. With no further time left to waste, he got up and left the pub, thinking he'd move his horses to another yard and forget about Farah's problems. She had her job back and had clearly decided to keep her head down. Even so, he wasn't about to leave his pampered nags in a place where there was even the slightest possibility of his inexperience in the racing game being exploited.

Disgruntled, Isaac couldn't have said why he turned his car back the way he'd just come. Instinct, he assumed afterwards. He could get to the motorway quicker if he drove through the village but something stronger than his own will forced him in the opposite direction.

His heart stuttered when he turned a corner and saw a car upended in a ditch, steam coming from under the bonnet. Someone had taken the corner too fast and come a cropper, and recently, too, by the looks of it. Isaac cut his own engine and went to help. There was no sign of the driver, who was presumably trapped inside the vehicle. There were no houses anywhere close by so the chances of the accident having already been reported were remote. He extracted his phone from his pocket and called the emergency services.

Ignoring the advice he was given to wait for help, he approached the car. Fuck, it was Farah! He could see her behind the wheel, blood spilling from a gash on her forehead, and she was unconscious. At least he hoped she was. He tried to wrench the driver's door open but it was stuck fast. The car was clearly too old to be fitted with an air bag and that omission could well have cost her her life.

Isaac thought quickly. The passenger door was buried deep in the ditch. He'd never get in that way. There was only one thing for it, he decided, looking about frantically. He found a boulder and brought it down as hard as he could against the windscreen. It cracked but didn't shatter and it took Isaac three attempts to break it, conscious all the while of showering Farah with fragments of glass. Perhaps he should wait but he couldn't hear any sirens. The emergency services would have to come some way, he assumed, and Farah still wasn't moving. Covering his hands with a jacket he grabbed from his car, he pulled the windscreen out, cursing when he still managed to cut the back of his hand, to say nothing of his expensive jacket, which was now ruined.

He reached in and touched Farah's neck, feeling relieved when he detected a regular pulse. But she was still out for the count and the smell of petrol inside the vehicle was too damned strong for comfort. He had to get her out but if she'd broken any limbs he could make matters worse.

What to do?

He called her name and she groaned but didn't open her eyes.

'Farah, wake up. You have to wake up!' He gently shook her shoulder. 'I know you can hear me.'

'Don't want to... Everything hurts.'

'Move your arms and legs for me, sweetheart.' He released her seatbelt and held her in place with one hand to prevent her slipping and perhaps hurting herself even more.

She mumbled and wiggled her fingers.

'Can you move your feet?'

'Hmm.'

'Come on, darling, you have to help me to help you.'

But she was largely unresponsive and he knew he'd never get her through the windscreen without her cooperation. Then a possibility occurred to him. He almost smiled as he looked at the driver's door from the inside. The old wreck predated central locking and the knob that locked the driver's door was engaged. Isaac didn't waste time wondering why, even if it seemed unlikely that she would lock herself in whilst driving familiar and quiet country roads.

Unless she had been spooked by something and felt threatened.

He popped the knob up, leaned over Farah's prone form and wrenched the handle open. The door creaked on its hinges when he pushed it back, bringing with it an influx of fresh air, which, combined with the hole where the windscreen should be, helped to dissipate the smell of fuel that resulted, presumably, from a ruptured fuel tank.

'Don't go anywhere.'

Isaac clambered through the windscreen, cursing when he ripped his jeans and felt a spurt of blood. He reached the driver's door as Farah partially regained consciousness, opened her eyes and groaned.

'What... How...'

'You've had an accident. I need to get you out of the car. Don't move. Let me do this.'

'Carry me,' she muttered. 'Like Daisy.'

Concerned at first that she wasn't making much sense, Isaac quickly caught on. He'd carried Daisy to her bed and she remembered. That was good.

He slid one hand beneath her bottom and the other around her shoulders and lifted her as gently as he could from the wrecked car. She cried out in pain or confusion but slid an arm around his shoulders and clung on for dear life.

Isaac carried her clear of her car and took her to his own. Opening the passenger door one-handed, he gently slid her onto the seat. Relieved to have her clear of the wrecked car, he slipped the seat belt around her semi-conscious form and went to the boot in search of his first aid kit.

'Where the hell are the emergency services?' he asked aloud.

Returning to Farah, he found her wide-eyed yet vacant, forcing him to reassess his hope that she hadn't been concussed. The gash on her temple was deep and still oozing blood.

Of course she had a damned concussion!

'Here, this will sting,' he said, gently dabbing at the blood and earning a squeal for his troubles. 'Sorry, darling, but it has to be done. The ambulance will be here soon. What happened? Can you remember? Did you lose control?'

'Puncture,' she muttered. 'Must have had a puncture.'

But Isaac knew that wasn't what had caused her accident. He'd looked at the tyres and they were all inflated, which he'd thought surprising, given the severity of the collision with the tree. A tree that had stemmed the progress of the car and probably prevented an even worse outcome.

Something else had to have caused the crash, he decided, recalling the black Rover that had shadowed him all the way to the Fox, and shuddering.

Before he could give the situation further thought, the sound of approaching sirens caused him considerable relief. Farah needed medical attention and she needed it now.

'Daisy,' she said, clutching Isaac's shirt with one hand. 'Don't tell her the truth. She worries.'

Isaac nodded. 'I understand. Don't fret. Leave her to me.'

Farah smiled and then groaned. 'Be careful!'

Isaac chuckled, touched that she was concerned for him, but whether she suspected Daisy of having designs upon his body or was warning him against darker forces, he had no way of knowing since an ambulance and the police arrived in tandem. Whilst the paramedics assessed Farah, Isaac gave a brief account of her accident to a female constable who spent more time ogling Isaac than she did making notes. No other vehicle was involved and so she didn't seem that interested.

'Insurance claim,' she said dismissively. 'Mind you, that vehicle looks dead on its feet anyway. Perhaps she did it on purpose.'

Isaac gave her a quelling look. 'They teach you to be *that* sensitive during your training, do they?' he asked acerbically.

'Oh, sorry. You quickly develop a cynical edge in this job. Goes with the territory. Is the lady a friend of yours? I just assumed...' She glanced at Isaac's Lotus and then back at Farah's wrecked jeep. 'I just assumed you were passing and...'

'Never assume,' Isaac said shortly. 'I'll arrange for the jeep to be towed. You can leave that to me.'

'Not part of our job description,' the woman said, turning to her colleague and saying something to him in an undertone.

Isaac googled local garages whilst Farah was still being assessed and arranged for the jeep to be collected. He gave specific instructions about what he wanted done once it had been towed away.

With the arrangements for the jeep's recovery in hand, Isaac returned to the ambulance.

'You need attention yourself,' one of the paramedics remarked, nodding at Isaac's various injuries.

'No need. Just scratches,' he said. 'Look after the lady.'

'We'll be taking her to the Royal Berkshire, in case you want to follow,' the guy replied. 'Do you know where it is?'

'I'll find it.' He leaned over Farah, who was strapped onto a stretcher and about to be loaded into the ambulance. 'I'll be along once I've seen Daisy,' he told her, bending to kiss her brow carefully on the uninjured side. 'Try and do as you're told in the meantime, if you possibly can.'

Farah groaned and closed her eyes, all the fight appearing to have drained out of her. For now.

* * *

Farah opened her eyes and saw halos of white lights. She felt light-headed and almost as though she was floating. The whiteness of her surroundings hurt her eyes, hurt everything, and she closed them again, wondering if she'd died and if this was the afterlife. If that's where she was, why did it have to be so damned white? she wondered.

'Ah, welcome back.' A friendly voice that she didn't recognise caught her attention and her eyes flew open again. 'Do you know where you are?'

'Somewhere white. Too white. And loud. And busy.'

'Ah, that would be because you're in the emergency department at the Royal Berkshire. Your car came off the road and you gave all of us quite a fright for a while there. You didn't seem to want to wake up.'

The person in scrubs addressing her, presumably a doctor since he had a stethoscope round his neck, indicated a chair on one side of Farah's bed. She cautiously turned her head and saw Isaac sitting there, looking large, and glamorous, concern etched into his features. Except she couldn't be absolutely sure that he was there in person and not a figment of her imagination. She was pretty sure he'd pulled her out of her wrecked car and carried her, much as he'd carried Daisy, but there again, her memory seemed determined to play tricks on her. Snippets kept filtering in and out and there was every possibility that Isaac's presence was wishful thinking on her part.

'Hey.' Isaac reached forward with a bandaged hand and touched her arm, his captivating smile tinged with genuine-seeming concern. 'Welcome back. You've been out of it for a while, sleeping on the job.'

'What...' She smacked her dry lips together and Isaac leaned forward to hold a plastic cup of water to her lips. She greedily sucked it in through a straw and closed her eyes when the cool liquid trickled down her throat. 'I can't remember much.'

'You have a nasty concussion but thankfully no broken bones,' her unnamed doctor told her. 'You were lucky. Anyway, we're keeping you in overnight for observation, but all being well, you should be able to go home in the morning, providing your man here can drive you. No work for a few days, though, and definitely no driving. Your body has suffered a trauma; you'll be bruised all over and need to give yourself time to heal.'

'Time to heal when I'm dead,' she muttered.

She heard Isaac chuckle. 'Nothing wrong with her sense of humour,' he said.

The doctor was called away and Farah found herself alone with Isaac. 'Daisy?' she asked.

'I told her you're going out to dinner with me.'

'You did what!' Farah sat bolt upright so fast that her head swam. So too did the room. She lay back down again and made do with grunting. 'What on earth did you say that for?'

'I had to tell her something.' Isaac's expression, unless Farah's concussion was playing tricks on her, looked just a little too self-satisfied. 'Her carer was there and I bribed her to stay the night. Told Daisy I'd persuaded you to come back to Brighton and catch a show.'

Farah blinked. 'And she believed you?'

'Of course she did. I can be very convincing.'

'When it comes to women, I'm perfectly sure that you can.' Farah felt ridiculously tired and fought to keep her eyes open.

'Daisy will think we're... we're...' What would Daisy think and why? It was hard to hold all her thoughts together.

'Can you remember why you came off the road?' Isaac asked gently.

Farah cautiously shook her head. 'Didn't I have a puncture?'

'No. Your tyres were all intact but they are about the only bits of your car that are, I'm afraid. It will be an insurance claim.'

'Damn!' she muttered. 'I loved that old heap. It belonged to my uncle. It served him well and had plenty of use left in it.'

She could see that Isaac wasn't convinced by her explanation but allowed her to keep her pride and didn't call her on the lie. It had been her uncle's run-around but she'd only kept it because she couldn't afford to replace it.

'I've had your jeep towed. They will be able to find out what went wrong.'

'It was well-maintained,' Farah insisted, yawning.

'Of course it was.' He bent to kiss her forehead, rather as though she was a child. If he insisted upon kissing her, then he might do a better job of it, she thought, feeling miffed. Short-changed. Angry and confused. And it was all his fault. She had never been confused about anything before meeting him.

'What are you still doing here?' she asked.

'I'll stay overnight somewhere local and drive you home when you're discharged tomorrow. We need to talk.'

She struggled to think why, then remembered Dale and Jonah. 'You don't think it was an accident, do you?'

'Right now, I don't know what to think. We'll have a better idea once the mechanics have looked over your car. Now sleep. You're all done in.'

Her eyelids drooped but she forced them open so that she could enjoy the sight of his rear end as he walked away from her. Even in torn jeans he looked like every girl's hottest fantasy. Farah sighed and closed her eyes, convinced once again that this really did have to be a figment of her imagination and that she would wake up alone and unfulfilled in her lonely bed the following morning.

* * *

Dale paced the length of his cottage, phone pressed to his ear, aghast at what he'd just learned.

'You didn't have to do that,' he protested, knowing that he was in no position to make waves but too shocked, and worried, to keep his mouth shut.

'If you'd been more careful then we wouldn't have had to,' a clipped voice responded. 'Now the interfering bitch has had a warning. Keep an eye on her and if she hooks up with Fernandez, let me know immediately.'

'She won't,' Dale replied with more confidence than he felt.

'She'd damned well better not.'

Dale breathed an audible sigh of relief. 'We need to lay low for a while,' Dale said. 'Let the dust settle.' *Or quit altogether.*

'Not happening. We own you and you do what we say. Is that clear?'

'Crystal,' Dale said, cutting the connection, then cursing and hurling his phone across the room. It hit the opposite wall and clattered to the floor in several broken pieces. 'Shit!' He fell into a chair and lowered his head into his splayed hands. 'How the fuck did it get to this?'

These people he'd got involved with sure as hell didn't muck about and he knew that Farah's *accident* had been as much a warning to him to toe the line as it had been to her. He couldn't help thinking that it had been clumsily arranged. Despite what he'd told his contact, he was pretty sure that there was something going down between Farah and Fernandez. He'd caught the way they'd glanced at one another during the auction and knew that they'd had lunch together at the Fox a few days previously. A busy man like Fernandez wouldn't spare a woman like Farah the time of day, despite her being the full package, unless there was a good reason to do so.

Jonah came into the cottage without bothering to knock, which further irritated Dale. Jonah worked for him, technically speaking, but they both knew who actually ran the show now that they were in bed together.

'What's the matter with you?' Jonah asked, helping himself to whisky and slumping down in a chair. He gave Dale's broken phone, scattered across the boarded floor, a scathing look. 'Throwing our toys out the pram now, are we?'

'Fuck off!'

'What's the latest on Farah?' Jonah asked in a disinterested voice.

'Concussion, so I hear. She's being kept in overnight.'

'And?'

'And what? Isn't that enough? She could have been killed and I didn't sign up to be a party to murder.'

'Bit late to develop a conscience,' Jonah remarked, taking a healthy slug of his drink. 'I hear Fernandez rode to her rescue.'

'Where did you hear that?' Dale had been careful not to mention the fact, even though he too had heard it.

'So much for them not being an item.' Jonah leaned back in his chair and crossed one foot over his opposite thigh. 'We might have to deal with that situation.'

'If you want to take on Fernandez then you're on your own,' Dale said forcefully. 'He is not the type of man to mess with.'

'Do as you're told,' Jonah said, sighing. 'You no longer call the shots.'

Jonah's presence in his cottage was more than enough confirmation of the fact. Dale watched him sizing the space up, as though anticipating the day when he would take it over. He was now the boss in all but name, and both men knew it, even if Jonah still toed the line in the yard.

Fuck it! Dale got up and refilled his glass. Getting so drunk that he didn't know which way was up held an appeal.

6

Isaac left the hospital, partially reassured regarding Farah's prognosis. It could have been so much worse. He'd lied to the nurses and said he was her significant other. His charm had worked; no one questioned that claim and the doctor shared his findings with him without reservation, telling Isaac how fortunate she had been.

Isaac set his chin in a grim line as he drove away from the hospital car park, dwelling upon Farah's lucky escape. The paramedics reckoned that she'd misjudged the turn and taken it too fast but Isaac wasn't buying that, not for a moment.

It didn't seem to have occurred to Farah that her accident had been no accident, not until he cross-questioned her about it. That was hardly surprising, given her concussed state. *Would she recall that the roads had been dry and that they were familiar to her?* She drove them every day. Despite the fact that her car was a heap, she was accustomed to its idiosyncrasies and even if she had been distracted, she still wouldn't drive recklessly.

Isaac admitted to himself that he had no real way of knowing if that was the case. She rode fast horses at breakneck speed for a living so perhaps she carried on her need for an adrenalin rush when behind the wheel – even a wheel attached to a slow, clapped-out car. It was possible but somehow he doubted it.

He went hot and then cold when he thought about what might have happened to her, had he not come along when he did. The fuel had been leaking. Anything could have caused it to ignite. Fuel tanks were positioned in front of the rear axles of modern cars, Isaac knew, and were protected by anti-puncture shields and some other accident-preventing gizmo.

Even so, he reasoned, as he continued towards the Fox, where he hoped to take a room for the evening, the key word was 'modern'. Farah's car clearly didn't qualify in that regard. Defective fuel lines – perhaps withered through age or neglect – routinely ruptured during accidents; an electrical spark was all it would take to ignite the leaking fuel and that would have been that.

Reaching the Fox, Isaac found an almost full car park and, upon entering the pub, an equally full bar. Jenny was on duty and spotted him immediately. She came straight over but there was no sign of her previous flirtatiousness. A hush fell over the bar as its occupants watched her, and obviously listened.

'What's all this I hear about Farah being in an accident?' she asked. The barman who had a crush on Farah ignored waiting customers, wiped his hands on a cloth and came to join them. 'Is she okay?'

Gotta love country living, Isaac thought, unsurprised that word had already reached the Fox but glad that the regulars cared enough to show concern. It was beyond time that someone other than incapacitated Daisy had Farah's back.

'Yeah, a bit battered and bruised. And concussed. They're keeping her in overnight for observation.'

'You found her?' The barman, Ben he thought he'd heard him called, made it sound like an accusation.

'Yeah, and just as well.'

'I hear that heap of hers was on the point of exploding and you rode to the rescue in the nick of time,' Jenny said, sending Isaac a flirtatious bat of her eyelashes. Having satisfied herself that Farah wasn't at death's door, she was back in full come-on mode. 'Looks like you got hurt yourself,' she added with genuine-seeming concern, nodding towards Isaac's hand that had been cleaned and bandaged by a paramedic. Her gaze drifted lower to his ripped jeans, through which the dressing on his thigh was visible. 'Need any help cleaning yourself up?'

Isaac laughed. 'I'll manage, thanks, but I do need a room for the night if there's one spare.'

'We're full,' Ben said.

'Sure, no problem,' Jenny said at the same time.

'Which is it?' Isaac asked with an easy smile that he shared between the two of them.

'We'll squeeze you in, lover, never fear. You're the hero of the hour. Of course, you might have to share.'

Isaac's horrified expression caused Jenny to roar with laughter and it took him a moment to realise that she hoped to be his roommate.

'Right,' he said, feeling rather foolish.

'Come and have a drink and tell us all about it. Does Daisy know?'

'She knows Farah won't be home tonight but not why. That's the way Farah wants it to stay.'

'She'll get to hear,' Ben said sullenly. 'She might be housebound but not much gets past her.'

'I won't take a drink right now,' Isaac said, craving privacy in which to catch up with his business affairs – the world of finance wasn't as idle as people supposed at weekends – and to decide what to do about the Farah situation. 'My need for a shower is greater.'

Jenny pouted, then grabbed a key from a board behind the bar. 'I'll show you up,' she said.

Several people whistled and raucous comments abounded as Jenny led the way to the narrow staircase accessed by a low, latched door.

'Don't mind them,' Jenny said, looking over her shoulder as she mounted the stairs. 'They've got one-track minds. Well, two actually. Most of them are wedded first and foremost to the racetrack.'

'Take it seriously, do they?'

'As a heart attack; trust me on this.'

Which caused Isaac to wonder just how far some of these hardened gamblers would go to ensure fiscal success. Tips, and not just about horses, would abound in that bar when tongues were loosened by alcohol. A lot of local lads drank there; he'd recognised some of them from the racetracks. No doubt exaggerated stories about clueless owners abounded too. He'd noticed everyone in the bar listening to what he had to say about Farah. Not all of them looked relieved that she had escaped relatively unscathed but none of them looked like the types to drive Range Rovers in a threatening manner.

What did such people look like? he wondered.

One or two of them looked highly suspicious of his presence in their midst, no doubt wondering why a high-flyer of his calibre was still hanging around. Perhaps he should have driven further afield and checked into an anonymous hotel, he belatedly decided, thinking he might be putting Farah at greater risk by showing an interest in her situation. But there again, his hanging about might cause the people behind the dangerous scam – whatever it was – to rethink their strategy.

'I thought a lot of your punters work in the industry,' Isaac remarked in a disingenuous tone. 'Surely they aren't supposed to bet.'

Jenny chuckled. 'My, for one so pretty you sure are naïve.' Jenny was puffing when they reached the landing. She inserted the key in a door and threw it open. 'There you go, sweet thing. Be it ever so humble...'

It would suffice, Isaac decided, glancing dubiously up at the low, sloping ceiling and making a mental note to duck if he needed the facilities in the dead of night.

'It's fine. Thanks for fitting me in,' he said, his tone making it clear that he knew they weren't fully booked. In all probability, he was their only guest. 'Your barman likes Farah?'

'That obvious, is it? He's been panting after her like a dog on heat for months but she barely notices him.' She watched as Isaac plonked the small bag he'd brought with him from his car, filled with basic essentials, on the bed. This wasn't the first time he'd been required to spend a night unexpectedly away from home and he'd learned to be prepared. 'I'll leave you to get settled. Come down if you fancy something to eat. The kitchen's open for another hour. Or call me if you need anything.' She gave another extravagant bat of her false lashes. 'Anything at all.'

'Thanks,' Isaac said, smiling at her because she was a good sort and he saw no harm in her. 'I'll be sure to do that.'

Left alone, Isaac checked his phone and responded quickly to the dozen messages that couldn't wait. Then he stripped off his soiled clothing and stepped cautiously under the shower that was too low for him. Everything in this place was too low but it had a certain rustic charm that Isaac appreciated.

The hot water felt good on his body and he stood under the spray for a long time, not caring if he got the dressings on his cuts wet, as he rotated his shoulders and worked out the kinks that had accumulated across his back.

He had only just dried off and towelled his hair when his phone rang. He padded naked back to his bed, remembering at the last minute to duck as he moved between the bathroom and bedroom, and recognised the number of the garage that had towed Farah's car. He'd given them a bonus for checking it out quickly. Hopefully, that's why they were calling.

'Yes,' he said abruptly.

'Mr Fernandez,' came a rough reply. 'You were right to have your suspicions about that car. It was no accident. The brake lines had been severed just enough so that the driver likely wouldn't have noticed, not in such an old vehicle. They had to be pumped at the best of times to be effective.'

Isaac nodded, even though no one could see him. It was as he had thought. 'Anything else?'

'Yeah, the fuel line had been loosened. She would have been losing petrol from the moment she turned the key, and even before then.'

'I see.'

'It must have been done not long before she drove it.'

'It couldn't have been done before? Say yesterday?'

'Nah, all the fuel would have dripped out. She'd have noticed that her tank was empty. The old heap wouldn't have started.'

'Sabotage?'

There was a long pause, during the course of which Isaac imagined the grizzly old mechanic rubbing his nose with an oily finger as he considered the possibility.

'Could be,' he eventually replied. 'Although why anyone would want to harm a wee slip of a girl...'

'Thanks,' Isaac said, aware that he'd got as much from the guy as he was ever likely to. 'Keep what we've discussed between us. I'll make it worth your while.'

'You already did. Don't worry, I'm no gossip. I like Farah.'

'You know her?' Isaac couldn't keep the surprise out of his voice.

'It's a small town. Knew her uncle. I told him that old heap had had its day before he popped his clogs. Shocked me rigid when Farah insisted upon keeping it. I did my best to ensure it was road-worthy but it was an uphill battle. Anyway, tell her Tom says hello and wishes her well.'

'Will do, Tom. Thanks.'

Isaac cut the connection and strolled to the window, thinking about what he'd just heard, none of which had come as any great surprise to him. Whatever was going down here in Lambourn, it amounted to a lot more than race fixing, he now accepted. Some heavy hitters were involved – the type of people who took no prisoners and snubbed out inquisitive bystanders as casually as the majority of people swatted irritating flies.

Just one problem: they hadn't counted on Isaac involving himself and he had connections most people could only dream about. He had intended to move his horses out of Lambourn and forget about a situation he didn't have time for, but Tom's account had changed everything. He scowled down at the car park, deciding then and there to take on Farah's problems and to make them personal. They *were* personal, given that his horses had been involved, and Isaac was no one's patsy.

Besides, he felt a connection to Farah that none of his dates had managed to inspire, despite their best efforts. He was convinced, if more conviction was necessary following the sabotage to her car, that she was in very real danger. She knew it, too, but he also suspected that nothing would prevent her from involving herself out of some misguided sense of responsibility. Isaac shook his head, determined to protect her from her own impetuosity.

He picked up his phone again, scrolled through his contacts and punched out a number. It was answered on the first ring. Isaac identified himself but didn't waste time on pleasantries.

'I need you to try and trace a black Range Rover. I have a partial index.' He reeled it off from memory. 'Likely registered in Lambourn or thereabouts but not necessarily.'

'I'm on it. Anything else?'

'Yep, get me all you have on a guy called Dale Drummond; he's the foreman at Guy Levant's racing yard in Lambourn. Check out the head lad, Jonah, as well. Don't know his surname.' But Isaac knew his man would find it in seconds flat. 'I need to know if either of them has had so much as a parking ticket in the last ten years. Oh, and look into Guy's connections whilst you're at it, too.'

'I take it you want this yesterday.'

'I do but I want it accurate. Sorry,' he added hastily, aware that he would have offended his investigator's sensibilities. 'Something's going on, Ray, and it's getting dangerous.'

'Want me to come down?'

'Perhaps, but not yet. Right now, you're more use to me doing what you do best behind your computer screens.'

'Right. I'll be in touch.'

The phone went dead. Still naked, Isaac pulled on the clean jeans and T-shirt from his overnight bag and pocketed his phone and wallet. His stomach rumbled and glancing at his watch he realised the kitchen was about to close. With a sigh, he headed for the door. It was either a case of enduring Jenny's flirting and the inquisition he'd get from the locals or starving.

Isaac enjoyed his creature comforts and had no intention of depriving himself of a decent meal. *How hard could it be to fend off one woman?* Besides, if he got chatting with the locals, there's no telling what snippets they might give away – intentionally or otherwise.

* * *

Farah opened her eyes and this time didn't find the white quite so dazzling. The throbbing inside her head had calmed to a dull ache but she felt rested and... well, alive, which was an improvement. She wiggled her arms and legs and winced, resigned to being bruised all over. Fragments of the accident came back to her, causing her to shiver. She'd been lucky. More than lucky. If Isaac hadn't...

Her gaze swivelled to the chair beside her bed, now empty. Had Isaac actually been there or was his presence a part of the weird flashes that had gone through her head on a looping kaleidoscopic prism? What time was it? What day was it? How long had she been here?

Her panic increased and a machine at her side started to beep.

'Ah, good morning.' A large, cheerful nurse appeared, pressed a button to stop the beeping and took Farah's vital signs. 'How are you feeling?'

'A good question.' At least Farah now knew that it was morning. 'Did I sleep all night? Was someone else here? What day is it?'

'That gorgeous man of yours had to be thrown out.' The nurse chuckled. 'Not sure what you did to land him but if I were you I'd keep him on a short leash. Anyway, he said he'd be back this morning to take you home, once the doctor's checked you over and given you the all-clear, of course. And yes, you did sleep all night. You needed to but we gave you a little something to help in that regard. And you've been here since late yesterday afternoon.' She noted something on a chart. 'Now, if that answers all your questions, I have one for you. Are you hungry?'

Farah shrugged, and winced when her muscles protested. She wasn't, not really, but knew they likely wouldn't let her go unless she ate.

'Something light would be appreciated. And hot tea,' she added, warming to the idea. 'If it's not too much trouble.'

'I'll organise it,' the nurse replied, plumping up Farah's pillows and bustling off, her wide hips swaying as they strained against the fabric of her scrubs.

The noise of a busy hospital ward buzzed through Farah's head as she lay back and waited. The woman in the next bed sent her a friendly smile but Farah closed her eyes, pretending not to notice. She was in no mood for comparing ailments, complaining about hospital food or talking about anything at all.

Instead, she needed some peace and quiet in order to try to figure out what had happened to her. Her head might be clearer but the lead-up to her accident – if that's what it had been – was still hazy. Flashes came back to her. A big car following her. She had dismissed it as irrelevant, thinking it was one of the owners leaving the yard. Now she wasn't so sure. There had been something sinister about it; she recalled thinking so at the time. Why, she could not have said.

Instinct, she supposed.

But she hadn't been forced off the road and the driver hadn't intimidated her by getting too close, so why did she feel it was so vitally important? She shook her head impatiently, wondering what Isaac was doing about it, if anything, and what he had found out. She suspected that he wouldn't have been idle but did he really intend to come and collect her? It was Sunday so perhaps he'd spare a few hours away from his computer screens to take her back to Daisy. Daisy, who never tired of lecturing Farah about the need to get a life for herself. Specifically, to get a man. One look at Isaac and she would have put two and two together and come up with seventeen. Farah chuckled, thinking she would have them married off in her mind by now.

If only!

Farah rolled her eyes. It hurt. Everything hurt whichever way she moved, a physical reminder of the fact that she was lucky to be alive. The seat belt, where it had dug into her shoulder and saved her from going through the windscreen, had left her with tender ribs and, no doubt, bruising.

An orderly appeared with her breakfast and placed it on a tray across her knees. Farah nibbled on a slice of toast and enjoyed the sensation of the weak, lukewarm tea trickling down her throat. She had only just finished when a harried doctor who looked far too young to be qualified came to check her over and give her the all-clear. The same cheerful nurse came to help her wash and dress. The effort drained Farah's resources and she felt like climbing back into the uncomfortable hospital bed. She squared her aching shoulders and fell into the bedside chair instead, waiting for Isaac to arrive.

The sound of several nurses laughing close to the entrance to the ward caused the nurse who was still with her to chuckle.

'If I had to guess, I'd say that's your young man getting my colleagues' collective hearts fluttering,' she said.

Before Farah could respond, Isaac's handsome face appeared round the edge of the curtains that the nurse had pulled when she'd helped Farah to dress.

'I could have been indecent!' Farah protested.

'I can see you're feeling better,' Isaac replied, grinning.

'I'm allowed to go home.'

'So I've just been told.' Isaac held out a hand and effortlessly helped her to her feet. 'You okay to walk to the car?'

'I am not an invalid,' she protested, turning to the nurse with a smile and thanking her for her efforts.

'My pleasure, honey,' she replied. 'You just take good care now and look after that young man of yours. He's a keeper.'

Farah blushed scarlet and didn't dare to look in Isaac's direction. Even so, she sensed that his grin had returned and wanted to kick him, or something, for being so smug. Instead, she linked her hand through the crook of his arm, worried that she really wouldn't be able to walk if she didn't lean on him. But developing the habit of leaning on Isaac Fernandez would, she knew, be most unwise.

'Do all discharged patients get the VIP treatment?' she asked, amused to see so many nurses making excuses to linger as they walked past them, all of them making cow eyes at Isaac.

'Only the cute ones, I expect.'

'Somehow, I don't think all these ladies are trying to impress me.' Conscious of the fact that Isaac was walking slowly for her sake, she tried to speed up but winced when her ribs protested.

'Take it easy. There's no rush. You're pretty bashed up and need time to heal. No charging around on horses for you for a few weeks.'

'What are you, my doctor?' she asked irascibly, immediately regretting her tetchy response. None of this was Isaac's fault – quite the opposite. 'I don't think I've properly thanked you for saving my life,' she said, her voice small and not quite steady.

He patted the hand that he'd cradled beneath his elbow. 'You are entirely welcome. The world would be a poorer place without you in it.'

It was her turn to chuckle. 'Does that line always work for you?'

He sent her a surprised look. 'No idea. I've never used it before. And, just for the record, I meant it. You have a certain style that's rare.'

'Oh.' That took the wind out of Farah's sails. 'I assume you're taking me back to Daisy's.'

'I am. You won't be able to keep the truth from her. It was all over the Fox when I got back there last night.'

'You stayed at the Fox?' She fixed his profile with an amused look. 'You spent a night under the same roof as Jenny and came out the other end unscathed.'

'I locked my door. And, just so you're aware, Jenny seemed very concerned about you.'

Farah nodded. 'She's one of the good guys.'

'But your friend the barman looked as though he wanted to use a blunt axe to remove my head from my shoulders.'

'He's a sweet kid but I don't encourage him.'

'I'm sure you don't. You could do a lot better.'

'I don't have time for dating. I work long hours, have to get up ridiculously early and, of course, I have Daisy to worry about.'

'All work and no play?'

'I could say the same about you but it wouldn't be true, I guess, given how often you're seen in the papers with some stunning babe on your arm.'

'Believe it or not, that's work too. There's no one special in my life.' He smiled at her and the simple gesture had the effect of turning her sore insides to mulch. 'Being in the public eye is all about perceptions. People see what they expect to see and draw their own conclusions.'

'A successful man who can attract the hottest dates must be a safe pair of hands for their investments?'

Isaac winked at her. 'Something like that.'

'What do the women get out of it?'

'Same thing. A boost for their modelling careers, or whatever it is that they're into. Basically, they get in the papers and get themselves noticed.'

Farah assumed they would like to be into Isaac on a permanent basis but decided against going there.

'Anyway, Daisy needs to know what happened to you.'

Farah's smile faded. 'My accident was no accident, was it?' she asked.

'No,' he replied, again patting her hand as they walked from the hospital and crossed the car park at a slow pace. His voice was a gentle caress but his expression was set in stone. When angry, Isaac Fernandez was one dangerous man, she decided. 'I don't think it was.'

7

Isaac could see that Farah was in pain but fighting it. Of course she was! Farah was tough, although probably not as tough as she imagined. Getting into his low car would be a test of the toughness in question. He should have thought of that and hired a taxi or something. He opened the door and took as much of her weight in his hands as he could whilst she slowly lowered herself into place.

'Got it, thanks,' she said through gritted teeth.

Isaac trotted round to the driver's side, climbed into the car and fastened her seat belt for her. 'You might want to hold it away from your body,' he suggested, watching her do so before starting the car and moving out of his parking space at a sedate speed the car hadn't been built for.

'Tell me what you think happened,' she said, as he waited for a gap in the traffic and moved onto the main road. 'I assume you have a theory.'

'I think it was sabotage,' he replied, anger radiating through his body. He glanced sideways to gauge her reaction but apart from swallowing, she took the news remarkably calmly. 'You don't look surprised.'

'I've had time to think and it might surprise you to learn that I'm not stupid.'

'I'm gobsmacked.'

She smiled. 'Seriously, though, I've driven that road a thousand times. I know it like the back of my hand.'

'I'd reached the same conclusion.'

'The brakes felt spongy. They always are but I did notice when I left the yard that they had got worse and thought I'd really have to do something about it.' She sniffed. 'I loved that old jeep. It was my last connection to my uncle.'

'Other than your memories,' Isaac replied softly. 'No one can steal them.'

'I'd like to see them try!'

Isaac chuckled. 'No one in their right mind would dare.'

'Was it the brakes?' she asked after a short spell of silence that Isaac felt disinclined to break.

'It was. Someone had tampered with them.'

'Oh.' She swallowed for a second time.

'But the fuel line had been loosened, too, which meant fuel was leaking out slowly and would likely have ignited, had I not called the emergency services and got you out of the car before it could happen.'

She gulped. 'You really did save my life.'

He took his left hand off the wheel and covered one of her own with it. 'You okay? Stupid question, of course you're not.'

'I had already worked out that someone was trying to warn me off. All I need to decide now is what I'm being warned away from. Presumably it's something to do with whatever's going on at the yard, which means...' She gulped. 'Which means that Dale must have spoken to someone about my suspicions. Either that or he took matters into his own hands.' She shook her head decisively.

'Whatever he's got himself mixed up with, I don't believe he's a killer. He wouldn't.' She blinked away tears. 'Would he?'

'It's hard to know what any person will do when backed into a corner. Even so, I do know that this was more than a warning, Farah.' Isaac glowered at the twisting road ahead of him as they neared the spot where the incident had occurred. Far from closing her eyes, Farah stared intently at the place where her car had gone off the road as Isaac slowed for the bend. 'If it had only been the brakes, that would have been a warning.'

She looked away from the roadside and nodded. 'Someone wanted me to go up in a blazing inferno,' she said, shuddering. 'But it wasn't Dale. I refuse to believe he'd go that far.'

'Right, then I fully intend to find out who's pulling his strings.'

'How will you do that? You stand out down here. Best leave it to me.'

'Do you want to die?' he asked, annoyed by her recklessness.

'I'll pretend that I believe my car gave out on me. No one will doubt it. Even by stable hands' standards, mine was an accident waiting to happen. It was an in joke in the tack room.'

'Even so, I—'

'I might suspect Dale and Jonah of... well, some sort of skulduggery to do with making a quick buck. Jonah is always short of money and Dale... well, Dale has expensive habits to feed. Even so, I am absolutely convinced that Dale wouldn't resort to murder.' She paused. 'I'm less sure about Jonah.'

Isaac nodded but was not convinced. He had learned early in his career never to trust anyone until they proved themselves to be trustworthy, never to believe what he was told without independent collaboration and never ever to take any situation at face value. And there was most definitely more to the current situation than met the eye.

'Here we are,' he said, pulling up at the side of Daisy's cottage.

He got out the car and went round to help Farah, who cried out when he gently extracted her from the vehicle.

'Sorry, didn't mean to jolt you.'

'Thanks,' she replied, briefly closing her eyes and blowing air through her lips. 'Ever thought of buying a more practical car?'

'Pots and kettles spring to mind,' he replied, grinning.

'I'll have you know that I was sentimentally attached to my car. Bet you can't say the same about your penis-extender,' she replied feistily, glancing back at his gleaming Lotus.

'Penis-extender?' He raised a brow in amusement. 'That's making a bit of an assumption.'

Farah felt her cheeks warm. 'Well, you know what they say about men who feel the need for flashy sports cars. They are almost always compensating for something.'

'I'll have to take your word for it.'

Farah giggled. 'Naturally.'

They entered the cottage to be greeted by Betty, the most loyal of Daisy's carers, whom Isaac had bribed to remain on duty. She beamed at them both, then took one look at Farah and her face fell.

'My goodness, darlin',' she said in a strong West Indian lilt, 'you have been in the wars.'

'You should see the other guy,' Farah quipped.

'What can I get you? Daisy's been asking for you.'

'You can get off now, if you like,' Isaac said, reaching for his wallet and slipping the woman a generous amount, over and above what had been agreed. 'I'll look after them both.'

'I'll bet you will,' Betty replied, her eyes sparkling. 'Not all bad news then, Farah.'

'You are incorrigible, Betty,' Farah said, laughing.

'If I knew what the word meant, I'd likely agree with you.' She flipped through the wad of notes that Isaac had given her and her eyes widened. 'Most generous of you. Thank you, kind sir.'

'You're welcome,' Isaac replied.

'Come on,' Farah said, once Betty had collected up her possessions and bustled off through the door that Isaac held open for her. 'We'd best face the inquisition.'

'Darling!' Daisy half rose from her chair in the sunroom when Farah and Isaac walked in. 'How was your evening out?'

'Oh, Daisy.' Farah cautiously hugged the older lady. 'I had a bit of an accident but as you can see, I'm absolutely fine.'

'I did hear.' Daisy's face was crowded with worry. 'Despite Isaac's best efforts to deceive me.' She sent Isaac a mildly condemning look. 'One phone call to the Fox was all it took to get to the truth.'

'Ben!' Farah and Isaac said together.

'He was concerned. I knew you must still be alive, otherwise Isaac would have had to tell me the truth and when he assured me you would be home today, I knew it couldn't be *that* serious.' She turned her attention to Isaac. 'I appreciate your efforts to protect my feelings but I prefer to know the truth. That way, it saves me from unnecessary speculation. I might be physically impaired but there's nothing wrong with my brain. At least not so far as I'm aware.'

'Duly noted,' Isaac said, accepting the reprimand with good grace.

'Blame me, Daisy,' Farah said, wincing as she lowered herself into a chair. 'I made him promise not to tell you.'

'Well, you're here and you can tell me now.' She wagged a crooked finger. 'All of it.'

'This requires tea,' Isaac said. 'I'll make some.'

He levered himself from his chair and took himself off to do precisely that, leaving the two ladies to talk in private for a few minutes. He stared out at the garden as he waited for the kettle to boil, trying to assess what he knew about a serious situation that really required police involvement and how much to reveal to Daisy. In the end he decided upon complete transparency. What little information Ray had so far come up with pointed to a strong local connection and Daisy, who did indeed appear to hear anything worth knowing without stirring from her cottage, might well be able to point them in the right direction.

A connection with much greater sway than the manager of a racing yard, he had already decided, despite the fact that Dale appeared to be up to his neck in it. It was possible that Daisy would know who the perpetrator – the person who would heartlessly order a young woman's vehicle to be terminally tampered with – might be and would relish the opportunity to point Isaac in the right direction, if only to prevent Farah from recklessly heading off on her own mission.

He made the tea with old-fashioned loose leaves, assembled cups, milk and sugar on a tray and carried it through.

'Here we are,' he said, interrupting a tête-à-tête between the two ladies.

'Is there anything you can't do?' Farah demanded with a small smile.

'Anyone can make tea,' he replied easily, placing the tray on the table in front of Daisy, thinking it unnecessary to remind her that he would likely have starved had he not taken over domestic duties at a young age in the unremarkable semi he'd grown up in.

Realising that neither lady had the strength to strain the tea and serve it, Isaac did the honours and then sat back with his cup in hand, watching the pair of them.

'Well, Isaac,' Daisy said in her slurred voice that made it hard to always understand what she was attempting to say. 'Farah has explained that my husband's car finally failed her but that isn't the complete truth, is it?'

Isaac glanced at Farah, who gave a reluctant nod. 'No,' he said, 'it was tampered with, causing Farah to lose control and veer off the road into a tree.'

Daisy inhaled sharply but otherwise remained relatively calm. 'That would account for the bump on the head,' she said, eyeing Farah's bruised forehead with total adoration in her expression.

'Isaac came along and rescued me, I'm told,' Farah said. 'I don't remember much about it.'

'The car's a write-off, I'm afraid,' Isaac said.

'Thank goodness,' Daisy said with feeling.

'I loved that car,' Farah protested.

'It had had its day, darling,' Daisy insisted. 'I kept trying to tell you that it was an accident waiting to happen.'

'Except this was no accident,' Farah pointed out.

'Indeed.' Daisy nodded, then glanced at Isaac. 'Your remaining in the area makes me think you know more than you're saying.'

'Perhaps, but first, why had you locked the driver's door, Farah?' he asked. 'I couldn't get it open so had to smash the windscreen to get to you.' He glanced down at the dressing on his hand. 'I thought the door had been warped shut in the accident, but in actual fact, it was locked. Just as well since I was able to unlock it from the inside, otherwise I'd never have got you out. Do you ordinarily lock yourself in on the drive home?'

'No,' she admitted, scowling in a clear effort to recall. 'But there was something... a car. I was being followed.'

'It is a public road,' Daisy said. 'Other cars are allowed to use it, darling.'

'I know but there was something about this one. Something that made me uncomfortable.'

'Did its driver get too close?' Isaac asked. 'Did you feel intimidated?'

'No. At least, I don't think so. It's hard to remember. Everything comes back to me in jumbled flashes, in no particular order. It's frustrating.'

She shook her head cautiously, implying that she still had a headache. Isaac nodded significantly towards the painkillers that the hospital had given her when she was discharged. The bottle had been abandoned on the table next to the tea tray. Farah snatched it up and swallowed one of the tablets with a swig of tea before sending Isaac a *satisfied?* look.

He grinned back at her, ignoring her fit of pique. The painkillers were, he'd been told, strong and likely to make her sleep. Sleep was what she needed right now. Sleep was nature's cure. Sleep was good. He also knew that she must be in considerable discomfort to have taken one without it being forced down her throat. She could teach a mule a thing or two about stubbornness.

'The car that was following you,' Isaac prompted. 'Was it distinctive? What do you remember about it?'

'Nothing specific, only that it made me feel uncomfortable and so I locked the doors. Then it turned off and I forget about it.'

'Was it by any chance a black Range Rover?'

Farah blinked up at Isaac. 'Yes, actually, it could well have been. It was certainly a large, dark SUV. How did you know?'

'It followed me all the way to the Fox, prior to your accident, and wanted me to know it was there,' Isaac said with a grimace.

'Did you see who was driving?' Daisy asked.

'Tinted windows, so no. All I could see was two men in the front, both of them bulky.'

'You were right to be worried then, darling,' Daisy said, smiling lopsidedly at Farah.

'I got a partial registration,' Isaac said, 'and have someone attempting to track it down. BGH something. Mean anything to either of you?'

The ladies exchanged a glance. Farah looked blank but Daisy's expression darkened.

'It's a personalised plate,' she said. 'We get a few of them around here although who the owners are attempting to impress is less clear to me. Anyway, that particular one belongs to Brian Hadleigh, a recent incomer and millionaire,' she said.

'Hadleigh?' Isaac asked, doing his level best to keep his feelings under guard. He knew him as a hard man to be reckoned with, a man with overall control of everything illegal in the part of London where Isaac had grown up. He hadn't supposed that their paths would cross ever again. He thought he'd put that phase of his life well and truly behind him. What the hell was he doing in Lambourn? Talk about a fish out of water. But whatever had brought him here, Isaac knew it couldn't be good news. 'Is he involved with horses?'

'He has his fingers in any number of pies,' Daisy said. 'There was a lot of talk when he moved down here from London about criminal ties, but as far as I'm aware he's never done anything to attract police attention since his move.'

'It would be the height of stupidity to follow someone in such a distinctive car, *with* a personalised plate, unless it was a warning,' Isaac said, deliberately not elaborating on Daisy's remarkably accurate gossip sensor, 'and anyone with half a brain and who knows even the most rudimentary facts about me would know that I don't back away from a fight.' *Especially when my nemesis chooses to provoke me.*

'He does have a couple of horses in training,' Farah said, 'but not at Guy's yard. He considered it but finished up going elsewhere. Guy was upset about that. Not sure what swayed Hadleigh's decision.'

'Even so, I don't see him taking such drastic measures over a little horse rivalry,' Daisy said, eyeing Isaac speculatively, as though she realised he was being deliberately reticent. 'I've met him a few times. Him and his wife of forty-odd years. He's charming but I didn't think much of her. She's too self-aware for my taste. Asked my carer if I take sugar, as though my incapacity prevents me from speaking for myself,' she added indignantly, producing a hoot of laugher from Farah. 'He has a couple of adult sons who come and go and several other tough-looking individuals constantly hanging around, which is probably who followed you. I doubt whether Hadleigh did it himself.'

'Very likely not,' Isaac agreed, furrowing his brow as several unsavoury possibilities flitted through his brain. If there was race fixing going on, he was pretty damned sure that Hadleigh would be pulling the strings from a safe distance. He wouldn't be able to help himself. If he'd taken his horses to another trainer, it would enable him to distance himself from the dirty doings at Guy's yard and come out whiter than white when the truth emerged.

When didn't he?

'He lives on a big, gated estate with acres of land just outside of Lambourn in the direction of Newbury. Bought it at auction from the previous owner who'd lost all his money in some sort of scam, I hear,' Daisy said. 'Anyway, word is he got it for a song because the other guy was desperate and now he lords it like... well, like the lord of the manor. His wife does anyway.'

'I'll get my people on to him. See what pops up.'

Isaac already knew what they would find but wasn't ready to share aspects of his colourful past with the ladies quite yet. He needed time to think about Hadleigh's involvement. One thing was for sure: Hadleigh hadn't left London for the sake of his health and had certainly not retired. Men of his ilk never did.

'Why would he go to so much trouble to tamper with Guy's

horses? That's the question.' Farah hid a wide yawn behind her hand.

'You need to rest,' Isaac said, standing and using her fatigue as an excuse not to answer her question. 'So I'll get out of your hair. Is there anything that I can do for either of you first?'

'Are you going back to Brighton?' Farah asked, failing to keep the disappointment out of her voice.

'For now,' he said, glancing at his watch. 'There's a meeting in the morning that I can't get out of. Lay low and rest, Farah, and don't trust anyone. Obviously, you can't work.' She opened her mouth to protest and then closed it again with no words emerging. Isaac could see it irritated her to accept that he was right and suspected that her bed had never seemed so appealing. 'Your carer will be back at her usual time, I gather,' he said, glancing at Daisy.

'You seem to have thought of everything.'

Farah made it sound like an accusation but Isaac knew her reaction was a manifestation of her frustration. She herself wasn't physically fit enough to help Daisy in the way that she normally did and it rankled.

'You are very considerate,' Daisy said, smiling at him.

'I'll walk you out,' Farah said, forcing herself to her feet and clearly trying not to wince when her ribs protested.

Isaac took his leave of Daisy, having assured himself that she was perfectly comfortable where she was and didn't need to go to her room, and then followed Farah into the hall.

'Tell me what you know about Hadleigh that you didn't say in front of Daisy,' Isaac said as soon as they were alone, sensing that there was something.

'He's a heavy gambler. Well, a player in all respects, come to that.' She rolled her eyes. 'Thinks he's God's gift to women.'

'He tried it on with you?' Isaac asked, scowling.

'More than that. He made me an offer he seemed to think I would struggle to refuse and was none too pleased when I did so.'

'Did he indeed. Can't fault his taste.'

'Not *that* sort of offer. Well,' she added, when he raised a cynical brow, 'perhaps his offer was all-inclusive; we didn't get that far. He has wandering hands, that's for sure, but I made it apparent to him that I wasn't interested, despite the fact that he flaunts his wealth and made it crystal clear that I'd want for nothing if I played nice.'

'So much for forty years of marital bliss,' Isaac replied, a cynical edge to his voice since he'd known that Daisy had got that big wrong. 'What precisely did he want you to do for him?'

'He said he'd heard my name spoken about in glowing terms when it came to horses. He wanted to open his own stud and asked if I'd help him get it off the ground.' She slowly shook her head. 'It didn't sound plausible to me and anyway, I don't know much about that side of the business, which he would have realised if he'd done his research.'

'Which made you suspicious?'

'Yep. Why a stud? I mean, he admitted that he barely knew one end of a horse from the other so why would he want to jump in at the deep end? Besides, I know he fell out with Guy about something. Guy said they couldn't agree terms, that Hadleigh refused to stump up his usual fees to train his horses, and made some disparaging remark about those with the most disposable income being the tightest with it. But... I don't know.' She paused to reflect. 'I got the impression that Guy felt he was being coerced and he was in a foul temper for days after that. He heard that Hadleigh had approached me and warned me away from him. Said he was bad news.'

'Well then, it could be that Hadleigh's beef with Guy runs deeper than we suppose and that he's getting his revenge any which way he can.'

'By turning Dale and perhaps Jonah against Guy?' Farah felt deeply troubled by that possibility. 'I don't see it myself.'

'What do you really know about Guy?'

Farah leaned a shoulder cautiously against a wall and folded her arms gently across her torso. 'He's a local lad who showed promise and who went abroad to train. He was in France for a while, rode quite a few winners before he gave up the struggle to make the weight, then came back married to Michelle and...' She unfolded her arms and spread her hands. 'The rest is history.'

'His wife's family supplied the money for his set-up?' Isaac's mind drifted towards the attractive Frenchwoman, to whom he had never really warmed. He recalled the open day. She had been there but looked as though she would prefer to be somewhere else. Isaac had tried to engage her in conversation but she'd failed to meet his eye, made an excuse to walk away, and their paths hadn't crossed after that for the rest of the day.

'That's what everyone believes.' Farah sent Isaac a speculative look. 'But you think it has something to do with Hadleigh?' She paused. 'All the stuff I've just told you – none of it came as a surprise, did it? I noticed how you managed to avoid Daisy's questions about Hadleigh just now. You're very good at deflection. So come on, give. What are you not telling me?'

Isaac held up both hands. 'I'll have my guy do some digging and see what pops up. We'll talk again then.'

'See, you're doing it again!'

He smiled at her frustration, then lowered his head and gently kissed her brow. 'Keep in touch and let me know if anything else happens. I'll delve into Hadleigh's background and see if I can find a connection between him and Guy. I'll be back in a couple of days.'

'Isaac—'

He turned with his hand on the door handle. 'Yes. What is it?'

'Thank you,' she said. 'I haven't been very gracious but I want you to know that I do appreciate your help, even if I'm sorry that you got dragged into the mess.'

His sexy smile appeared to resonate with her and her cheeks flooded with colour. Good! She wasn't quite so impervious to his charms as she pretended to be. 'My pleasure, darling,' he replied. 'And you didn't drag me into anything. Dale did that when he interfered with my horses.' He winked at her. 'See you very soon.'

8

Brian Hadleigh leaned back in his chair, listening to his sons as they tried to justify their clumsy handling of the Farah Ash situation. Doing his level best not to let his volatile temper get the better of him, he already knew he was fighting a losing battle in that regard.

'We fixed her car. She don't drive fast enough to kill herself,' Mark protested. 'You told us to give her a warning and that's what we did.'

Brian shook his head, wondering how he could have bred two such imbeciles. If he'd been that stupid on the way up, he wouldn't have lasted five minutes. He'd been too soft with them, he accepted. Once he'd earned a few bob and was in a position to indulge them, he'd wanted them to have the best of everything, all the things he'd had to go without when he'd been a kid. But he hadn't had much time for them in their formative years, he'd been too busy establishing himself as a hard man who no one crossed, and so had failed to instil in them a healthy respect for the value of money, which he now accepted had been a miscalculation.

Everything had come too easily for them and they traded on the fear that their surname engendered. They'd enjoyed lording it around the manor and knocking a few heads together when called for, but they hadn't had to depend on their wits to stay ahead of the opposition. Thinking wasn't their strong point and they were better at taking orders. They were, he hated to say it, despite their gym-enhanced bulk, weak and soft.

'She got the message,' Henry added in defence of his brother, breaking the awkward silence that Brian had permitted to develop.

Brian threw back his head and resisted the urge to yell with frustration. 'She *almost* lost her fucking life, you morons, and if that had happened it would have brought the filth piling in. You know they're just waiting for an excuse to turn us over.'

'There's nothing to connect us to—'

'There's always something. And worse, Fernandez rescued her.'

'We was gonna get her out ourselves but when he turned up…' Henry shrugged and let his words trail off.

Brian couldn't believe what he'd just heard. 'You were going to let her see your ugly mugs. That was your brilliant master plan?' Brian shook his head. 'We're trying to keep a low profile out here in the sticks.'

Brian tried not to think about the Albanians who had taken over most of his patch and forced him out of London. It brought bile to his throat whenever his mind dwelt upon that humiliation and did his ulcer no favours. He wouldn't admit it to a living soul, but they scared the shit out of him and Brian didn't scare easily. They were a new breed of thug who enjoyed inventing increasingly violent forms of torture, from which women and even kids were not excluded.

There was no code of conduct within the ranks of the current generation of villains.

'The girl's already suspicious of the activities at Levant's yard,' Brian reminded his sons, striving to remain calm. His doctors had warned him about getting overexcited and causing a spike in his blood pressure. All well and good but the fucking doctors didn't have to deal with these wankers on a daily basis. 'If you two turned up at the scene of her supposed accident, she ain't stupid enough to think it a coincidence. Now Fernandez is in her corner. He took her to hospital, stayed overnight at the Fox and picked her up this morning. Now why do you suppose he did that?'

'Because he wants to get into her knickers, I expect,' Mark said, smirking. 'Can't say as I blame him.'

'God give me strength,' Brian muttered.

'You told us to make it look accidental and we did,' Henry protested, sharing a bewildered look with his brother. 'Anyway, she won't be able to work for a while so she'll have to keep her nose out of our business.'

Brian looked at them both: handsome, muscle-bound kids without much between the ears. His wife had mollycoddled them, which hadn't helped, and although they were now both in their twenties they still ran to Mummy and complained if Brian got heavy with them. All for a peaceful life, he'd let Marion have her way in the past, aware that she wouldn't make waves about his series of affairs, pretending not to know that Brian regularly played away, provided her boys didn't feel the sharp side of his tongue. Or worse.

In retrospect, that had been a mistake, too, he conceded. Marion would do as she was fucking well told. She'd long ago lost interest in sleeping with him but her taste for spending his money had never waned. Be that as it may, her fussing over the boys had made them soft targets. If anything happened to Brian then the Albanians would disrespect the fragile truce and move in within days to take over what was left of his empire, well aware that Mark and Henry didn't have the nous to control it. He'd spent a lot of time and effort making his business affairs seem legitimate, on the surface, and he had absolutely no intention of letting the Albanians get their greedy mitts on arguably the most profitable little earner he'd ever devised.

No, sir – no way.

He'd diversified into property but the bulk of his income still came from supplying drugs. And one or two other interesting little sidelines: old scores that he was now in a position to indulge himself by settling. In the meantime, Brian sat here in the Berkshire countryside in his mini-palace, playing the part of the country squire and watching the plod chasing their tails as they failed to pin anything on him. It was amusing. In a way, he supposed, the Albanians had done him a favour but being forced out and losing face still rankled.

With the incompetence of these two morons, the local filth might well get their wish, turning Brian into a laughing stock in the process. The Farah situation – the fact that she'd realised something wasn't right at the yard and had the courage to tackle Dale over it – was a concern. The fact that she now appeared to have linked up with Fernandez was downright worrying. He and Fernandez had previous. Isaac hadn't always been a high-flyer and he knew how to fight dirty.

He hoped that for once his sons had got it right and that Fernandez had only stuck around because he had the hots for Farah. But somehow he doubted it. The idiots had attracted the interest of a wealthy and determined guy who Brian most definitely didn't want to have poking his nose into his affairs since he had his own plans for the wanker.

'There's some collections to be done,' he said, dismissing his sons with a flap of one hand before he completely lost it. 'Get up to town and see if you can do that without screwing it up.'

'Aw, Pa,' Mark whined, 'I had plans for tonight.'

Henry took one look at the rigid set to Brian's features and tugged at his brother's arm. 'Come on,' he said. 'Let's get it done, then we can play.'

Alone, Brian leaned back in his chair, trying to assess the damage. It had been a mistake to try to send Farah a warning, he now realised, especially when it was his sons he'd entrusted with what should have been a simple task. He hadn't thought he needed to spell it out to them but should have known better. Her heap of a car had been an accident waiting to happen for months and that particular message was far too obscure. It would be looked upon as precisely that – a long overdue accident from which she was lucky to have escaped – just so long as no one looked too closely at the wreckage. That shouldn't have happened but with Fernandez now involved, and if he learned that these days Brian lived in the area, he would get suspicious and definitely start digging.

'Fuck it!' Brian picked up his glass and flung it at the wall. The expensive crystal shattered into a thousand shards and tumbled onto the Turkish rug that Marion had insisted upon and which had cost Brian an arm and a leg.

A physical warning in a dark corner one night, Brian decided, returning his thoughts to Farah, would have better fitted the bill. He should have insisted upon it.

He sighed when the door opened and his wife stormed through it.

'What the hell?' She looked at the broken glass and sighed, having the good sense not to harp on about it. 'What have you said to the boys?' she asked instead. 'They look like they've had their arses slapped with a wet haddock.'

Brian eyed the woman who had once been the love of his life with icy disdain. She'd let herself go, piled on the pounds and over-done the plastic surgery in an attempt to reclaim her lost youth. She'd been a real looker during the youth in question, a knockout, and Brian had pulled out all the stops to impress her. Now her face was frozen into a permanent scowl and she couldn't smile even if she felt so inclined, which she never seemed to. Was it any wonder that Brian looked elsewhere for his leisure activities?

'Don't start, Marion,' he said, holding up a warning hand. 'I ain't in the mood.'

'I don't care what you get up to, Brian Hadleigh. As far as I'm concerned your floozies are welcome to your inadequate dick. But don't take your bad temper out on the boys. Nothing they ever do meets with your approval, which ain't fair. You know, all they care about is impressing you.'

Brian was still smarting about the 'inadequate dick' quip. He'd never had any complaints before.

'If they want to impress me, they need to use what passes for the brains they were born with.' Brian again flipped a dismissive wrist. 'Ain't you got no shopping to do?'

'Aw, don't be like that, Bri.' Marion's attitude changed in the blink of an eye, as it so often did when she realised he'd got the hump. He wasn't a comfortable man to be around when that situation arose and he'd often had to give her a backhander, just to remind her who was the boss in their marriage. He didn't subscribe to all the equal rights bullshit that people harped on about nowadays. A man wasn't a man if he wasn't the undisputed king of his own castle. 'I know they ain't the brains of Britain but they're good lads deep down.'

'Very fucking deep,' Brian muttered, watching Marion's wide backside dispassionately as she bustled from the room.

Once the door closed and he was assured of privacy, he picked up his mobile and called a number from his contact list. 'We need to meet. Tonight, at the usual place. Yeah, I know,' he added, listening to what the guy said to him. 'We have a fucking situation and it's getting out of control.'

* * *

Isaac drove fast all the way back to Brighton, his head full of all the stuff he ought to have done but had neglected in favour of Farah's more pressing situation. He wondered when any situation had last taken precedence over his work and couldn't think of a single occasion. He couldn't decide if that spoke of commendable dedication or of being a workaholic who needed to get a life.

There was something about the situation at Guy's yard that he found deeply unsettling. The desire to grab Dale by the scruff of the neck and shake him until his teeth rattled and he told the truth had grown harder to resist each time he looked at Farah, battered and bruised and lucky to be alive. That was the only course of action that would have occurred to him but with success had come a cooler head, the ability to worry over a problem before acting on it and the willingness to box clever.

His rescuing Farah couldn't remain a secret and he fervently hoped that public knowledge of his involvement in her affairs would protect her from the ruthless individuals who had tampered with her car. The Hadleighs' presence in the area was deeply disturbing and highly suspicious. If they wanted to have another crack at Farah, he knew there was little he could do to prevent it, as things stood. At least for the next few days her injuries would prevent her from leaving Daisy's cottage but the security at the place was virtually non-existent.

He ground his jaw, surprised by the degree of his determination to protect her personally. She had worked her way around his defence mechanisms and succeeded in procuring his attention in a way that none of his dates ever had – perhaps because she hadn't tried to. She was vulnerable yet stubbornly assertive, focused and determined, attractive in a natural manner that was responsible for his growing awareness of her.

In short, she was different, desirable, and way out of her depth if the Hadleighs were indeed behind the shenanigans at Guy's yard. She needed his protection whether she realised it or not. Isaac gripped the steering wheel a little tighter, wondering what he could do to increase the ladies' security without frightening them.

There had to be something.

His phone ringing intruded upon his introspective, somewhat alarming thoughts.

'Damn!' he muttered when Cindy's name appeared on his screen. She was the supermodel whom he had escorted to a function recently and was due to take to another that night. He'd forgotten all about it.

'Hey,' he said, pressing the button on his steering wheel to take the call.

'Hi, stranger.' Cindy's velvet voice purred down the line. 'I was expecting to hear from you before now.'

'Sorry, got called away.'

'Kristen told me when I rang your office. I know you don't like me interrupting your busy days by ringing your mobile too often.'

Isaac wasn't sure what to say to that so he remained silent. As always tended to happen, that silence worked for him and Cindy felt obliged to fill it.

'Hope I didn't interrupt anything important.'

'Seven-thirty tonight,' he said, choosing not to give a direct response to such a probing question. 'I'll pick you up.'

'I look forward to it.'

'That makes one of us,' Isaac said aloud, after he'd cut the connection.

He had thought Cindy to be as ambitious as him and that she understood the rules. They could be of service to one another, professionally speaking, but it seemed that Cindy now wanted to take their arrangement to a personal level. She was the most fun of all the women he dated and he had been toying with the idea of making their relationship exclusive. They could be the ultimate power couple, headlines guaranteed. But since meeting Farah, feisty, fresh-faced, brave, stubborn and opinionated, being constantly in the limelight had lost its appeal.

The damned woman had a lot to answer for, he decided.

Arriving at his office in a terrace of Regency-era houses in a Brighton crescent overlooking the sea, he was trailed into his office by both Kristen, his glamorous PA, and his junior partner, Patrick. Kristen carried her tablet and reeled off a list of people waiting for calls back from the boss in person. Patrick simply looked amused and didn't say a word until Kristen had left them.

'Playing hooky again, boss?' Patrick asked, going to the coffee machine in the corner of the expansive room and making Isaac a much-needed Americano.

'Thanks.'

Isaac plonked himself behind his desk and picked up his cup.

'Wanna talk about it?' Patrick asked, sitting across from Isaac with his own coffee and sending him curious glances. 'It's not like you to let the kiddies run the ranch, being the hands-on type that you are. Talking of hands-on, woman trouble, is it?' Patrick flapped a casual wrist. 'Nah!' he said, answering his own question. 'It has to be something more serious than that to make you go AWOL.'

Patrick and Isaac had worked together since Isaac had first started up, trading from his laptop, driven by blind ambition from a bedsit on the wrong side of Brighton. He'd graduated from university, and turned down all the job offers that came his way from the head-hunters who lurked in the college halls, pouncing on the brightest of the bright. He had known even then that he could do better on his own and set out to prove it, falling back on his affinity for figures and a fierce determination to make something of himself.

Patrick had grown up in the lap of luxury and left Oxford with a first in mathematics and a desire to prove himself the hard way. He too turned down all the offers of gainful employment that came his way from established organisations and instead joined Isaac's start-up investment company – little more than a pipe dream. In those early days, it couldn't have been any tougher. Patrick's familial connections had saved them from going under when the odd eccentric sent them crumbs out of a sense of duty, or pity, no doubt expecting to lose the lot. When Isaac's instincts had the opposite effect, it was enough to set them on their way.

Patrick's family had threatened to disown him when he refused to take the easy option. They rubbed shoulders with the rich and titled and couldn't have a son of theirs mixing with a chancer from a dodgy part of London's East End, no matter how intelligent he happened to be. Appearances mattered in their world, as did backgrounds. They'd changed their tune pretty quick when Isaac started to make a name for himself. Relatively impoverished nowadays, it was Patrick, Isaac knew, who kept his family's collective heads above water.

Patrick could make figures sing and dance for him but he lacked the flair for leadership, the willingness to assess risks and embrace them, that had seen Isaac eclipse his rivals and rapidly become the go-to man for investment advice. A friendship, a bond, had grown between the two men. They tended to work and play together and there was little about Isaac's private life that Patrick didn't know. Isaac trusted him absolutely and didn't hesitate to explain what had kept him in Lambourn for so long.

'Geez!' Patrick sucked air through his teeth as he assessed what Isaac had just told him. 'What the fuck...'

'My sentiments entirely. Suggestions are welcome.'

'Hot, is she, this Farah chick?' Patrick asked, grinning.

Isaac smiled in spite of himself and simultaneously shook his head. 'Glad to see you've got your priorities right.'

'Glad to see you haven't lost the ability to avoid questions you'd prefer not to answer.' Patrick's grin widened as he rubbed the designer stubble decorating his chin. 'Come on, give. What's really happening?'

'That is what I would very much like to know. But what I can tell you is that Brian Hadleigh has taken up residence in the area and it was almost certainly his Range Rover that tried to intimidate me.'

'Who's Brian Hadleigh?'

Isaac sighed. 'Ah, of course, you wouldn't know, not being well-acquainted with the hoi polloi.'

'I talk to you, don't I?' Patrick protested.

'Right, if you have to. All joking aside, though, Hadleigh is bad news. Your stereotypical East End gangster who took no prisoners. Into everything, he was. Drugs, prostitution and fuck knows what else.'

'Your paths have crossed, I take it.'

Isaac leaned back in his chair and grimaced. 'You could say that. He's supposedly retired now but I don't believe a word of it. You can bet that he's still got his grubby fingers in all sorts of dodgy pies, even if he does now play golf with the police commissioner and gives enough of his ill-gotten gains to worthy charities to make himself appear respectable.'

'So have Ray check him out.'

Isaac shook his head. 'He won't find anything that Hadleigh doesn't want him to find. The man has brains, I'll give him that.' Isaac grinned. 'If he'd been born into a family like yours, he'd likely be a captain of industry by now. In a way, I suppose that's what he is.'

'Yeah, well, most so-called captains of big corporations know how to dodge bullets. Why do you think I didn't want to get involved with all that crap?'

'Point taken.' Isaac nodded. 'Anyway, Hadleigh has two sons, and they are as thick as the proverbial pig-shit. All brawn but none of their father's brains. No one dared to question their parentage when we were growing up, not publicly, but we all wondered.'

'How do you know all this?'

'How does anyone know about the Krays?' Isaac lifted one shoulder into a careless shrug. Some truths were best left buried. 'Hadleigh's name was known and feared throughout the East End. Everyone either worked for the family in some capacity or other or knew not to mess with them.'

'But not you? You didn't work for them.'

Isaac shuddered. 'I'm a leader, not a follower.'

Patrick pondered for a moment. 'If Hadleigh is intent upon going straight, at least ostensibly, why get involved in tin-pot horserace fixing?'

'That, my friend, is the vital question.'

'If Hadleigh wants to play the part of the country squire, and if he's as clever as you imply, he'd know better than to mess in his own backyard. London is one thing. It's large and violent, he has all the right connections there, probably greases the right palms and can get lost in a crowd. Either that or use intimidation to get out of trouble. I don't suppose there's anywhere for him to hide in the country where everyone knows everyone else's business, even if he is buying his way into local society.'

'You're willing to give a violent individual the benefit of the doubt?' Isaac asked, flexing a brow in surprise.

'Not at all, but you do appear to have tunnel vision on this one, which isn't like you. Do you have a history with Hadleigh? Clearly, you despise him.'

'A friend of mine at school sold drugs for him in the playground.

I told him not to get into it but... well, the same old story.' Isaac's explanation was true, and probably enough to satisfy Patrick, but it was far from what lay at the crux of Isaac's disagreement with Brian Hadleigh, which was decidedly personal. Too personal even to share with Patrick. And still unresolved. 'The rewards were too good to be resisted. Anyway, he finished up getting hooked on free samples and took a fatal overdose.'

'Tragic, but hardly Hadleigh's fault. If he hadn't supplied, someone else would.'

Isaac picked up his gold Cartier pen and flipped it between his fingers. 'I know that. Hadleigh was at the top of the tree and wouldn't have known Simon's name, or cared about him one way or the other. It's just the way things were back then, and still are to some extent. But still, whenever my path crosses with a ruthless individual like Hadleigh, who got rich on the back of other people's weaknesses, it makes me so fucking angry.'

'Understood.'

Isaac drew in a long breath. 'Hadleigh might be as pure as the driven, but given that it was his Range Rover shadowing me, I somehow doubt it.'

'Why not just move those pampered nags of yours to another yard, insist that Farah be taken on to continue with their care, and forget all about something that doesn't concern you?'

Isaac scowled. 'Run away, you mean?'

'A tactical retreat with all your limbs intact.'

'Not happening. They involved one of my horses and that makes it personal. I don't go looking for trouble, Patrick, as well you know, but I won't be anyone's patsy. Nor will I back off if trouble comes knocking at my door.'

Patrick gave a placatory wave. 'I know, but I had to try.' He paused. 'It's more likely something to do with the bookies' stringers who you say have been hanging around the gallops.'

'I know.' Isaac's mobile rang. 'It's Ray,' he said, checking the display and taking the call. 'Yeah, Ray, what do you have for me?'

Isaac put the call on speaker so that Patrick could hear.

'That partial number plate you asked me to check.' Ray paused. 'You know who it belongs to, right?'

'Yeah, but I needed to be sure.' Ray knew of Isaac's history with Hadleigh. 'So what else have you got?'

'Word is, Hadleigh still runs his patch in town and his lads do the heavy lifting. But his patch has shrunk significantly. The Albanians have taken over a big swathe, which might account for Hadleigh reinventing himself in the country.'

'He's saving face?'

'Something like that. Word on the street is that the Albanians wanted his entire operation but Hadleigh was willing to start a war rather than let that happen. Anyway, terms were agreed. The Albanians are vicious bastards and would have welcomed a fight, but Hadleigh still enjoys a huge amount of support in the East End and I guess they had the sense not to go that far.'

'A criminal with heart,' Patrick said derisively.

'Compared to the Albanians, trust me he is. Anyway, there's a fragile truce right now.'

'And Hadleigh can't help diversifying into illicit country pursuits, like race fixing,' Isaac suggested.

'I can't find anything to back that assertion up, but I'll keep digging.'

'What about Dale Drummond and Jonah whatever his name is?'

'Jonah Mitchell. Came over from Ireland two years ago. Everyone's friend, great with horses... Sorry, Isaac, that probably doesn't tell you anything you don't already know but I can't give you what's not there. He has no criminal record as an adult in this country but there are sealed records in Ireland relating to a juvenile conviction. I'm attempting to get those records unsealed.'

'I won't ask how,' Isaac said. 'Wonder if whatever he did is the reason why he came to England?'

'Possibly. Now then, Dale Drummond is an interesting character. He does have a criminal record. Two convictions for drink driving, the most recent two years ago. He got a three-year ban.'

Isaac nodded, even though Ray couldn't see him. 'I got the impression that he was a little too fond of the sauce. I've smelled it on his breath more than once.'

'Did he hurt anyone when he got done for drinking?' Patrick asked.

'Good question,' Ray replied. 'He did. It was early afternoon. He failed to stop when a lollipop lady held up her sign outside of a school. He hit a little boy who didn't get out of the way in time. Broke both of his legs.'

'Did it make the news?' Isaac asked, leaning back in his chair, his mind whirling with possibilities.

'Only locally and then only briefly.'

'So someone hushed it up.'

'That's what I'm thinking,' Ray said. 'I'm attempting to trace the family. I'll get back to you on that. What I can tell you is the kid came from a single parent set-up. They lived in local authority housing but upped and left soon after the boy came out of hospital and no one knows where they went.'

'Sounds like they were paid off,' Patrick said, earning a nod of agreement from Isaac. 'I mean, no offence, but a single mum would ordinarily be all over the press, demanding justice or else would be encouraged by ambulance-chasing lawyers to bring a civil suit against Dale, which they would have won. But she didn't go for it. Can't help wondering why.'

'Right,' Ray agreed. 'Makes you wonder who got to the mother, but I'm on it. They can run but they can't hide.'

'What about Guy Levant?' Isaac asked.

'Well now, there's a boy made good that you ought to be able to identify with, Isaac.'

'Why do you think he sent his pampered babies to that yard?' Patrick asked, earning himself the finger from Isaac.

'Hey, rude gestures count as staff harassment,' Patrick protested. 'I just might sue.'

'Good luck with that,' Isaac chuckled.

'Anyway, if I have your attention,' Ray said. 'Guy was a jockey in his own right, which you know. Did well for himself in France—'

'Met and married a rich Frenchwoman and the rest, as they say, is history,' Isaac finished for him, thinking once again that he'd never really taken to Michelle Levant. Not that he'd had much to do with her. She was a good-looking woman but remote, unapproachable.

'Not quite,' Ray replied. 'The lovely Mrs Guy Levant, Michelle, was a stable girl.'

'What?' Isaac looked at Patrick askance and shook his head. 'That can't be right. He tells everyone that he got lucky and married a rich owner's daughter.'

'Well, he's telling porkies. She was actually an up-and-coming three-day eventer. Had a lot of potential in that sphere, apparently, but gave it up when she married Guy and moved to England.'

'She trades in eventing horses here in England. Finds them for people who need something specific, I think.' Isaac allowed himself a moment's contemplation. 'So, we have a successful new trainer who's telling lies about the source of his financing, a foreman who bought his way out of a serious situation and a head lad who has a questionable past buried in Ireland.' He paused. 'Do we have anything more on Michelle Levant's background? I know I didn't ask you to look but given the situation...'

'I'm on that as well. Give me a little time.'

'You have it. Thanks, Ray.'

'I haven't forgotten the bookies' runners, or the bookies they work for. I imagine I shall uncover a whole host of nasties with that lot. I'll get back to you.'

'Good man.'

Isaac cut the connection and glanced speculatively at Patrick. 'Well,' he said, 'any inspired thoughts and I'm ready to hear them.'

'Seems to me that no one at that expensive yard of yours is who they appear to be.'

'Very insightful!'

'Still think you should move your horses, and Farah, out of harm's way. Doesn't mean you can't carry on digging. I know you want to but I also sense that you want to keep the girl safe.' Patrick chuckled. 'Don't tell me that a female has finally breached the barricades around that frozen heart of yours.'

'Get a life!' Isaac threw a paperclip at his partner.

'It was only a matter of time,' Patrick continued, oblivious to Isaac's frown. 'You have a low boredom threshold and have never really taken to the red-carpet treatment. You do it because you think you should.'

'Thank you, Dr Freud. Now, unless there's something you need to discuss about the business, I need to do some work.'

'Okay.' Patrick stood, still grinning like he'd just discovered the meaning of the universe. 'I know where I'm not wanted.'

'Since when?' Isaac replied, not looking up from the emails he'd just pulled up on his screen.

9

The first day into her recuperation and Farah was already bored out of her mind. *Who knew there could be so many hours in one day?* Ordinarily, there weren't enough of them to get all the tasks she needed done. She felt stiff all over, her head ached and she was having trouble breathing. She had been warned to expect all of those restrictions but, unused to ill health, they rankled. She was fractious, unable to settle to anything and was short-tempered, even with Daisy.

'Settle down and read a book, darling,' Daisy said with commendable patience when Farah complained for the tenth time about her enforced idleness. 'Or we could watch a film together. We haven't done that for a long time.'

'I'm sorry, Daisy.' Farah stood and crossed the sunroom in order to kiss her aunt, wincing when she stood up too quickly and her ribs protested. 'My ailments are only temporary and yet I can't stop whinging. You on the other hand endure yours with commendable stoicism.'

'I don't really have much choice, do I?'

It was the closest that Farah had known Daisy ever get to

complaining and she felt thoroughly ashamed of herself for raising the subject. 'I wish it could be otherwise, Daisy. You don't deserve what life has thrown at you.'

'Yes, well, we seldom get our just desserts in this world. Let's hope the hereafter has more potential.'

'Don't talk that way! It's upsetting.' Farah resumed her position on her chair and tapped her fingers impatiently on her knee. 'I just wish I knew what Isaac has found out and that he would share those findings with me. I feel like a spare part.'

'What makes you suppose he's found out anything?'

Farah sent her aunt a disbelieving look. 'He isn't the type to let something like this continue, especially if it involves his precious horses. He will take it personally and try to figure out what's going on.'

'You think he will cut you out?'

'He seems to think that I need protecting.' Farah rolled her eyes. 'What century does he think we're living in, for god's sake? Women can take care of themselves nowadays.'

Daisy focused her gaze on Farah's scraped face and said nothing.

'Yes, all right, I might be banged up physically but my brain is still in full working order,' she said indignantly. 'I'm a big girl, not one of the hot-house flowers he dates who wilts at the first sign of neglect. And besides, I know the yard a lot better than he does. There's the outside possibility that I might even be able to make the odd helpful suggestion, *if* he deigns to tell me what the hell's going on and which direction he'd like me to look in.'

'He's been gone from here for less than a day, darling. He does have a business to run. Give him a chance.'

'I suppose,' Farah said ungraciously.

Daisy smiled her lopsided smile. 'The way you spoke in such

denigrating terms about his women, you make it sound as though you would like to be one of his dates.'

'Ha! Can you see me prancing up a red carpet and posing for the cameras? Credit me with a little more depth than that.' She grinned. 'Quite apart from anything else, I have no idea how to walk, elegantly or otherwise, in those stiletto heel thingies.'

'Perhaps Isaac has tired of that sort of thing.'

'Not a chance.' Farah gave a mirthless laugh. 'He revels in all the attention. Women don't have the monopoly on vanity, you know.'

'He told me that he does it for business reasons.'

'Ha!'

'You know that he came from a poor background and made something of himself through his own efforts.'

Farah smiled. 'I don't often read the gossip mags,' she admitted.

'Whereas I have nothing better to do with my time.'

'Oh, Daisy! You know I didn't mean it like that. Take no notice of me. I'm just feeling fractious. We're at Newbury later this week. Well, some of the horses are and I should be, too, but I won't be.'

'Then watch it on the box with me. I never miss it, as you know.'

'Yes, I...' She paused at the sound of the door knocker, her heart palpitating but not because it might be Isaac. She was more concerned about the possibility of receiving less welcome visitors. 'Are you expecting anyone?'

'No, it's probably for you.' Daisy's expression turned mischievous. 'I expect Isaac has come to put you out of your misery.'

'You are a meddling old woman!' Farah scolded, smiling as she wagged an admonishing finger at her aunt.

She stood and made her way slowly to the front door, feeling every one of her twenty-seven years, and then some. Everything hurt when she moved too fast, and even when she didn't. She wondered how long bruising took to heal, aware that she was good for nothing as things stood – especially not riding feisty horses or even warding off unwelcome visitors.

She opened the door, expecting to see the postman or, worse, Ben from the pub, using her accident as an excuse to get up close and personal. Instead, she got the shock of her life to see her boss standing there.

'Guy!' she cried stupidly.

'Hey, Farah. I couldn't believe it when I heard about your accident and needed to make sure you're still in one piece, give or take.' He eyed her bruised face with genuine-seeming concern. 'Geez, you were lucky!'

Farah opened her mouth to tell him it had been no accident, but then quickly closed it again without speaking. She had agreed with Isaac that they would keep what they knew to themselves. She could trust Guy but she was pretty sure he didn't have any secrets from Dale and would never believe her if she raised her suspicions about him and Jonah. In fact, he would take Dale's side and that would be the end of a career she loved.

Again.

'Come in,' she said, opening the door wider. 'Daisy will be pleased to see you. She doesn't get many visitors.' Wondering why she felt the need to babble, she led the way into the sunroom. 'Look who's come to pay us a call,' she said brightly.

'Guy!' Daisy lifted a hand and Guy gave it a gentle squeeze.

'How are you, Daisy?'

'The same as ever.'

Guy took a chair but declined Farah's offer of refreshment. 'I can't stay long. I took a detour on the way back from the gallops.'

'How's Dickens' fetlock?' Farah asked. 'Is he back in work? Will he be fit in time for Goodwood?'

Guy laughed and held up both hands. 'Always working. Relax! Dickens worked this morning and was full of himself. He should be fine, and I know this isn't what you want to hear but the yard is still functioning, just about, without you.' Farah's face fell and Guy clearly realised he hadn't been particularly tactful. 'We all miss you and worry about you, of course, so I came to see if there was anything I could do to make your life easier.'

'She will need a new form of transport,' Daisy remarked in a disingenuous manner that made Farah both frown and smile. She couldn't expect Guy to provide her with a car and wouldn't accept, even if he offered.

'She's needed that for years. I'm frankly surprised that your old jeep didn't give up the ghost before now, Farah.'

'I loved that car,' she replied stubbornly.

'I might have something I can lend you, once you're fit enough to drive, until you can sort your insurance claim.'

'Thanks, but don't worry. I'll figure something out.'

Farah knew she sounded ungracious but thoughts of someone deliberately attempting to kill them would be enough to unsettle the most stoic of people. It also increased her determination to discover what was so lucrative that the perpetrators were willing to resort to murder in order to cover it up. In spite of everything, she refused to believe that Dale would go that far.

Guy chatted to Daisy for ten minutes but when her eyelids began to droop, he took the hint and stood up to leave. In the hallway he paused and turned to Farah.

'I don't like what happened to you, Farah,' he said, looking highly perturbed and most un-Guy-like. Ordinarily, nothing fazed him.

'I'm not mad about it myself,' she replied with a casual shrug.

'Has anything else... I mean, have you had...' His words trailed off and he scratched his ear in a distracted fashion. Farah had never known him lost for words before and seeing him in such a state of indecision served to increase her concerns.

'Have I what?' she asked.

'It's just that one or two unexplained things have happened at the yard and, as you know, I do like to have a place for everything and everything in its place.'

'What do you mean, unexplained?'

'Well, entries for races not going in, although Michelle swears they were submitted.'

'Cock-ups happen, Guy, even to control freaks like yourself.'

'I know, but they never have before and now, suddenly, there's been a whole spate of them. It's... I don't know, almost like someone resents my success. I haven't been here for years so I'm an upstart in the eyes of some of the established trainers, and that breeds resentment.'

Farah widened her eyes, not having to feign surprise. 'You think one of the other trainers is out to trash your reputation?' She probably sounded as sceptical as she felt. 'Of course there are jealousies and petty rivalries but I can't imagine anyone going quite that far. How would they do it? Tamper with entries, I mean. They would have to have supersonic cyber powers or...'

'Or tame lapdogs in positions of authority at the various race-courses.' Guy nodded glumly. 'I know, and put into words it sounds kinda out there. I get that.'

'Have you talked to Michelle about your suspicions?'

'No. I don't want to worry her. She has a lot on her plate. Her eventing horses have never been in higher demand but she still insists on doing my paperwork. Says we're a team. She sends her love, by the way.'

Farah was tempted to argue the point. Michelle was a first-class horsewoman but aloof and didn't invite friendships, not with the hired help at any rate. Unlike Guy, she believed in maintaining boundaries.

'Why did you ask me if anything else had happened? You know

everything that goes on before it happens.' *Was he on a fishing trip at Dale's behest?* she wondered, dismissing the idea before it could take a firm hold. Guy wouldn't be a party to anything underhand and, friend or not, Dale would be out on his ear if Guy even suspected him of dishonesty. She was as sure as she could be that if Dale was up to something, Guy knew nothing about it. 'As you say, my car was an accident waiting to happen. Perhaps it's as well that it has. Now I will have to get something boring, safe and reliable.' She summoned up a smile for Guy. 'And where will the fun be in having a vehicle that always starts on the first turn of the key?'

Guy laughed. 'We've all had to adapt. Anyway, everyone sends their love and are anxious about you. I'll let them know that you're on the mend.'

'I should be back at work next week.'

'Hold on a minute! You don't set foot in that yard until the doctor's signed you off. Are we clear?'

'But—'

Guy cut off her protest with a raised hand. 'I'm serious, Farah. No one's indispensable, not even you. And if you come back before you're ready, I will be in trouble with my liability insurers.'

'I'm a liability now, am I?' she asked, folding her arms cautiously over her bruised ribs, her offence not entirely feigned.

'You know better than that.' He chuckled at her fit of pique. 'I'll call again in a few days and see how you're doing.'

Farah waved him off, still unable to decide why he had really called, or if there had been an ulterior motive. He certainly seemed to think that things weren't as they should be at the yard, and she was pretty sure that missed race entries were not what had got him so worked up. But she hadn't wanted to press him until she was surer of her facts. The situation was delicate. Dangerous. Having her life threatened had, she realised, made her suspicious of everything and everyone. Even so, she would mention the episode to Isaac, if and when he deigned to contact her again.

* * *

Brian met Dale Drummond in an out-of-the-way pub not frequented by the racing fraternity, mid-way between Lambourn and Newbury. Dale looked haggard, the effects of years of drinking too much reflected in his sallow complexion and the network of red lines decorating his nose and cheeks. Brian watched him approach the table that he'd appropriated in a quiet corner of the bar, looking sullen. But not so sullen that he hadn't already bought himself a pint and a whisky chaser. He was still banned from driving following the accident that Brian had made go away but that didn't prevent him from borrowing one of the yard's jeeps and driving himself all this way.

It didn't prevent him from drinking and driving either. Brian sighed, thinking some people never learned.

'Where's Jonah?' Brian asked, when Dale pulled out a chair and sat down.

Dale shrugged. 'I didn't know he was invited.'

'Well, he knew and he's late.' Brian tapped the face of his gold Baume & Mercier watch for emphasis. 'I thought you'd come together.'

Brian knew that Jonah was playing a petty game of one-upmanship. A non-drinker when it suited his purposes, playing chauffeur would have given Dale carte blanche to get paralytic. He almost smiled, enjoying seeing his underlings falling out with one another. It kept them dishonest.

Jonah arrived at that moment, swaggering into the pub as though he owned it. Brian admired his style. Dale was weak and too reliant on the sauce but Jonah had drive, ambition and a total lack of a moral conscience. If his own boys possessed even half of Jonah's natural assumption that they had a right to own the world, his organisation would be in much better shape. He might not even have given in to the Albanians and instead instigated a turf war. *But what was the point when there were no safe hands to pass it all on to?*

But still, he had Jonah. He'd taken a personal interest in his welfare and he would go far.

Brian would make sure of that.

'Hiya, lads,' Jonah said, seating himself and making a big show of glancing at Dale's two drinks before placing a solitary glass of mineral water on the table in front of him. 'Nice night for it.'

'What happened to Farah?' Dale asked, glancing moodily at Brian. 'Was that really necessary? She could have been killed. It's only good luck that she wasn't.'

'She's been warned and will be out of the way for a while, which gives us the opportunity to progress our plans,' Brian said, unwilling to admit that he agreed with Dale and that his boys had well and truly cocked things up. Family loyalty ran deep in his world, no matter how moronic the family members in question happened to be. It had to look as though Brian had sanctioned the warning just the way it went down and that he was fully in control, otherwise he would lose face. If that happened Dale might actually develop a backbone and jump ship. Or worse, reveal what little he knew to those in a position to do something about it.

Brian couldn't take that chance.

'What plans?' Dale asked, taking a long swig of beer, glowering at Brian over the rim of the glass with open suspicion. 'I wish someone would tell me what the fuck's going on? Pulling horses from races ain't the crime of the century and doesn't mean you have to nearly kill a stable lass to stop her from asking awkward questions.' He frowned. 'I told you I could handle her. What you're doing, going in heavy-handed, makes no sense and will only make her more suspicious.'

Brian tended to agree but he wasn't about to admit that he wasn't the one pulling the strings. 'You ain't here to make sense of anything but to do as you're told.' Brian's voice had turned hard. Cold. 'If it weren't for me, you'd be likely keeping a jail cell warm right now. Either that or spending the rest of your life paying that family for what you did to that little boy. Never lose sight of the fact that you're... well, a loser.'

'What do you need from us?' Jonah sent Brian a warning look that advised against pushing Dale too far.

'Fernandez's horse is entered in Goodwood, right?'

'Yeah, Force has qualified for a two-mile handicap.'

'I'm told he has a good chance.'

Dale shrugged. 'Better than good. That horse is a speed machine.'

'Well, then, he needs to fail a dope test once he wins or places,' Brian said calmly.

'What the fuck!'

Dale and Jonah spluttered simultaneously the exact same words and Brian could see that even Jonah, who had no morals whatsoever, was shocked. Ask him to give another fella, or even a woman, a slap to keep them in place and he wouldn't bat an eyelid but doping a horse was, it seemed, asking too much of him.

'Don't look holier than thou, either of you,' Brian sneered. 'It's a bit late for that. Just do as you're told.'

'It will ruin Fernandez's reputation,' Jonah said, tapping a finger thoughtfully against his crooked teeth, 'which I guess is the idea. Someone has an axe to grind, so.'

'It will ruin Guy as well,' Dale said quietly, downing his Scotch in one swallow and looking vaguely surprised when he discovered that his glass was empty.

'You realise that Fernandez has linked up with Farah and you can bet she's shared her concerns with him,' Jonah added. 'He ain't the sort of person you'd want to cross without preparing your ground thoroughly.'

'He's a man like any other. Besides, Farah will be out of action for a week, possibly two. Certainly until after the Goodwood meeting. Just do what needs to be done. A cyber trail will lead the authorities directly to Fernandez's door, implying that the doping took place at his insistence.'

'Holy fuck!' Dale muttered into his beer. 'He's really pissed someone off.'

Brian believed in leaving meetings on a high before those attending could pick holes in what had been decided. Not that these two had any part in the decision-making; they were there to do as they were told. Even so...

He finished his drink and stood up. 'You know what to do,' he said. 'Sort it out between yourselves. We won't speak or meet again until well after the race.'

And with that, he walked out of the pub without a backward glance.

* * *

'That was fun.' Cindy leaned the side of her face against Isaac's shoulder as the limo he'd hired for the night sped towards Cindy's flat. 'We got some valuable press coverage. Will you come in for a nightcap?' she purred, her meaning transparently obvious. 'We can talk about how to take advantage of it.'

'Thanks, but no, I have an early start tomorrow.'

'But it's Saturday.'

Isaac nodded. 'No rest for the wicked.'

She pouted and stroked his arm. 'Still, it was fun tonight.'

Isaac nodded for a second time, despite the fact that he had been bored out of his skull, making inane social chit-chat for the majority of the evening. He was no longer convinced that he needed to keep up the rigmarole in order to attract high-flying clients. Certainly not at any price. He had more than enough already and had reached the point where he was turning would-be investors away.

He climbed from the limo when it pulled up outside Cindy's apartment block, again declined her invitation to go inside, gave her the obligatory hug and retreated to the relative safety of the car's warm interior. As soon as the driver moved away, Isaac worked his phone. His first call was to Ray. He had missed two calls from him that evening so figured he must have unearthed something important.

'What have you got for me?' he asked, not bothering with any preamble.

'I'm waiting outside your place,' Ray replied. 'I found some stuff that we need to talk about in person.'

Isaac glanced at his watch. Ray, he knew, was a night owl, which was why he hadn't hesitated to return his call at one in the morning. But Ray wanting to meet in person at such an hour raised red flags.

'I'll be there in ten,' he said, cutting the call.

A biker dressed in black leathers dismounted the Honda he'd been straddling when the limo pulled up outside Isaac's residence. Ray removed his helmet, grabbed a messenger bag from his pannier, which Isaac knew would contain his top-of-the-range, highly encrypted laptop, and followed Isaac into the deserted ground floor of his house, which also served as his office and was a hive of activity during daylight hours. Right now it was eerily silent, just screens permanently tuned to money markets the world over, flashing constantly as prices changed, casting shadows over the adjacent walls.

Isaac's gaze was automatically drawn to the screens showing the Asian stock markets, despite it being Saturday. Old habits.

He made for the stairs, indicating to Ray that he should follow him up to his living quarters. He offered his investigator a drink, already aware that he would decline. He was stick thin and in all the years that Isaac had availed himself of the man's services, he had yet to see him eat or drink anything.

Isaac switched on a couple of lamps and gestured towards a stool at the kitchen island. He popped open a bottle of water for himself and took the stool across from Ray, watching as he unpacked his precious laptop and fired it up. His fingers flew over the keys and he gave a grunt of satisfaction as he came to the screen he wanted.

'Jonah Mitchell's juvenile conviction was for GBH,' Ray said conversationally.

'Bloody hell!' Isaac's eyebrows disappeared beneath his hairline. 'How old was he at the time? What happened?'

'He was sixteen and beat another stable lad to a pulp. He never said why; nor did the victim.'

'A nasty individual, then.'

'Oh yeah. There was no way he'd get work with horses in Ireland after that. The records were sealed but it's a small community. The word would have spread about his volatility.'

'But no one on this side of the pond would have been able to check?'

'Only if they took the trouble to ask but I'm told the man has a natural flair with horses. He worked for another trainer before moving on to Guy so if Guy checked anywhere it would have been with Bevan.'

'Bevan is a highly respected trainer,' Isaac said, nodding. 'Always in the news. His word would have been enough to satisfy Guy, I expect.'

'Well, there you are, then.'

'Someone handy with their fists would always find a warm welcome in Hadleigh's world,' Isaac said thoughtfully. 'But I'm less certain about Dale.'

'I've found the mother of the little boy who Dale knocked down,' Ray said. 'Spoke to her on the phone. Didn't think she'd want to talk about it, not if she'd been paid off. Which I'm pretty sure she has been, by the way. She lives in Southampton. I googled her address. She owns a three-bed semi worth close to half a mil outright.' Ray glanced up from his screen. 'We're talking about a woman who worked as a cleaner before her son's accident and claimed every benefit she was entitled to, as well as some that she wasn't. Now she doesn't work. I haven't tried to hack into her bank account. I will if you want me to but I don't think it's necessary.'

'I think we can draw our own conclusions, even if we can't link Hadleigh directly to her.'

'Ah well, you could be wrong about that. Anticipating her disinclination to give anything away, I got inventive and phoned her pretending to be an associate of Henry Hadleigh's. I figured the sons would have been more likely to deal with her, given that their father likes to keep his distance. Anyway, I asked her if everything was all right and if there was anything she still needed. She harped on about her son still walking with a limp and never being able to play football again. She also complained about selling out too cheap and speculated about the press interest in her case, if she chose to bring it up again.'

Isaac sat forward. 'She was trying to screw Henry for more dosh through you? Blimey, I wonder if she realises what thugs she's dealing with,' he said, thinking of the heavy-handed manner in which they'd dealt with Farah.

Ray nodded. 'Seemed that way to me.'

'Well, if we can definitely put Dale in Hadleigh's debt then it's not a huge leap to assume that he's exploited Jonah Mitchell's violent tendencies for his own purposes too.' Isaac took a swig of water from his bottle and wiped a dribble away from his chin with the back of his hand. 'But what precisely those purposes are we have yet to discover. Even so, it appears to involve the manipulation of my horses and is serious enough to warrant a life-threatening warning to Farah, who has suspicions about dodgy goings-on but doesn't actually know anything specific.'

'These people clearly don't fuck about, Isaac.'

'Yeah, I got that part.' He glanced across at Ray. 'But you didn't come round here at this time of the morning to tell me stuff you could have talked about on the phone. So, come on, give. What else have you got?'

'Guy Levant.'

Isaac groaned. 'Don't tell me he's bent too.'

'Nope, not as far as I can tell. He seems kosher to me. Everything you told me about him pans out. He really was a jockey who made it big in France, *but...*'

'Come on, Ray.' Isaac tapped his fingers impatiently against the kitchen surface. 'Don't make me torture it out of you.'

Ray waved a bony hand in the air but kept his eyes focused on his screen. 'I think Hadleigh and his thuggish sons are involved up to their grubby necks in whatever's going down, but I think... no, I *know* that Hadleigh isn't the one calling the shots.'

'Blimey!' Isaac blinked. 'From what I recall about Hadleigh's reputation when we were kids, he was always top dog. Definitely not one to take orders from anyone else.'

Ray sent Isaac a devious little smile. 'Not even from his daughter?' he asked.

10

'Daughter?' Isaac blinked. 'I wasn't aware that he had one.'

'Nor was Hadleigh, it seems, until about five years ago.'

'Who is she? Anyone I know?'

Ray allowed a dramatic pause, during the course of which Isaac felt an overwhelming sense of foreboding. Whatever was going down was, he now sensed, connected somehow to him. Isaac's sixth sense was usually accurate, accounting for his business success. He had learned to trust it and follow his instincts. Farah, it seemed, had been lucky to escape death because of something he was unaware he'd done. People were sometimes disappointed in the return on their investments but that went with the territory and he was absolutely certain that none of his disillusioned clients had felt the need to turn murderous in some obscure and vindictive desire to extract revenge.

'Michelle Levant.'

'What!' Isaac's entire body jerked as he blinked repeatedly at Ray, convinced that he must have misheard him. 'But how? Who? Why, come to that, and what has it all got to do with me?'

'She's your half-sister.'

Isaac's mouth fell open but no sound emerged for several seconds. 'My mother's child?' he asked in a hollow tone.

Ray nodded. 'Looks that way.'

Isaac ground his jaw. 'Yeah, it most likely is. My old man worked for Hadleigh back in the day, using his native Spanish and the other languages he spoke to coordinate Hadleigh's foreign interests. That's how I know so much about the way he operated.'

'There's no mistake, Isaac. I triple-checked my facts before bringing this to you.' Ray paused. 'I'm sorry.'

'There's no need to be. It's not your fault. I know Hadleigh had a thing for my mother but...' Isaac paused, his mind whirling. 'How old is Michelle and how come she's French?'

'She's pushing forty and was adopted in France. Your mother went there to have the child and put her up for adoption.'

'So, she's five years older than me.'

Isaac stared off into the distance and tapped the fingers of one hand against his opposite forearm, lost in the past. Remembering all the times that Hadleigh had called to see his mother when his father was out of the way. Wondering how his father had felt about it all. He must have known and was volatile, his hot-blooded temperament often getting the better of him. He was a proud man, too, and macho with it.

'He would not accept my mother's adultery without beating her lover to a pulp and then turning his fists on her. But, of course, Hadleigh was untouchable.' Isaac paused to rub his chin. 'He'd have had to be suicidal to call him on it.' Isaac stood and paced the length of the kitchen, thinking the matter through. 'Hadleigh always did have an eye for the ladies and took whatever caught the eye in question; he considered it to be his right. Went with the territory, but a child. Phew! Holy fuck!'

'Did you use to take foreign students into your home?'

'Not students, so much. More contacts of my father's from

across Europe. He had his fingers into any number of dodgy pies and sometimes people needed a bolt hole. I never knew why at the time but have a much better idea now, looking back.'

'From what few sketchy facts I can piece together, your mother went to stay with a French family, had the baby there and the child-less couple adopted her. Your father forgave your mother because he realised she'd been coerced.'

'Right.' Isaac nodded decisively. 'Hadleigh took whatever he wanted and Pa wasn't stupid enough to confront him over the matter. But he also wasn't prepared to raise Hadleigh's bastard as his own, I imagine.'

'That's kinda what I thought,' Ray said sympathetically.

'The affair carried on, or resumed, I'm guessing. I remember Hadleigh being a regular caller when I was a toddler and the old man was away on jobs for Hadleigh.' Isaac shrugged. 'Perhaps there was genuine affection on both sides. Hadleigh was the man, back in the day, and probably gave my mother the life she craved. It's pretty damned obvious now.' Isaac took a deep breath. 'Anyway, how did Michelle track Hadleigh down? And, more to the point, how do you know all this?'

'I hacked into Michelle's email when I got suspicious about her,' Ray replied nonchalantly, as though it was the most natural thing in the world. For him, it likely was. 'She was adopted by a family in Lyon. She took riding lessons, hung around the stables like pony-mad girls tend to do, mucking out in return for rides, that sort of thing. Proved to be a natural at it by all accounts. But she was ambitious, held back by her adoptive parents' modest means. So she pushed them for information about her birth mother. Her adoptive mother knew the truth about Hadleigh and eventually came clean.'

'And Hadleigh bought it?' Isaac asked sceptically.

'She was tenacious, wouldn't give up when he told her to get lost and turned up on his doorstep one day, challenging him to take a DNA test to prove it one way or the other. So he eventually did.'

'Fucking hell!' Isaac breathed. 'He must have seen something in Michelle, remembered the adopted baby, otherwise he'd have told her to scarper. That makes me kinda related to Hadleigh in an obscure sort of way.'

'Yeah, well, we can choose our friends.'

'I still don't get... well, any of this.' Isaac scowled at his kitchen cabinets. 'Why the vendetta that's starting to feel increasingly personal? If she wanted me to know who she is, or recognised my name when I put my horses with her husband, why not just come right out and tell me?'

'Would you have believed her?'

'I might have needed a bit of convincing. You have no idea what stratagems people use as an excuse to get close to me. But if she had evidence then yeah, why the hell wouldn't I believe her?'

'You were close to your mother?'

'What the fuck has that to do with anything?'

Ray shrugged a bony shoulder. 'Not sure. All I'm saying is that if she knew who her mother was before she died and kept an eye on things, she could have seen that close relationship and perhaps resented it.'

'I spent the majority of my time protecting my mother from my father's fists,' Isaac said, grinding his teeth at the memory.

'Well, only Michelle can answer your questions. All I know is that she met Guy not long after she and Hadleigh acknowledged one another and recognised her own ambition reflected in him.'

'It was Hadleigh who financed Guy's yard?'

'Right. He saw in his daughter a ruthlessness and driving desire to succeed, no matter what the cost, that is singularly lacking in his sons.'

'But they didn't announce their relationship. Why not?'

Isaac thought about Michelle, trying to decide if there was any family resemblance between them. Nothing obvious sprang to mind. She was a good-looking woman but aloof and Isaac had never shared more than a few passing words with her. She had never made a point of instigating a conversation with him, now he came to think about it. In fact, although he'd caught her staring at him once or twice, she also seemed to go out of her way to avoid him, much as she had done at the recent open day. He hadn't wasted much time bothering to decide why.

Now he had his answer.

The woman disliked him, resented his success and was out to ruin his reputation out of some warped sense of revenge.

But how?

'That was at her insistence.' Ray paused. 'I get the impression that she's working her way through the list of people she wants to punish because her life in France went wrong and she needs someone to blame. And I think she has Hadleigh dancing to her tune.'

'That'll be a first,' Isaac grunted. 'I'm high on her list of most wanted, it seems, but I'd still like to know why. My mother's long dead and my father scarpered years ago. I have no idea where he is. Probably in bed with Spain's criminal fraternity, so what Michelle thinks she missed out on is hard for me to fathom, always assuming that's the way her mind is working. Or why she holds me responsible when I wasn't even around at the time of her conception, come to that. We didn't have a normal family life, so it's not as if she missed out. We constantly had the old bill knocking at the door. It wasn't exactly a bed of roses so it sounds as though she was better off in France, where at least she got to enjoy horses.' He scowled. 'Why do people always think the grass is greener?'

'Well, now, that's the question. Or a ton of questions, come to that, but I do agree that she has it in for you.'

'Perhaps, but she can't have married Guy in the hope of getting to me. I only acquired my horses a couple of years ago, long after they were married.'

'I reckon... no, I know from reading her emails that she saw it as fate when you picked her husband's yard.'

'She sounds unhinged.'

'I rather think that she is,' Ray agreed, tapping away at his keyboard. 'Do you have any foreign investors?'

Isaac blinked. 'Of course. Loads of them. Why?' A flash of inspiration caused Isaac to frown. 'Don't tell me. Someone she knew in France invested with us and lost money.' He lifted one shoulder. 'It happens if they insist upon going for high-risk stocks, which we tend to advise against but people get greedy if they experience a little success and refuse to listen. It's a bit like gambling... well, it is gambling and it's addictive.'

'Her adoptive father went to a seminar where you were represented. In Paris.'

Isaac nodded. 'I recall doing those in the early days and hated it. No need to now. We can be more selective.' Isaac sighed. 'So this deranged woman blames me for her adoptive father's losses, does she, or could there be some other underlying cause?'

'The man killed himself, Isaac.' Ray glanced up from his keyboard. 'She found him hanging in his garage.'

'Christ!' Isaac scrubbed a hand down his face. 'Even so, how I can be culpable?'

'Michelle was eighteen at the time. She'd planned to have a career in three-day eventing and was hotly tipped to make it big-time. Instead, she was required to abandon her dreams and get a job so that she could look after her adoptive mother. She lost golden opportunities to ride decent horses and—'

'—Blames my mother for the circumstances of her birth and me for her thwarted ambitions.' Isaac scowled again, this time at the walls. 'It surprises me that she doesn't blame Hadleigh too.'

'According to their email exchanges, he swears he knew nothing of your mother's pregnancy and would have taken her in himself if he had.'

Isaac flexed a brow. 'And she believes him? I can't imagine anything making him take a DNA test if he hadn't known. And if he did know, he wouldn't have wanted a child that might look like him anywhere near his wife, who's a bit of a dragon. I'm sure she knew of Hadleigh's affairs but wouldn't have wanted to see the result of one of them staring at her across the breakfast table every day. Hadleigh would have known that too.'

'Well, you'd know more about that than me. What I can tell you is that it seems they are cut from the same cloth, those two. Both ruthless and vindictive – streaks they undoubtedly recognised in one another.'

'Streaks that Hadleigh admires, wishes he could see in his sons and looks to exploit in his daughter.' Isaac nodded slowly. 'I get the picture and would simply remove my horses from the yard and walk away, but for the fact that I really, really want to know what I've done.' Isaac clenched his jaw. 'And more to the point, why it was necessary to try and kill Farah in order to exact revenge on me, which I assume this is all about.' He turned to face Ray. 'This is now personal, Ray, and I need answers.'

Ray chewed at a fingernail. 'Have you thought of forcing her hand?'

Isaac swung on his heel and turned to face his investigator and friend. 'What do you mean by that?'

'Well, it seems to me that you now have the upper hand. Michelle has been careful to keep her background a secret and didn't expect you to get suspicious and start delving.'

'Right,' Isaac said, nodding pensively in agreement. 'I doubt if even Guy knows. In fact, I'm sure he doesn't. If he did, he would have pushed his wife to reveal her true identity to me. He's not the devious type and wouldn't have been able to act normally in front of me if he knew the truth.' He paused. 'I very much doubt he knows that Hadleigh is her biological father either. I suspect Guy is being used as a means to an end by a very manipulative female. She saw an opportunity to get to grips with decent horses again *and* to get her revenge.'

'Very likely. Which means you can somehow use what you know about her to play her at her own game.'

Isaac pursed his lips. 'If I knew what the hell that was.'

'Bound to be something to do with horses,' Ray said, stating the obvious. 'Most likely *your* horses.'

'Something that will destroy my reputation, but that won't happen by pretending a perfectly sound horse is lame.'

Ray removed one hand from his keyboard, a rare occurrence, and waved it at Isaac in a dismissive manner. 'Above my paygrade. I only talk to computers. Horses are a complete mystery to me. All I know is that one end bites and the other end kicks – horses, that is, not computers.'

'Right. That about sums it up, if you discount the fact that horses eat their pampered heads off and cost a fortune to maintain.'

'Hey, if you can't afford it then why do it?'

'I sometimes wonder that myself.' Isaac resumed his chair and allowed his chaotic thoughts free rein as he attempted to make sense of what he'd just learned. 'Did you find out anything about the bookies we suspect?' he asked. 'Given what we now know about Michelle, there's no doubt in my mind that she's the brains behind the operation, but it's not beyond the realms of possibility that she's inveigled one of the bookies into helping her do... well, whatever sting it is that she hopes to pull off.'

'Bob Ellis has been in the trade a long time and inherited his bookies' business from his father, and grandfather before him. As far as on-course bookies go, he has a good reputation and I can't find any skeletons in his cupboard. Well, nothing serious. The odd cashflow problem but they've never lasted for long. But Dave Fenton is another story.' Ray pressed a few buttons and grunted when he found the screen he was looking for. 'He "inherited" his business from an old timer called Paul Dakin. His name was synonymous with fair betting, if that's not a contradiction in terms, but he suddenly threw in the towel without warning and Fenton sprang up in his place.'

'Perhaps he got fed up and retired.'

'He was fifty-something.'

'Even so, he might have been unwell. Is he still alive and kicking?'

'Yep, retired to a bungalow in this neck of the woods.'

Isaac grinned. 'And you just happen to have the address.'

Ray sent Isaac an injured look. 'I hope you are not questioning my cyber-sleuthing skills.'

'Wouldn't dare,' Isaac replied, holding up a placating hand, still grinning.

Ray scribbled an address on a Post-it note and handed it to Isaac before switching off his laptop and packing it away. 'Well,' he said, 'that's all I have for you thus far.'

'Which is more than enough. Plenty of food for thought.'

'Let me know if you need me again once you've visited Dakin, which is what I know you intend to do,' Ray said, donning his biking jacket and hitching his laptop bag over his shoulder.

'I will, thanks,' Isaac said, opening the door and leading the way down the stairs.

He let Ray out, locked up behind him and returned to his sitting room. It was now very late but he wasn't tired and knew he had too many possibilities circulating in his brain to make sleep possible.

He'd drunk little that night so poured himself a Scotch and sat in the dark, savouring it as he contemplated what he'd learned.

He speculated upon his mother's long-standing affair with Hadleigh; something he had always known about or suspected, but had put to the back of his mind. She had been besotted with her handsome Spanish husband, overlooked the affairs that he took precious little trouble to cover up, and made endless excuses for his criminal activities. Isaac had cottoned on when he hadn't been much older than ten that the endless stream of women his father seemed to hook up with, even when Isaac was with him, were not just the friends that he made them out to be.

He had known, without having to be told, not to mention them to his mother, who preferred to turn a blind eye. He now accepted that as a young man he had also known that his mother was in love with two men at once.

The beatings that his father dealt out to his mother for no apparent reason weren't so easy for Isaac to understand or to ignore and he gradually came to resent the man whom he had once looked up to and admired. *Perhaps the undeserved beatings were the catalyst that had forced her into the arms of a man who treated her right?* The violence that Isaac had grown up surrounded by had been one of the reasons why he had applied himself at school and used his intellect to make something of himself, rather than following in his father's questionable footsteps.

In a way, the old man had done him a favour, he reluctantly conceded. *Had he not been quite so handy with his fists...*

Isaac winced, recalling the many beatings he himself had endured when trying to protect his mother. Until he grew big and strong enough to fight back, which was when his father was force-fully persuaded to quit the family home.

Permanently.

Ironically, not long after that, his mother was diagnosed with terminal cancer. Isaac expected her to ask for her husband and he wouldn't have been able to refuse her dying wish. Instead, she seemed content to have Isaac and a series of carers looking after her and finished her days in a hospice with Isaac at her side, free from the strains of a violent relationship.

At least he had been able to do that much for his mother and gained a degree of peace from the fact that she died in... well, peace.

'Tomorrow,' he said aloud, draining his glass and standing, ready for bed, 'or should that be today, I will get to the bottom of this mess and hopefully discover what it is I'm supposed to have done to antagonise a half-sister I didn't even know I had.'

11

_____

Farah found her enforced idleness impossible to cope with and became increasingly fractious as a consequence. She particularly resented the fact that Isaac hadn't reported in. Convincing herself that he was holding stuff back from her, she eventually gave up all restraint and called him.

'Hey,' he said. 'Is everything okay?'

'Why wouldn't it be?' Her voice sounded sullen, even to her own ears, but she couldn't seem to help herself. She knew he had been out on the town the previous night – his picture was all over the online newspapers – and she felt peeved that he could even contemplate enjoying himself whilst she was stuck at home, worried and unsettled. She couldn't remember the last time she'd had a night out that didn't involve a quick glass of wine at the local but it hadn't seemed important to be missing out on the glamorous life before now.

'It's kinda early to be calling, especially on a Sunday.'

'Not for me,' she replied, glancing at the clock and wondering if she'd woken him. Wondering too if he'd woken alone. Probably not. 'It's gone eight in the morning. I've usually been up for over two hours by now, regardless of what day of the week it is. Just because you didn't get in until sparrow fart...'

'What a charming turn of phrase.' His chuckle resonated down the line, deep and earthy, chasing away a little of her resentment – if that's what she had been feeling. 'Anyway, I was about to call you.'

'Right.'

'Are you always this disbelieving?'

'Did I say I didn't believe you?' Farah vaguely wondered when she had been reduced to the level of playground behaviour.

'Can you get someone to take care of Daisy today?' he asked, not deigning to fall to her level of immaturity. His question took Farah unawares but had the effect of further lifting her depressed mood. If Daisy needed day care then presumably Isaac had need of her company.

'Yes, I guess. Why? What do you have in mind?'

'I've found out a few things. Tell you what, get yourself ready, make the arrangements for Daisy and I'll collect you in a couple of hours.'

'Okay... I think. Want to tell me what this is all about?'

'Not on the phone.'

'Very cloak and dagger.'

Farah felt the remnants of her antagonism giving way to amusement. Isaac, this tough individual who took no prisoners in his professional life, appeared to want her help and she would not repay him by being surly. This was as much about her own survival as it was about his and they needed to work as a team.

Keep telling yourself that.

Besides, she never seemed to feel bored when he was around. He kept her on her toes and made her feel safe in the middle of a situation that she knew to be a minefield of corruption and deception.

'There's stuff going on and we haven't scratched the surface yet so we need to get up to speed and start fighting back. It sounds melodramatic but I do not exaggerate. Believe me on this.'

'I do actually,' she replied, thinking of Guy's odd visit. 'And I have news of my own. Anyway, I'd best sort Daisy out. See you in a bit.'

She hung up and set about working the phone, ensuring that Daisy's needs would be adequately catered to for the rest of the day. Daisy herself seemed remarkably chirpy when she learned that Farah would be spending the day and, as Daisy herself put it, perhaps the night, too, with Isaac and asked few questions about the makeshift arrangement. Farah wanted to put her straight by pointing out that this was work, but she didn't want to worry Daisy either, so left her conceptions uncontested, part of her wishing that spending the night with Isaac could actually be based in fact.

As good as his word, Isaac arrived two hours later in a Mercedes hatchback, looking fresh and vibrant in jeans and a white shirt that he wore untucked. The weather was fine and a pair of sunglasses was perched on top of his head – every woman's wildest fantasy walking towards her door with a smile lighting up his rugged features.

'Hey,' Farah said, opening the door to him, aware of her insides performing Olympic-standard somersaults as she drank in the sight of him.

She, too, was wearing jeans but had replaced her work T-shirt with a vest top that sculpted her body, over which she wore a loose shirt. The bump on her head looked bigger and the bruising was emerging in a rainbow of clashing colours. She hadn't attempted to cover the damage with make-up and wondered what Isaac would make of her indifference in that regard. Perhaps he wouldn't even notice and wasn't likely to care much either way, even if he did.

'Hey yourself,' Isaac replied. She thought at first, when he hesitated, that he was going to hug her. *Don't be ridiculous!* He didn't, of course, and made do with smiling instead. 'How are you feeling?'

She gave a self-deprecating shrug, winced when various body parts objected to the simple gesture and pointed to her damaged face. 'Probably better that I'm not at work. Wouldn't want to frighten the horses. Quite literally.'

Isaac laughed. 'Now you're just fishing for compliments.'

'Am I?' She was genuinely surprised by the suggestion. 'Come on through. I'm sure Daisy would like a few minutes of your valuable time before we take off to wherever we're going.'

'I have all the time in the world for Daisy.'

And he set about proving it by sitting across from her and chatting as though they'd known one another for years rather than days. Farah admired that trait. There was a genuineness about him that set people at their ease. Most good-looking guys seemed to think that a quirk of nature set them apart from the rest of the population. Not so this hunk of male perfection. Even so, Farah needed to remember that he was not here for her but was looking for answers. So was she, and she wasn't about to fall in line with just about every lady he met and waste time fantasising about unrealistic possibilities.

Eventually, they left Daisy dozing in the capable hands of one of her carers.

'Slumming it today, are we?' Farah asked, eyeing his modest Merc with amusement.

'Blending in,' he replied, winking as he opened the passenger door for her.

'Yeah, I guess that other thing does rather stand out, to say nothing of causing noise pollution.'

Isaac chuckled as he climbed behind the wheel and fired up the engine. 'That's one way of looking at it.'

'Sorry if I've insulted your status symbol.'

'I don't get emotionally attached to machines,' he replied, moving away from the kerb and turning the car in the direction of the motorway.

'Mind telling me where we're going?'

'You first. You have news for me?'

Farah felt a pang when Isaac stopped to allow a string of race-horses to cross the road towards the gallops. They weren't from Guy's but she recognised their yard's livery and slid down in her seat, not wanting any of the riders to recognise her.

'They've gone,' Isaac said, sympathy in his tone. 'You can sit up now.'

'Sorry.' Farah flashed a sheepish grin. 'Not sure why I did that.'

'Ashamed to be seen with me?' he asked in a teasing tone.

'Mortified.'

Isaac moved the car forward, laughing at her. 'Well, that's me told.'

'I had a surprise visit from Guy yesterday,' Farah said into the ensuing silence.

'What's so surprising about that? He's your boss and yours is a close-knit yard. I've seen the way that he looks after you all so it's only natural that he'd want to know how you are, especially given the severity of your accident.'

'Perhaps but... I don't know. I got the impression that he was on a fishing trip. He asked me if there was anything going on at the yard that he ought to know about. Well, he didn't put it quite that bluntly but something has obviously raised his suspicions.'

'He believes that your crash was no accident?'

Farah waggled a hand from side to side. 'Not so sure about that but he seemed... well, worried about something.'

'With just cause.'

Farah's mouth fell open when Isaac calmly told her what his investigator had discovered.

'Michelle?' she asked stupidly. 'Guy's Michelle? Is he absolutely sure of his facts?'

'I've never known him to get things wrong. Besides, he hacked into her email and got most of his information from there.'

'Even so.' She absently plucked at her lower lip. 'Do you really think it's possible – that your mother had this Hadleigh man's child, I mean, and you've never known?'

'Yeah, I wouldn't write anything off when it comes to Hadleigh, no matter now implausible. And since it all happened five years before I was even born, there's no earthly reason why I would know.'

'I see.' She paused. 'I think. Although I don't, not really.'

'Join the club, baby.'

'Why did your father not go and punch his lights out?'

'My father was very handy with his fists, but only used them on those who were smaller and weaker than him.' Isaac's expression turned dark and unreadable. 'Hadleigh was *the man*. Untouchable. You didn't mess with him. He took what he wanted and the rest of the world had to put up with it.'

'Sounds charming,' Farah replied with a derisive sniff. 'And it was his sons, Michelle's half-siblings, who you think ran me off the road.'

'I do,' Isaac replied with a grim nod.

'Do you think they are aware of Michelle's true identity?'

'I would imagine so. They don't have much brain power, but they do know how to keep shtum and not talk about their father's business.'

'Wouldn't it make them resentful? Their father pouring plaudits on their long-lost half-sister, I mean. Equality of the sexes has, I would imagine, passed their sort by and they won't like being eclipsed by a woman, surely.'

'Possibly, but they don't have the balls or the brain power to outmanoeuvre their father. Don't make the mistake of imagining that he will ever retire – not completely. And he will always have to be in absolute control of what remains of his empire.'

Farah nodded absently and allowed a long pause whilst she tried to make sense of a senseless situation. 'But how can Michelle hold you responsible for what happened to her?' she eventually asked. 'It sounds as though she had a perfectly normal upbringing in France and has nothing to feel resentful about.'

'Well, that's the question I will eventually put to her.'

'If you're going to confront her, why are we driving away from Lambourn?'

'Oh, I expect I will confront her, but I sense that she's a vindictive character, so I need to have some ammunition of my own to throw at her before I do face up to her.'

'You want to know what she's planning to do, I imagine.'

Isaac nodded. 'Especially if she's using my horses to try and destroy my reputation.'

'Funny you should raise questions about her character. I've never been comfortable around her. I put it down to the fact that she's as withdrawn and disinterested in the yard as her husband is outgoing and interested in the people who work for him. I thought she was one of those women who doesn't like other women, so I kept out of her way. But then again, perhaps I picked up on her grievances without actually realising it.'

'Is she too old to forge a career in three-day eventing?' Isaac asked. 'That was what she was forced to give up when her adoptive father topped himself and, I'm thinking, forms the bedrock of her resentment.'

'She is a remarkable horsewoman,' Farah replied without hesitation. 'No one who's seen her on horseback could deny it. She can get horses to dance for her in a way that I'll never manage.'

'And Guy could sponsor her, so why...' Isaac indicated to overtake a slow-moving truck, articulating his thoughts as he did so. 'Perhaps she enjoys nurturing a grudge? Perhaps she's afraid of failing and so uses that grudge as an excuse not to try?' He gave a one-shouldered shrug. 'I have no doubt that she will enjoy telling me how I am responsible for ruining her life when we finally get to discuss the subject.'

'I dare say.' Farah let out a long breath. 'So, where are we going now?'

She listened as Isaac told her what his investigator had discovered about the two bookies who interested them. 'Did you know Paul Dakin before he sold out to Fenton?' he finished by asking.

'No, I can't say that I did.' Farah screwed up her eyes in an effort to recollect. 'I don't get time on course to take much notice of the bookies. You get to recognise names and faces, though, but I can't recall seeing Dakin's out there.'

'It was five years ago, about the same time as Guy and Michelle married. Could be a coincidence but I don't believe in them.'

'Okay, so I assume you have an address for Dakin and we're going to see him.'

'We are. He lives down on the coast, not far from me.'

'Then why drive all the way to Lambourn, only to drive back again?'

'Hey, I thought you'd like to hear what he has to say. Besides, you know more about the racetrack goings-on than me and if he's reticent, you might be able to charm him into opening up. Anyway, I knew you'd be climbing the walls so thought I'd give you an airing.'

Farah laughed in spite of herself. 'Very gracious of you.'

'That's me,' he replied, chuckling.

Isaac drove fast yet economically and the rest of the trip down to the coast passed with just spasmodic conversation between them. Farah was surprised when she didn't feel the need to fill the regular silences. They were comfortable rather than tense and she felt remarkably at her ease ensconced in a small car with this Adonis. She would have given a lot to know what thoughts passed through his quick brain but was given a small insight into his life when his phone rang several times, always something to do with the world of high finance despite the fact that it was a Sunday.

'No such thing as a weekend in your line of work,' she remarked. 'A bit like mine, I suppose. Horses still expect to eat, even on bank holidays and at Christmas.'

'Yeah, it can be pretty full-on but I thrive on the pressure.' He paused. 'Or did. I reckon it's a young man's game though, which would explain why brokers burn out in their thirties and forties.'

'Well, I guess you're reaching the pinnacle of your career then.'

He sent her a jaundiced sideways look. 'Perhaps it's time to do something else.' He surprised her by the sincerity behind his words, and she suspected that he had surprised himself too. She was pretty sure that he hadn't given conscious thought to retiring. 'You can have too much of a good thing.'

'You'd be bored out of your skull within weeks,' she told him. 'Men who are driven to succeed don't really know how to relax.'

'Oh, I don't know. I could buy a boat and sail round the world. Or,' he added, glancing at her, 'set you up with your own yard and you could teach me all there is to know about horses.'

'Ha! I know my limitations. I'm no trainer.' She chuckled but still felt the full force of the compliment since she sensed that it hadn't been made entirely spontaneously. 'Bet that's the first time a woman has turned down any proposition of yours.'

'I'm not in the habit of propositioning them,' he replied, applying more attention to the road than it had thus far warranted.

Farah wondered if she had somehow struck a nerve and so didn't pursue the subject. She fell into contemplations of her own, the smooth progress of the car causing her eyelids to droop. She jerked awake again when the motion abruptly stopped. Blinking sleep from her eyes, she found that they had pulled up outside a small bungalow on a hill overlooking Brighton.

'Sorry,' she said, swiping at her eyes with the back of her hand. 'I must have dropped off. Is this it?'

'Not to worry. Your body's still recovering from massive trauma. I'm not even sure you should be out of hospital but I know it would be a waste of breath to say so. Anyway, yes, this is Dakin's salubrious residence.'

'Not much to show for a life of bookmaking,' she remarked, turning her nose up at the unprepossessing sight: a small, rundown bungalow in a terrace of small bungalows – each indistinguishable from its neighbour. 'Clearly, the profession doesn't pay as well as the world has been led to believe.'

'Evidently not.' Isaac opened his door. 'Shall we go and ask Mr Dakin about the downturn in his circumstances?'

'If he's at home. There doesn't seem to be much sign of life.' Farah nodded towards the grimy net curtains, which didn't move when she climbed awkwardly from the car. She ignored the protest raised by her injured ribs but needed to take a moment to feel secure on her feet, which infuriated her. She was not the insecure type. 'And will he talk to us, even if he is in? Perhaps you should have called ahead.'

'And given him an opportunity to warn whoever's intimidated him?'

Farah blinked as she walked round the car to join Isaac on the pavement. 'You think he's been coerced into selling up?'

'I do.' Isaac took his turn to stare at the dilapidated bungalow. The old windows were peeling paint and probably allowed draughts to creep round the warped frames. Double-glazing had passed this place by. The roof looked in need of attention and the front garden was made up entirely of a dry patch of grass, not a plant in sight. 'Bookies always win long term; it's a known fact. So either Dakin had an expensive habit or somehow got taken for a ride.' He grinned. 'Pun intended. Anyway, after you.'

They passed through a gate swinging drunkenly off one hinge and approached a sloping porch situated precariously over a front door with a glazed panel. Isaac pressed the bell but when no sound emerged he fell back on thumping his fist against the wood. He was required to do so three times before the door was eventually wrenched open and a small man whose wrinkled face put Farah in mind of a gnome peered up at them.

'Yeah. What do you want?' he asked belligerently.

'Paul Dakin?' Isaac replied.

The man sniffed. 'Depends who's asking.'

Isaac introduced himself and Farah. Dakin peered myopically at Farah and his expression cleared. 'I've seen you at the tracks,' he said.

'You would have. I work for Guy Levant.'

'Right. This is about horses, I suppose.' He sent Isaac another belligerent look. 'I'm out of that game now, so I'm not sure what you think I can tell you.'

Isaac slipped him a fistful of notes. 'A moment of your time is all we ask.'

The notes disappeared faster than a rabbit down a burrow into the pocket of the baggy corduroy trousers Dakin wore. 'Come in.'

He nodded over his shoulder and led the way down a dingy and narrow lino-covered hall into a dirty kitchen. There was a small table beneath the equally dirty window, cluttered with used crockery and surrounded by wooden stools. Farah didn't relish the thought of sitting anywhere in this hellhole but Isaac, for all his satirical elegance, didn't appear to harbour similar qualms. He plonked his backside on one of the stools and made himself at home. Farah reluctantly did the same and was relieved when Dakin didn't offer them anything to drink. The thought of putting her lips to any of his crockery, even if he thought to wash it first, made her stomach turn.

'Well, what do you want?' Dakin asked, leaning against the sink and folding his arms defensively across his skinny chest. He leered down at Farah in her skimpy vest and she instinctively covered herself by pulling her shirt across her torso. 'I ain't got all day.'

'Fine,' Isaac replied, scowling when he obviously noticed the direction of Dakin's gaze, 'we won't take up much of your time in that case. I can see you're busy. So tell us, why did you give up your valuable on-track pitch?'

'Valuable?' Dakin rolled his bleary eyes and the smell of alcohol exuding from him as he opened his mouth was overwhelming in the small kitchen. 'Was once, but not no more. Too much competition from the power houses. Can't compete with online betting and guaranteed best odds. Ain't an even playing field no more. Of course, racegoers still like to have a punt on track. They get a thrill from it, but the majority of dosh goes online. Breeds addicts if you ask me, 'cause it can be done secretly. No one does ask me, of course, but it's a fact for all that.'

'You didn't make a decent living from it?' Isaac asked.

Dakin glanced round his kitchen and gave a derisive snort. 'I'll let you figure that one out.'

'Then if it was so bad, how did you manage to sell your pitch to Fenton?'

A modicum of fear flickered across Dakin's ferret eyes. 'Have you any idea how much it costs to get a pitch and how much it costs to run it if you do manage to get a decent one? Of course, you'll be thinking of the likes of Royal Ascot and Cheltenham, where available pitches are rarer than hens' teeth, the competition to nab one if it does come up is totally corrupt, but if you manage to score then even an inept bookie in a bad spot can make a killing. But take an evening meeting at say Kempton on a wet Wednesday night when only the most hardened of punters leave their warm firesides and you're lucky to break even.'

'Even so, you did it for a long time,' Isaac said. 'If it wasn't working out then you could have sold up and done something else.' He fixed Dakin with a laser gaze. 'So come on, earn those notes you just pocketed.'

'Why are you so interested?'

'Why are you so reluctant to tell us?' Isaac shot back.

'Ain't none of your concern.'

Isaac peeled two more fifties off a roll in his pocket and held them just out of Dakin's reach. Dakin looked at them, licked his cracked lips and appeared to have a brief struggle with what passed for his conscience.

'My son has a rare form of leukaemia.'

'I'm sorry,' Farah said, speaking for the first time.

'So am I. Me wife and me split years ago but that boy was my moon and stars. Still is and I'll do whatever it takes to keep him alive.'

'You paid for private treatment?' Isaac asked.

'Course I did, once the NHS ran out of options. What father wouldn't? The wife heard of this experimental treatment in Switzerland. I sold everything I had but couldn't raise the funds. Then, out of the blue, Fenton's representative approached me with an offer above the odds for my pitch.'

'Didn't that strike you as odd?' Isaac asked.

'What it struck me as was an answer to my prayers and I didn't ask too many questions. I took the dosh and gave up a business that's too tightly regulated nowadays anyway. Course,' he added with another sniff, 'the money weren't enough. It soon got eaten up with extra charges but at least me boy is still breathing and has a chance.'

'Who else knew about your boy's condition?' Isaac asked.

'Most of the on-course bookies. We have a sort of camaraderie going. We're rivals, not exactly friends, but we do watch one another's backs.'

So, Farah thought, *any one of them could have let slip about Dakin's financial straits.*

'You mentioned Fenton's representative. He didn't approach you direct?'

'I'd never heard the man's name before, and never met him either. All the negotiations were done between me and these two guys.'

'Two guys?' Isaac leaned forward. 'Describe them.'

Farah had never met Hadleigh's sons – the two men who had supposedly driven her off the road – but she had heard them described before. And she was hearing that same description right now, in this shabby kitchen. She sent Isaac a *what the hell* look but could see that he was as much in the dark as her.

Isaac asked a few more questions but when it became obvious that Dakin had nothing more to tell them, he handed over the notes he'd been waving about.

'Do not tell anyone else about this visit,' Isaac said in a mordant tone. 'I shall know if you do and you won't like the consequences.'

'Hey, don't threaten me! Who the fuck am I gonna tell? Does this dump look like a hub of social activity?'

Isaac nodded, hoping to hell that they understood one another. 'Let me know if anyone comes asking the same questions we have,' he said, handing Dakin his card. 'I'll make it worth your while.'

'Yeah, yeah.' Isaac's card disappeared into the man's pocket. The same pocket where Isaac's fifties now resided. 'Mr Popular, that's me.'

Isaac wished him luck with his son's treatment and they left the dingy bungalow.

Farah greedily drank in the fresh, salty air as soon as they stepped outside and left the fetid smell of neglect and depression behind them.

'What's going on, Isaac?' she asked, turning a bewildered look upon the financier.

12

Isaac opened Farah's door and waited for her to ease herself into the car. It was obvious that her injuries protested and she couldn't hold back a slight groan – a sign of weakness she would probably prefer for him not to have seen. Isaac knew all there was to know about pride, about putting on an act to defy those who would see him fail, and understood the determination that drove her.

He drove away from Dakin's depressing residence with an unmitigated sigh of relief that he sensed was shared by his passenger. It had reminded him a little too graphically of the squalor of his own childhood, but for the fact that his home had at least been spotlessly clean. He noticed the grimy curtains at the front room window moving as the man watched them depart and wondered what he would do about Isaac's visit.

'A very good question and one that would be best discussed over lunch,' Isaac said, replying to the query that Farah had posed the moment they'd left the bungalow. He turned the car in the direction of a cliffside pub that he knew did a decent Sunday roast. 'You okay?'

'It's impossible not to feel depressed. And I feel sorry for the guy. Never thought I'd say that about a bookie.' Her expression was as surprised as her tone of voice. 'Why would Michelle, or Hadleigh for that matter, want a bookie with a trackside pitch in their pocket? And more to the point, why did you feel the need to threaten him? It's obvious that he's now out of the game.'

'But not out of the sights of the people who did him over and he will likely run to them, telling tales about our visit, hoping for another payday. He watched us drive away and probably tried to get our number. Good job he's short-sighted.'

'How do you know?'

'Didn't you noticed the way he squinted?'

'Can't say that I did. He told the truth about his son, though. I saw a ton of pictures of a child on the mantelpiece in the front room as we walked past it. It was like a shrine. Spooky but kinda sweet.'

'I did too but it doesn't necessarily mean that the child's ill. He could be alive and well and living a full and active life as an adult. The illness thing might be what he was told to say if anyone like me came asking questions.'

Farah frowned. 'Do you think he's really that devious?'

'If he was strong-armed into giving up his pitch, which would have been more valuable than he let on, even with online competition and all the regulations he referred to, then he will have a weakness that Hadleigh identified and played on.'

'Are you always this suspicious?' Farah asked.

Isaac glanced sideways at her and grinned. 'In my line of work, it pays to be sceptical.'

'So, what do you think that weakness might be?'

'That's something for Ray, my investigator, to look into. I'll get him to check on the son's supposed illness too. If that pans out then I'll give him the benefit of the doubt.'

'If you're unsure then why did you give him your card? Now he, or whoever's pulling his strings, will know who you are.' She paused. 'Who we are?'

'You think they wouldn't connect the dots from a description? I want to rattle them. So far, they've been patient and organised, apart from arranging your little trip off-road, that is, but if we let them know we're coming after them it just might panic them into making an error.'

'Or going after Daisy to get to me. If Dale is working for them, he will have told them about my circumstances.'

'I've thought of that. I have a nice ground-floor apartment that's currently empty down here in Brighton with a lovely view of the sea. Since you aren't working right now and Daisy could do with a change of scenery, do you think she'd agree to—'

'You'd be better advised to ask if *I'll* agree,' Farah replied hotly. 'You seem to have it all worked out but didn't bother to run it past me first. I do have a life, you know.' She flapped a hand. 'It might not seem like much to you but—'

'Sorry,' he said contritely. 'I've been making plans on the hoof and haven't had time to consider your feelings. You have to believe that I want to keep you both safe and I knew you wouldn't agree if I asked you first.'

'Is this how you do business?' she asked, a cynical edge to her voice. 'Does it work?'

'Usually.' He shot her a sideways grin and returned his attention to the busy road, crawling with holidaymakers in no particular hurry. 'No one knows I own that flat and Hadleigh won't find you there.' He sent her a pleading look. 'Do it for Daisy,' he said persuasively. 'It will only be for a few days. I have a feeling that this situation will resolve itself in that period of time.' Isaac set his jaw in a firm line. 'I will ensure that it does but I need to know that you and Daisy aren't in the direct line of fire. Daisy can't protect herself and right now, nor can you.'

'All right, I'll run it past Daisy. But,' she added, pointing a finger at him, 'I will not sit meekly at home letting you take all the risks. Either we're in this together or Daisy and I stay put and take our chances.'

'You drive a hard bargain, woman.' Isaac grinned at her. 'I'm trying to be chivalrous, in case you hadn't noticed.'

'Well, don't be. It isn't helping. We're no longer living in the dark ages, you know.'

Isaac pulled up into the pub's car park, content to have got his way and to let her have the last word. To let her think she was calling the shots. Unlike Hadleigh, he was all for equality of the sexes but what he'd just told her was the truth. She was temporarily debilitated, Daisy permanently so. Which made them vulnerable and Farah must realise it but getting her to admit it was another game altogether.

The pub's gardens were already crowded since a lot of customers had chosen to eat outside at the bench tables. Kids appeared to be everywhere, kicking balls against the wheels of parked cars and running riot, mostly unsupervised, in the children's play area.

'Come on. Hopefully the bar will be a child-free zone.'

She laughed. 'I admire your optimism.'

Isaac cut the engine and they both climbed out of the car. He noticed Farah wince as she slowly stood upright and wished there was something he could do to ease her pain. There were a lot of things he would like to do with Farah but chased that line of thought away. Now wasn't the time and it definitely wasn't the place.

Perhaps there never would be a right time. They came from different worlds and yet the better he got to know her, the more he wanted to be a part of her world, away from the cut and thrust and fierce competition of the financial sector. A man could only spend so much money during the course of his lifetime and Isaac, not yet forty, was already a millionaire several times over.

How much was enough?

They managed to get a table in a fairly secluded part of the pub with a view over the cliffs to the sea below that was, for once, calm and deceptively benign. A good day to be out in a boat, Isaac absently thought as he examined the menu, toying with the possibility of purchasing one.

Once they had drinks in front of them and had placed their order, Isaac reapplied his mind to the interview with Dakin.

'It was Hadleigh's sons who did the negotiating with Dakin, wasn't it?' Farah asked, anticipating the turn his thoughts had taken.

'I'd bet money on it.'

'But why would Hadleigh, or more to the point Michelle, need an on-track bookie in her pocket? And why wait all these years without making Fenton earn his keep?'

'If she has waited,' Isaac said, sipping his lager straight from the bottle. 'There's no saying what schemes she has percolating.'

'Is she attempting to line her own pockets, though? She has a rich, guilty daddy in Hadleigh ready to satisfy her every whim, does well with buying and selling eventing horses, so why...' She pondered for a moment and then turned worried eyes upon Isaac. 'You think she's using Guy for some reason and plans to leave him when he's served his purpose? That would destroy Guy. He worships the ground she walks on.'

Isaac spread his hands. 'It pains me to say that I have no idea what she had planned in the past but I'm pretty sure I'm now her main target. Whether she's been building up to have a pop at me all these years or whether I'm just a convenient distraction that she can't bear to pass up is a question that I fully intend to get answers to.'

Farah leaned her elbow on the table and the side of her face on her cupped hand. 'Even so, we knew that much before going to see Dakin, that she wants to get back at you, I mean, so we're not much further forward, are we?'

Isaac grinned at her and said nothing.

'What are you scheming, Mr Fernandez?' she asked, frowning suspiciously.

Their food arrived at that moment, which allowed Isaac time to consider his response. 'I have absolutely no idea,' he settled for saying once the waitress had left them and he'd picked up his cutlery. 'It's a waiting game now.'

'Don't believe you,' she taunted, grinning across the space that separated them. 'You're not the passive type.'

'True.' He tasted his beef, shrugged when he found it not up to standard but couldn't be bothered to send it back. He cut into a potato instead. 'Since you ask, I have Ray doing more digging into Michelle and her adoptive parents. I looked into my online records, too, for about the time that her adoptive father was supposedly recruited into one of my schemes.' He paused, fork poised midway to his mouth. 'There is no one by the name of Blanchett registered. I checked twice and I can assure you that our record-keeping is tight and one hundred per cent accurate. It has to be. On-track bookmaking isn't the only strictly regulated industry.'

Farah abandoned her fish, placed her cutlery aside and leaned towards him. Isaac wished the hell that she wouldn't. Every time she did so, he was treated to an up-close view of her cleavage. The fact that she wasn't aware and wasn't doing it deliberately made it ridiculously erotic. To say nothing of distracting.

'Her father's loss of income was nothing to do with you?'

'Nope.' Isaac picked up his knife and fork again. 'Unless he traded under a different name, I've never had dealings with the man.'

'Then why did your investigator imply otherwise?'

'A very good question,' Isaac said slowly. 'His information is usually spot on so I didn't bother to ask him where he came across it. He probably wouldn't tell me anyway. He can be annoyingly secretive about the places he hacks into, which is his favoured modus operandi.'

'Then why does Michelle have such a massive hard-on for you?'

Isaac grinned. 'Well now, there's a question.'

'Stop it!' Farah threw a chip at him as her cheeks flushed with colour. 'What we need to do is to talk to someone who knows Michelle better who might be able to throw some light on the subject.'

'I agree. As I say, I'm having Ray look into the Blanchett family's background but in the meantime, I was wondering about Dale.'

'In what respect?'

'Well, the way he flew off the handle and fired you when you asked questions; that smacks of a desperate man who's in too deep with nasty people and is feeling the heat.'

'I agree. Dale was a contemporary of my uncle's and I've always looked upon him as... well, as a surrogate uncle. He's always looked out for me, which is why I confided in him, expecting him to support me, yet his behaviour was so out of character.'

'Think he'll talk to us and consider swapping sides?'

'It's risky,' Farah said after a brief moment of contemplation. 'I don't think he's naturally a bad man, but we know his drinking got him into this mess. Hadleigh covered it up for him and now owns Dale. And Hadleigh helped Dale, in all probability, because his daughter asked him to.'

'If he knows we're on to him, he'll do one of two things. He'll either decide that I'm powerful enough to protect him, or he'll run to Hadleigh and tell him we've been asking awkward questions.'

'Which is why you jumped the gun and left your card with Dakin?'

Isaac waggled a hand from side to side in a considering fashion. 'It never hurts to cover all the bases.' He fixed her with a serious look. 'Which course of action do you think Dale is more likely to take?'

'If you'd asked me that a month ago, I wouldn't have hesitated to defend him and insist he was on the good guys' side. But now... well, now I don't know what to think. Hadleigh and his crew are a nasty bunch of thugs, and I include Michelle in that category. You have to be either brave or a little crazy to cross them.' She leaned her chin on her clenched fist and sent him a speculative look. 'Which are you, Isaac?'

As Isaac considered his response, he felt a great sense of privilege to be alone with this attractive, brave and complex woman. A woman who knew what she wanted from life, and it didn't require millions in the bank to make it happen. Could Isaac say the same about himself? Making more money for money's sake seemed increasingly pointless, even if the amount he'd garnered gave him immense satisfaction and a feeling of self-worth. He could so easily have followed the example set by his father and if he'd done so he would likely now be one of Hadleigh's minions, doing as he was told, never allowed to express an opinion. Always striving to stay one step ahead of the law.

Even with her battered face devoid of make-up, Farah was a knockout and to his eyes, far more genuine than the plastic women he dated on social occasions to bolster his social standing and impress male clients. He sensed that Farah would turn her pert little nose up at such shallow behaviour and Isaac was starting to see a point of view that she had not actually expressed.

'Well?' she prompted.

Her voice reminded Isaac that he hadn't responded to her question. 'I never was one to give in to bullying,' he said. 'Bullies tend to rely on... well, brute force and their reputations as hard men. I prefer to use this.' He pointed at his head for emphasis.

Neither of them had finished their food but they let the waitress clear their plates and both declined the dessert menu.

'You can have too much of a good thing,' Isaac remarked as they waited for the woman to return with the card machine.

'Thanks,' Farah said as they stood up to leave.

'Not a patch on the food served in the Fox,' Isaac replied apologetically as they left the pub. He booted a football back to a small child before it could bash Farah's legs and knock her off balance.

'You missed your vocation,' she remarked.

'Think of the trillions those prima donnas get paid for kicking a ball about.' He grinned. 'Perhaps you're right and I should consider a career change.'

'I think it's a little late for that.'

'Ouch!' He placed a hand dramatically over his heart. 'You know how to wound a guy.'

His response made her smile, which pleased him. She had a lovely smile and should use it more often. 'You're a big boy. You can take it.'

'Come on. I'll show you the apartment I have in mind for you. I think Daisy will enjoy the change of scenery.' He paused, waiting for some kids to clear away from the back of his car before he reversed from his spot. 'I think you both will. Lots of bracing walking to be had across the cliffs. Sorry,' he added contritely. 'I realise Daisy can't walk far but I'm guessing that you will enjoy it.'

'There's nothing to stop me pushing her along.'

Isaac rather thought that her bruised ribs might put paid to that idea but kept his thoughts to himself. He knew she was wary of his suggestion and reluctant to be forced out of her home by the thugs who had tried to kill her. She was a feisty individual who didn't like the idea of running from a fight and felt as aggrieved as Isaac did at the thought of his horses somehow being manipulated for an as yet unexplained purpose.

She didn't realise how dangerous her situation was, Isaac knew. His views might be old-fashioned but he absolutely didn't want her or Daisy making targets of themselves. Isaac knew just how ruthless Hadleigh could be and had qualms about facing him himself – qualms that wouldn't prevent him from taking him on. There were long overdue scores to be settled.

Be that as it may, Isaac was under no illusions. Hadleigh didn't fight fair and Isaac would have to use his superior brain power to get the better of him. The odds were stacked against him, he knew, and if Hadleigh recognised Farah as his weak point he wouldn't hesitate to use her to get to Isaac. The old concept that villains left women and children out of their nefarious doings was an out-of-date fallacy.

There again, he was just as likely to shoot Isaac in the head in broad daylight in front of a dozen witnesses, so confident was he that he'd walk away from any charges. Isaac didn't know what had really driven him out of London, other than the rumours about the Albanians. True or not, he would still be involved in dodgy dealings and likely already had useful locals in high places in his pocket.

'Good idea,' Isaac replied as he drove with swift efficiency in the direction of Brighton marina.

'This is... different,' she said, after they'd travelled slowly in silence for a while and she'd taken an interest in her surroundings. The sunshine had brought out the crowds and Brighton seafront was teeming with people, as was its beach. He wondered if she would balk at the thought of being swamped by hordes of meandering tourists, being accustomed to the quiet country life, but she showed no outward signs yet of running away.

'Here we are,' he said, pushing a remote on his key fob and

waiting for the entrance gates to the apartment compound to swing open.

He parked up but Farah was unnaturally quiet when they left the car.

'You get a good view of the fishing fleet, such as it is, coming in and out of the marina early most mornings. Hope you don't mind the smell of fish.'

He led the way into the communal entrance hall and unlocked the front door to the spacious apartment that he hoped she would agree to call home for a few days. She glanced with a decided lack of interest around the large, modern open-plan space with seating arranged that allowed unimpeded views over the sea and towards Roedean ladies' college on the cliff edge behind them.

The sun had come out and sparkled off the sea as it gently lapped against the breakwater that protected the boats in the marina from the English Channel's unpredictable moods. There was a small beach just beyond the breakwater and the sound of children splashing about, their laugher and tantrums ringing out, brought an unexpected smile to Farah's face.

Clearly, she liked children and he wondered if she dreamed of one day having a family of her own. It was not a prospect that had thus far inspired Isaac, despite the best efforts of some of his dates to persuade him otherwise. Recollections of his own traumatic childhood had still not left him. Perhaps they never would but until such time as they did, as far as he was concerned, bringing children into this uncertain world was one massive responsibility that he would prefer to evade.

'They're searching for crabs,' she said, stepping out onto the terrace and peering at the kids scrambling about with buckets on the rocks, slipping and sliding on the slimy seaweed, often pushing one another. She barely spared a glance for the gleaming boats moored in the marina. 'I remember my uncle bringing us all on beach holidays like this one and we spent hours digging for... well, I'm not sure what we were actually looking for but I do remember that competition was fierce and we had a lot of fun.'

Isaac shook his head, smiling at her sense of priorities. Any other woman to whom he'd offered such luxurious accommodation would be keen to explore the entire apartment. It somehow didn't surprise him that Farah was more interested in reliving happy memories from her childhood.

'Come on. I'll show you the bedrooms.'

There were three, and two bathrooms. Farah immediately decreed that the largest, with an en-suite, would suit Daisy.

'There are no steps so it will be easy for her to get into the shower. We'll need to get a stool for her, though. She can't stand.'

Silently, Isaac reached into the spacious cubicle and pulled down the folding seat attached to the wall.

'Ah, right. That's perfect.' She smiled at Isaac. 'You've gone to a lot of trouble and I'm not very gracious, am I?

'You'll do,' Isaac replied, tugging playfully at a lock of hair that had escaped her ponytail.

She sent him a speculative look and then preceded him from the bedroom, almost as though she couldn't put distance between them quickly enough. Isaac permitted himself a wry smile, thinking that was a first. Ordinarily, the women he dated were only too happy to linger in bedrooms with him.

He followed her into the open living area, where she was examining the titles on the spines of the books shelved along one wall.

'Do I make you uncomfortable?' he asked, leaning his shoulder against an archway and folding his arms across his chest as he watched her.

'What? No. Of course not.' She gave a false-sounding laugh, which belied her denial. Was it his imagination, a product of wishful thinking perhaps, or was the air between them fuelled with sexual tension? Damn it, this was all his fault! His thoughts took that detour whenever they dwelt upon Farah, which was both inconvenient and unfair to her. 'It's just all a bit cloak and dagger, that's all. I'd like to say that you're overreacting but given what happened to me, I guess I need to give you the benefit of the doubt.' She spread her arms expansively. 'If it was just me then I'd take my chances but... well, Daisy is my responsibility, she hasn't got that much time left and I want her to enjoy the rest of her days.'

'I know.'

She wandered about the room, picking things up at random and putting them down again, clearly unsettled.

'If you don't like the apartment, I can arrange a hotel...'

'God no! Thanks, this will be fine, if it is only just for a few days.' She stopped her restless pacing directly in front of him and sent him a concerned look.

'Then what?'

'I've been thinking about your suggestion of approaching Dale and I would advise against it,' she said, a slight frown marring her bruised brow.

'Okay. Mind telling me why?'

'Because I've never seen him like this before.' She let out a long sigh. 'He's in over his head and running scared, Isaac. Scared enough to sack me, when he's often referred to me as the daughter he never had.'

'If he's sold himself to Hadleigh then he has good reason to be scared.'

She nodded as she tapped the fingers of one hand on her opposite forearm. 'The only reason I can think of for him turning on me is because I got too near the mark with my questions and it was his clumsy way of protecting me from whatever's going down.'

'Perhaps, but that only leaves me with Michelle and I don't want to approach her from a position of weakness.'

'Have you considered Ryan?'

'Ryan?'

'Ryan Coultard, the stable jockey.'

'Oh right, sorry. I'm with you now.' It was Isaac's turn to frown. 'You think he's involved?'

'Frankly, I have no idea, but I've always got along with him well. He seems like a straight shooter. If they're race fixing, I honestly believe he wouldn't get involved. Then again, if anyone had told me that Dale would, I'd have refused to believe it, so I'm not really much help.'

'Everyone has their pressure point. Secrets that men like Hadleigh have a way of ferreting out and exploiting in order to turn them but yes, if you think he'd be a good starting point, I'll corner him and have a word. Better not to confront him at the yard, though. Any idea where he lives?'

'He lodges in the village. There's a woman who lets rooms out to jockeys.' She reeled off the address. 'He rides out most mornings if there isn't a race meeting. The best time to catch him would be at about eleven, after exercising, when he'll head back to his lodgings for breakfast.'

'Okay, then that's what I'll do.'

'Be careful, though, Isaac. I don't mean to tell you your business but exercise caution when you speak to him, just in case...'

'In case he's up to his neck in it too. Don't worry. I'll have Ray look into his background, see if there are any skeletons that Hadleigh might have exploited.'

'Good.'

She turned away from him and stared intently at the view. He wondered what had taken her attention and it took him a moment to notice her shoulders shaking.

'Hey, what's up?' He gently grasped the shoulders in question and turned her to face him. 'Have I upset you? If so, I didn't mean to say anything that would...'

Tears streamed down her face and she seemed incapable of speech. Wordlessly, Isaac grabbed a sheet of kitchen paper from the surface behind him, handed it to her and watched as the tears abated and she mopped them up.

'Sorry,' she said, sniffing inelegantly. 'I don't know what's wrong with me. I'm not usually so feeble.'

'Farah, you were almost killed, you're in more pain than you're willing to let on *and* some of the people you trusted most seem not to be what you've always thought they were. Even so, you're more worried about Daisy than you are about yourself. Of course, you're upset. Anyone would be. Don't give it another thought.'

'I hate all this,' she said on a long sigh.

Somehow her head finished up resting on his shoulder; Isaac wasn't sure how.

Except that he knew very well.

He was the one who'd gently grasped her waist and pulled her against him. She didn't seem to mind and slid her arms round his waist with a soft sigh of capitulation. He kissed the top of her head as he soothed her back with long, practised sweeps of his hands, conscious of her heart beating an irregular tattoo against his chest and of her breath coming in increasingly short gasps. He wasn't being fair to her, taking advantage of her emotional distress, and yet he couldn't seem to help himself.

Something that felt so right couldn't possibly be wrong. Could it?

Isaac thought about dead cats, the starving masses in Africa, inequalities based on race – all the things that men were supposed to think about to distract them from inappropriate arousal. This time it wasn't working and she wouldn't be able to help feeling the evidence. He expected her to pull out of his arms but she remained right where she was and no longer seemed quite so distressed.

Keep telling yourself that you're performing a public service, Fernandez!

She looked up at him, a question in her eyes at that precise moment, shattering Isaac's feeble hold on his self-control. With a shake of his head as he admitted defeat, he lowered his head and slowly claimed her lips in a drugging kiss that she participated in fully, no holding back. His tongue plundered her mouth like a parched man dying of thirst but she met him halfway and tangled her own with it, greedy and determined. Isaac was sure as hell dying of something, he decided, and it went by the name of frustration.

He broke the kiss but kept his arm round her waist, smiling down at her.

'I'd apologise for taking advantage of you,' he said, 'but for the fact that it wouldn't be sincere.'

'No apology necessary,' she replied, looking a little dazed. 'I'm as much to blame as you are.'

'That I very much doubt.' He led her to a chair and held her arm as she lowered herself slowly into it. 'And just so that you know, I've wanted to do that since first setting eyes on you.'

'No need for false compliments, Isaac. I don't suppose there are many women who would stop you from kissing them. You can take your pick.'

'So can you, darling. So can you.'

'Hardly.' She waved the compliment aside.

'So little self-confidence,' he replied, tutting.

'That's as may be,' she said, recovering a little of her old spirit, even if her eyes were still red-rimmed and puffy from crying. 'But unlike you, I'm selective!'

13

'Don't tell me what to do! You forfeited that right when you abandoned me forty years ago.'

Michelle folded her arms across her torso in a gesture of frustrated annoyance and paced up and down in front of Hadleigh's fire. Despite everything, she still couldn't think of him as her father and would definitely not address him as such. Nor did she buy his assurance that he hadn't known of her mother's pregnancy. It was clear from the way he spoke about her that he'd been infatuated and would have noticed her condition, to say nothing of her abrupt disappearance abroad.

Fernandez, her mother's husband, had told Hadleigh that she'd gone on a prolonged visit to his family in Spain. Michelle blew air through her lips, well aware that Hadleigh was too sharp to have bought that explanation, unless it suited his purpose. It was far more likely that he simply hadn't wanted to take on his own bastard. Or worse, he'd paid her mother to get rid of the inconvenience of an unwanted child.

Hadleigh thought she'd forgiven him for his neglect but nothing could be further from the truth. She was biding her time, using Hadleigh for her own purposes, but when she was done with him that would be the time to drop him in it and disappear into the sunset, an exceedingly wealthy woman in her own right; past grievances avenged.

'Don't come the hard woman with me,' Hadleigh replied, not cutting her any slack. Michelle liked that about him. Even if she didn't like the man himself she could still approve of his vicious streak. A person only had to look at world politics to see that being mealy-mouthed and willing to compromise achieved diddly-squat. It was the dictators, those with the courage of their convictions, who prevailed.

Hadleigh admired Michelle, she knew, and felt guilty about the way she'd been treated, but he still didn't let her walk all over him. Guy, on the other hand, was a soft touch, as were most of the other men in her life.

All so weak, so eager to please. It made her sick to the stomach.

Guy had been full of sympathy when she'd tearfully told him about her adoptive father topping himself. Good job he didn't know that Michelle had enjoyed a private party when she'd found him dead. Such a weak individual, allowing a small setback to destroy him, but Michelle had learned from her adoptive mother's example. Men were malleable, if handled properly. Guy had come along at the right time and she hadn't hesitated to use him for her own purposes.

'We have a good thing going here, to say nothing of an agreement.' Hadleigh's hard tone recalled Michelle's wandering attention. 'I won't pass it up simply because you're worried about missing your chance to get even with your precious half-brother. We both want that and will see to it in due course.'

'Ha! There's nothing precious about him. I despise the man. He lords it about, thinking he's the big I-am just because he's made a success of himself and never sees what's under his nose.'

Hadleigh chuckled. 'Just as well, but need I remind you that he is not our priority?' Michelle tossed her head and sent Hadleigh a scathing glance. 'I'll take that as a *no*. Now, is everything in place for the next delivery?'

'Of course.' She treated Hadleigh to a disdainful look that she knew neither of his weakling sons would dare to bestow on him. 'I do know what I'm doing.'

'Just as well 'cause we're in too deep to give up now. Anyway, we can't.'

Michelle thought she saw a brief expression of fear flit across Hadleigh's features but it was gone so quickly that she wondered if she had imagined it. She found it hard to believe that anything or anyone scared Hadleigh and felt absolutely sure that he'd exaggerated the violent tendencies of the people they were associated with.

'Okay,' she said, 'but bear in mind that this is the last time, then you have to keep your side of the bargain and help me bring Fernandez down.'

'Don't threaten me, darling. I won't take it, not even from you.' His icy expression gave way to a mean smile. 'However, it will be my pleasure to give you a helping hand in that regard. His mother, your mother, was a lovely woman but the Spanish bastard she married was a hard devil who knocked her about. I reckon Fernandez takes after his old man. He certainly takes no prisoners in the world of business so I know where he got his ruthless streak from.'

'He can't have been that ruthless, his old man, that is, if he overlooked his wife's indiscretions,' Michelle said flippantly, curious to see how Hadleigh would respond to the challenge. No one dared to question a word he said, she knew, but it would do him the world of good to discover that he'd met his match in his own daughter. 'What sort of hard man does that make him?'

'One who preferred to continue breathing,' Hadleigh replied, his voice taking on a brittle edge that made even Michelle a little afraid of him. 'But don't worry, a deal's a deal. Isaac'll get his. I tried to give him a hand when he was starting up but the little turd threw the offer back in my face and disrespected me. I don't forgive slights like that.' Hadleigh glanced at his watch. 'Now, the old lady will be back soon and if you don't want her to see you here and ask questions, you'd best be getting along.'

'I don't mind answering her questions,' Michelle said, grinning. 'It's about time she knew that I'm her stepdaughter.'

'If that's a threat and if it's supposed to scare me, think again.' Hadleigh's voice was hard but the suggestion of a smile shaped his cruel mouth. 'The day has yet to dawn when any woman gets the better of me. Even the one I was daft enough to marry.' He allowed a significant pause as he drilled her with a look. 'Even you.'

'Right.' Michelle knew when to back off. 'Fernandez was seen in the village this morning and Farah has disappeared, leaving Daisy alone,' she said, idly tapping her fingers on the arm of her chair.

'So?' Hadleigh shrugged a meaty shoulder. 'He might suspect that my idiot sons exceeded their instructions but he's flailing in the dark when it comes to everything else. I expect he's whisked Farah off somewhere to sympathise and work his way into her knickers.' Hadleigh chuckled. 'Can't say as I blame him for that. She's a looker. I'd have been tempted myself, back in the day.'

'A looker? Well, I suppose, if you like the pale, insignificant, wholesome type,' Michelle replied dismissively, irritated to think that Hadleigh might have got it right. She had been planning to leave Farah out of things but she'd just signed her own guilty verdict and Michelle would find a way to implicate her when the shit hit the fan. She disliked any woman who took the spotlight away from her.

Hadleigh barked an ugly laugh. 'She's younger than you, darling, and none of the schemes percolating in that vindictive brain of yours, will alter the fact.'

'What makes you think I give a shit?'

'You're a chip off the old block. Your old man don't like being eclipsed either.'

'Dale seems to have settled down,' Michelle remarked, picking up her bag. 'He was in a hell of a state after your boys stupidly drove Farah off the road but he's come to his senses now and appears to be toeing the line. The fact that he doesn't know of my involvement means I can watch him without rousing his suspicions.'

'I know he's behaving himself. Who do you think talked him round?'

'Jonah's as right as ninepence and Guy is still as ignorant as pig shit. It's only interfering little Farah and my brother that we have to worry about.'

'Do. Not. Do. Anything.' Hadleigh wagged a meaty finger at Michelle as he emphasised each word as a separate sentence. 'Not without my say-so. Don't fuck this up, Michelle. I won't be able to protect you if you let your own hang-ups get in the way of business. Do we understand one another?'

'Of course. And just for the record, I don't need your protection. I've gotten along just fine all these years living off my wits.'

'Good to know,' he replied, clearly not willing to show any of the remorse she'd hoped to see.

Hadleigh stood and followed her to the door. He didn't touch her, nor did he offer her insincere words of affection. She liked that about him. There was no bullshitting. He was proud of her, it showed sometimes in his eyes, but he was also ruthless and focused on the business in hand.

That was okay because so too was she.

* * *

Farah grinned, enjoying herself as she drove Isaac's Merc far too
fast back to Lambourn. He had insisted that she borrow the car to
get herself and Daisy about until such time as she could claim on
the insurance for her jeep. He hadn't taken no for an answer and,
truth to tell, Farah hadn't protested too hard. She had forgotten
what fun it was to drive a decent car and fully intended to make up
for lost time. In the passenger seat beside her, if Isaac was
concerned about her rather reckless driving, to his credit he gave no
indication and appeared to be falling asleep.

'How are you getting back?' she asked. 'There won't be room for
Daisy and all her paraphernalia and you and me. Besides, we won't
leave until the morning. I dare say you have money to make before
then.'

'Don't worry about me,' he replied, his eyes closed and seat
pushed back as far as it would go to accommodate his long legs.
'I've made arrangements to be picked up.'

'I'll just bet you have,' she muttered under her breath.

She noticed him in the periphery of her vision opening one eye
and sending her a jaundiced look. She decided against an apology,
even though he probably deserved one. He had been very considerate, given up a lot of his time and appeared genuinely concerned
about her and Daisy being caught up in something unsavoury. And
she was repaying him by being less than gracious.

She sensed that there was more to his history with Hadleigh
than he had let on, that this crusade was personal for him in ways
that eclipsed the manipulation of his horses. Well, of course it was
personal! He had just discovered that he had a half-sister, fathered
by a man whom he intensely disliked. And all Farah seemed
capable of doing was challenging his every suggestion and generally making his life difficult.

Her problem was that she was drawn to him on a level over
which she had precious little control. Her common sense flew out

the window whenever she was anywhere near him and that infuriated her. Just because he was a pretty face... Just because he'd taken up the cudgels on her behalf... Just because he'd kissed her *and* pretended that he'd wanted to from the word go. That was what had gotten to her, she knew. There was no need to lie. She'd seen pictures of the women he dated; he seemed to have an entire stable of them and she couldn't match up to any one of them.

Nor did she have any desire to.

But she wouldn't be treated as a plaything, a novelty sideshow to amuse himself with simply because he was bored. Unlike some she could name, she had a brain and wasn't afraid to use it. Well, when he wasn't around she didn't have any problems in that respect, she conceded, but his presence seemed to short-circuit the brain in question. But if she tried to explain that she could be useful to him, that they were partners in this investigation, both with vested interests, then he would point out that impulsively speaking her mind to Dale had almost got her killed. Worse yet, she couldn't deny it. It was infuriating because he always seemed to be right.

Now he'd lent her a luxury flat and a car that didn't need to be coaxed into life. It was a taste of his own life, a high life, to which she was not accustomed and never wanted to be. And it left her indebted to him. He assumed that whilst she was safely tucked away in Brighton, he would be able to get on with his investigation unimpeded and not tell her what was going on. Her grip on the steering wheel increased with her determination not to be sidelined. He should not have lent her a fast car, she decided, biting back a mischievous smile, if he didn't want her to follow her own line of investigation.

What direction that line would take she had yet to decide. All she knew was that whatever was going down, it centred around horses and that was her world.

Not his.

'Like the car?'

She thought he'd been sound asleep and his voice gave her a start. 'Don't do that!'

'Do what?' He looked genuinely baffled. 'Talk to you?'

'Sorry.' She shook her head. 'I was miles away and thought you were asleep. You startled me, that's all.'

'I can understand why you're so jumpy. You've been through a lot.'

He spoke in a matter-of-fact tone that implied understanding rather than sympathy or, worse, patronisation. She was grateful for that. She had no plans to be a victim – not for a second time. She would take Daisy with her back to the coast but she had no intention of staying there and taking up knitting.

Someone had tried to kill her and she was damned if she would allow Isaac to fight her battles as well as his own.

* * *

Michelle drove slowly back to the yard, in no particular hurry to be fussed over and petted by her husband, almost as though she was one of his pampered equines. Keeping up the pretence of being besotted with him was rapidly wearing her down. Only the reminder that they were finally approaching the finish line and the pretence would soon be over kept her motivated. She was nothing if not tenacious when it came to getting her way. Her own fractured childhood had taught her the value of patience as well as how to bear a grudge.

She thought longingly of the fireside beside which she would much prefer to be languishing; the arms in which she would much prefer to be ensconced; the lively conversation interspersed with laughter and love-making, and sighed.

'The sacrifices I make,' she muttered.

She parked her car in the open barn where all the vehicles were kept, plastered a smile on her face and let herself into the cottage that she shared with Guy through the kitchen door.

'Hey, there you are.' Guy turned from in front of the range, spatula in hand, and smiled at her. 'I was getting worried. Dinner's almost ready.'

'Thanks.' She walked up behind him and wrapped her arms around his waist, her disdainful expression lost on him since he continued to prod at whatever he was cooking instead of turning to kiss her, as he would ordinarily do. She felt mildly concerned by his uncharacteristic behaviour but was too distracted by her own turbulent thoughts to dwell upon it. 'Something smells good.'

'Sit yourself down. I'll dish it up.'

Michelle made all the right noises about the food which, admittedly, did taste good but she barely registered what she put in her mouth. Instead, her concerns regarding Guy steadily worked their way to the forefront of her mind. He was withdrawn, obviously worried about something and Guy never worried. He said it was a destructive emotion, that things had a way of working themselves out and worrying was a waste of energy. It was probably one of the horses getting ill, or something equally trivial, but she hadn't come this far only to drop the baton at the last hurdle.

'Is something wrong?' she asked, as they cleared away and stacked the dishwasher. 'You're very quiet tonight.'

'Just a bit concerned about Farah,' he replied, turning to face Michelle, his brow creased with a level of worry that exceeded mere concern. *Shit, was the entire male population of Berkshire getting wound up about a bump on the head?* Michelle wondered, hiding her contempt behind a sympathetic expression. *God give me strength!* 'I called to see her yesterday. Her face is a mess, Michelle, and she's obviously in a lot of pain. She's damned lucky to be alive.'

'I didn't know you were planning to call. I would have come with you.'

Guy looked mildly surprised. 'I didn't think you'd want to. You never take much interest in the girls who work here.'

Michelle felt miffed by the suggestion of a complaint that was entirely... well, valid. But still, Guy didn't ordinarily criticise anything that she did and now, did he but know it, was definitely *not* a good time for him to start.

'That's your side of the operation – the training, I mean,' she replied, quelling the edge that sprang to her voice. 'We agreed when we set up here that we'd play to our strengths and not infringe upon one another's territory. It would be a recipe for disaster if we were in one another's pockets twenty-four seven.'

'I know, but—'

'I spend a lot of time and energy on my eventing horses, finding the right ones for my clients, getting them over here and selling them on for a commission. The business turns a decent profit and supports the training side. Without it, we'd be struggling.' *And don't you forget it!*

'I wasn't criticising you, darling.'

Oh yes you were! And Michelle wasn't about to let him get above himself. 'Anyway, Farah's face will heal and perhaps now she'll purchase herself a decent vehicle. Sentiment is all very well, but that heap of her uncle's was an accident waiting to happen.'

Michelle knew she'd let her temper get the better of her when Guy turned to fix her with a mildly suspicious look. 'How did you know she drove her uncle's jeep and was sentimentally attached to it?' he asked.

'Oh, I heard her mention it once, I think, when someone was teasing her about the car. Why? Does it matter?'

'I don't suppose so.' The worry lines left his face and he held out a hand to her. 'How about an early night?'

She knew precisely why he wanted one and wasn't in the mood to play along. 'Sorry,' she said, placing a hand over her stomach and wincing.

'No!' He looked crestfallen. 'Your period?'

'Yep.'

'You didn't say.' He sighed but his expression cleared. 'That's where you've been, isn't it? I did wonder. You didn't want me to see how upset you are but really, darling, you don't need to hide your feelings from me. We can share the pain.'

'It only happened today and I haven't had a chance to tell you.' She bit a lip to prevent herself from smiling. He was *so* easy to manipulate that there was almost no fun in it. 'And you're right, I needed a bit of time to myself but I'm fine now, really I am.'

'Damn!' Guy fell onto a kitchen stool and dropped his head into his splayed hands. 'Perhaps the time has come to consider IVF.' He held up a hand to prevent her from protesting. 'I know you want to conceive naturally, darling, but it's been five years and, well… nothing.'

That would be because Michelle hadn't come off the pill. No way was she bringing a child into this crazy world, especially not after the way she'd been treated like an inconvenience. Besides, she didn't like children. They demanded attention, whined and complained all the time and always wanted the best of everything.

A child would also spoil her figure and take the attention away from her.

But she knew that Guy dreamed of having a family and when she had identified him as the man she needed to help her see her scheme through, she'd been forced to pretend that it was her dearest wish too.

'I'm disappointed too but let's give it another six months, then we will go down the IVF route. I promise.' She plonked herself on his knee and wrapped her arms around his neck. He smelled of horses and cooking oil but needs must. 'I have a feeling that if we stop being so anxious it *will* happen. You still hear stories about IVF babies having various internal problems, learning difficulties and God alone knows what else and I so want our child to be perfect.'

'Okay.' Guy gave a weary sigh but didn't kiss her, as ordinarily he would. Instead, he tipped her off his lap and headed for the door. 'I'll do evening stables myself,' he said.

'Shit,' she muttered, hoping that she wasn't losing control of him – not now, when matters were finally coming to a head.

She reached for her mobile and called the one person whose voice of reassurance she needed to hear at that moment.

14

Isaac knew that Farah and Daisy were safely installed in his Brighton Marina flat, hopefully well away from danger. He knew because he had checked on them himself, pretending to want to know if there was anything they needed. Since he'd had the fridge and freezer fully stocked, the bookshelves were bursting and every TV channel known to man was available to them, as well as fast-speed internet, he wasn't surprised when they assured him that they were spoiled for choice.

More to the point, Daisy seemed to be enjoying herself enormously. Farah, not so much. He had sensed her reluctance to be away from the action and knew that she'd only agreed to this enforced holiday for Daisy's sake. Perhaps it had been a mistake to provide her with a car but there was no way she could return to Lambourn and get into trouble, he had convinced himself. That would require her to leave Daisy alone, which was something she would never do.

Now, on Monday morning, late to his desk at arguably the busiest time of his week, he was finding it hard to concentrate on the financial markets. That had never happened before and he wondered if it should concern him more than it actually did. Lack of attention could lead to costly mistakes. Patrick picked up on his distraction and remarked upon it.

'Woman trouble?' he asked, grinning. 'It's about time one of those lovelies played you at your own game.'

'I wish it was something that easy to resolve,' Isaac replied absently.

'Easy for you, perhaps. Us lesser mortals have to work at these things.'

'Right.' Isaac grinned, aware that his partner was as popular with the opposite sex as he himself was.

Patrick wandered back to his own office, leaving Isaac with his thoughts. He had Ray beavering away, delving deeper into Michelle's background as well as that of Fenton, the bookie who had taken over Dakin's trackside pitch.

'Why the hell do they need an on-course bookie in their pocket?' he wondered aloud, tapping the end of his pen absently against his teeth.

His intercom buzzed, intruding upon his unproductive morning and introspective thoughts.

'Yes,' Isaac said brusquely.

'There's a detective here to see you, Isaac,' Kristen's voice purred.

'A detective? What does he want?'

'To speak with you.'

Isaac's first thoughts turned to Farah. God forbid that someone had got to her. Common sense told him that he would have heard about it if that was the case long before the police got round to calling. Even so, he had to know for sure. 'Send him in,' he said curtly.

The door opened shortly thereafter and Kristen led two men into the room. Isaac stood to greet them, taking a moment to assess his visitors. The elder wore a smart suit and tie, making Isaac, in designer jeans and open-neck shirt, feel underdressed. The second man was a great deal younger. He was also suited and booted but clearly suffered from budget restraints, as evidenced by his cheap attire.

'Gentlemen,' Isaac said, nodding at Kristen to leave them, even though it was obvious that her curiosity was piqued and she would have much preferred to remain. The younger policeman turned to watch Isaac's statuesque PA leave the room, making no attempt to hide his appreciation of her physical attributes. Isaac was pretty sure that sort of behaviour was frowned upon nowadays by the politically correct brigade and even if it wasn't, an officer of the law ought to exercise more restraint. He decided that he didn't much care for the younger man, an emotion that was clearly reciprocated given the scathing manner in which the detective's gaze roamed around Isaac's opulent office before coming to rest on Isaac himself.

Envy, Isaac wanted to tell him, was a destructive emotion.

'How can I be of help to Brighton's finest?' he asked instead.

'I'm Detective Inspector Rice and this is DC Burke.' They both flashed their warrant cards but Isaac could see Rice taking everything in about Isaac's high-tech office as he did so. 'Hope this is a convenient time.'

'More convenient than you could possibly know,' Isaac replied. 'I was looking for an excuse to skive off.' He directed them towards an arrangement of chairs in front of the fireplace and took one himself, content to wait for them to get to the point.

'We're investigating a murder, sir,' Rice said, seating himself and adjusting the fall of his trousers with fastidious care. DC Burke remained standing, as though to intimidate, notebook poised. Isaac almost smiled. To the best of his knowledge he had done nothing wrong. He definitely hadn't murdered anyone and it would take more than a wet-behind-the-ears DC to intimidate him into making a confession, even if he had.

'Someone I know, presumably,' Isaac replied, crossing one leg over his opposite thigh, 'otherwise you wouldn't be here.'

'Does the name Paul Dakin mean anything to you?'

Isaac's feet hit the floor with a resounding thud and he leaned towards the DI, scowling. 'It does. I visited his home just yesterday and left... left my card with him. Presumably that's what drew you to me.'

The DI nodded. Isaac's mind churned with increasingly troubling possibilities, even as he anticipated the nature of the detective's next question.

'May I ask why you called on him, sir? I'm struggling to think of any reason why a man of your stature would have any reason to be involved with Dakin.'

'He was once an on-course bookmaker.'

'We already know that.' The DC's surly voice earned him a look of disapproval from the inspector and he wisely closed his mouth again before making matters worse.

'I have three horses in training with Guy Levant in Lambourn whose performances have been disappointing.' Isaac spread one hand, his conscience bothering him since he was almost certain that his visit had been responsible for the murder, even though Dakin hadn't told him anything he could use to further his investigation. *What did Dakin know that had made it necessary for him to be permanently silenced?* 'I was clutching at straws, I suppose, and was curious to know why Dakin had suddenly sold up. I mean, we all know that bookies don't lose in the long run and despite all the regulations, those pitches are still like gold dust.'

Isaac's explanation sounded weak even to his own ears but if the DI doubted him, his bland expression gave nothing away about the nature of his thoughts. He absolutely didn't want to admit that Farah had been with him and drag her into this mess. It would mean revealing her whereabouts and right now he didn't trust anyone not to sell her out. Call him paranoid but this business, whatever it was, was bigger than he'd realised and a damned sight more dangerous. People who were willing to commit murder if there was even a suggestion of a threat to their security, their anonymity, wouldn't think twice about wiping Farah out.

Or Isaac either.

'What reason did Dakin give for selling out, just as a matter of interest?' The first signs of scepticism had entered the inspector's voice.

'He needed the money to pay his son's medical expenses.'

Burke gave a nasty little laugh. 'He had you over. He don't have any kids.'

A look from the inspector again shut Burke up but this time Isaac wasn't buying it. They were playing 'good cop, bad cop' and were so damned good at it that Isaac had only just caught on.

'In that case, Constable, I guess he's taken his reasons to the grave with him.'

'Did you take anyone else with you on this spontaneous visit?' the inspector asked.

'I fail to see what that has to do with anything,' Isaac replied mildly, careful not to sound defensive. 'I can assure you that Dakin was alive and well when I left him at about midday yesterday.' He paused. 'What time was he killed, as a matter of interest, and how?'

'Between midnight and two in the morning. Someone hit him over the head with a blunt object,' the inspector said wryly.

'Well then, I can't help you any further,' Isaac said, standing to indicate that the meeting had come to an end. Rice stood, too, but didn't look as though he was finished with his questions. Presumably he didn't want to remain seated and be looked down on, even though Isaac had half a head over him when standing and could still achieve that ambition.

'Can you account for your whereabouts during those hours, sir?'

Isaac flexed a brow. 'Am I a suspect?'

'It's routine. You were one of the last people to see him alive so it has to be asked.'

'I was here, upstairs in bed. Alone, unfortunately.'

'So no one can vouch for you?'

This time Isaac was ready for the young constable's acerbic interruption and met his gaze with equanimity. 'My alarm. I live above my office, and have a state-of-the-art system. I set it when I go up at the end of the day and can only come downstairs again if I turn it off. You can check with the alarm company. They will be able to tell you if it was turned off at all during the time period that interests you.'

'We will.'

Burke made a meal out of noting down the alarm company's particulars when Isaac produced their card. His attitude was starting to rankle but Isaac figured that was the entire point and so refused to show a reaction.

'Do you have any idea why Dakin would lie to you about his reasons for giving up such a lucrative pitch?' Rice asked.

'I didn't know he had lied until you told me. I bought his story about his son. I saw a number of photos of a boy on the mantelpiece in his front room. Dakin spoke to me in his kitchen but I saw the pictures when I walked past the open door. A bit like a shrine so they were hard to miss.'

'Are you sure?'

Isaac stared at the inspector, who was starting to get on his nerves. 'Of course I'm sure. You must have seen them there.'

'Actually, no. The place had been turned over and there were no pictures. Absolutely nothing of a personal nature.' The inspector rubbed his chin, looking pensive. 'Very odd. Very odd indeed. I don't think it would be worth any self-respecting thief's time to rob Dakin. It was fairly obvious from the outside that he didn't have anything worth nicking, so why bother to take the pictures you say you saw?'

'That's your field, Inspector, not mine.' Isaac paused. 'Do you suppose that the killer was looking for something? Perhaps he woke Dakin, who came to investigate, thereby signing his own death warrant.' *Signing his own death warrant? Did I really just say that?* Isaac wondered if he was cracking up under the strain of his workload.

'Dakin was still dressed in street clothes.'

'Implying that he was a night owl, or had arranged to meet his killer and let him in.' It was Isaac's turn to pause. 'Presumably you found his mobile. That will reveal a great deal.'

'We can't find one registered to his name,' the inspector replied, making the admission with obvious reluctance.

'Well, I can assure you that he had one. It was charging on the side in his kitchen when we were there yesterday.' *Shit*, Isaac thought, aware that the inspector had caught the slip of the tongue. Isaac knew better than to correct it, thereby drawing attention to the fact that he hadn't been alone. That would get him wondering, Isaac knew. If he had someone to vouch for his account, why not say so? They were bound to think that he was covering something up. 'It was most likely a pay-as-you-go and before you ask, no I don't have the number but presumably you'll be able to find someone who does.'

Not that it would do them much good, Isaac knew. Calls to and from pay-as-you-go phones were harder to trace, which was why they were so popular with the criminal fraternity.

'If you think of anything else.' Rice extracted a card from his wallet and handed it to Isaac. 'I can be reached on those numbers at any time.'

'Good luck with your investigation, Inspector.'

Isaac opened the door to his office and Kristen sprang to her feet to show the policemen out.

'Everything all right, Isaac?' she asked solicitously once she had done so.

'Just fine,' he replied, returning to his inner sanctum and closing the door behind him.

He picked up his mobile and dialled Ray's number. His investigator answered on the first ring and listened without interrupting as Isaac explained the nature of the detectives' enquiry.

'Sounds to me,' Ray said, when Isaac ran out of words, 'that your Mr Dakin, the slimy little bastard, saw an opportunity to extract dosh from Hadleigh by grassing you up, thinking it would earn him some brownie points. Instead it got him killed and has put you in Hadleigh's sights.'

'The same possibility occurred to me,' Isaac replied. 'And now that I know the story about a sick son was all a load of cobblers, I have to say I'm feeling a bit confused.'

'Yeah, about that, I was going to call you. Dakin has never been married and I can't find that he ever had kids – at least none that he acknowledged.'

'But he had his story off pat, like he'd been expecting to be asked at some point. He even implied that other on-track bookies knew about his son. And all those pictures on his mantelpiece were a convincing touch.' Isaac paused to rub the stubble on his chin. 'Why would the killer go to the trouble of taking them?'

'You might be better advised to ask why they were there in the first place.'

'You think he had an unnatural interest in pubescent boys?' Isaac asked, feeling sick to the stomach.

'If he did, would he display that interest quite so openly?'

'Good way to deflect suspicion.'

Ray grunted. 'Perhaps. Anyway, good job you had Farah Ash

with you. I mean, your father's connection with Hadleigh is bound to be common knowledge in police circles so that will make you a suspect, despite all your success. Perhaps they think the success in question is founded on the proceeds of crime. It's the way their minds work.'

'Yeah well, I refrained from telling them that Farah was with me.'

Ray sounded as though he was choking down the phone. 'What the fuck...'

Isaac explained where Farah was now and why he didn't want to draw attention to her.

'Got to you, has she?' Ray chuckled. 'How the mighty have fallen. Never thought to see this day.'

'Get a life!'

'Don't need to when I can live my love life vicariously through you.'

'Yeah, good luck with that one.' Isaac's expression sobered. 'Just one thing. I told the inspector that I was tucked up in bed at the time of the murder.'

'But you weren't?' Another groan.

'I used the escape route. Just reassure me that if they check with the alarm company, which they will, they won't cotton on.'

'Not a chance in hell, Isaac.' Ray's confident tone permitted Isaac to breathe freely for the first time since the detectives' departure. 'Mind telling me where you were, and who with? Like I say, I need to get my jollies somehow.'

'Not happening.'

But not for the reasons that Ray probably supposed. He wasn't about to make himself look a prat by admitting that he'd spent over an hour of the time during which Dakin was being bashed over the head with the ubiquitous blunt object, sitting outside his own apartment in Brighton Marina. What had drawn him there he couldn't have said but he hung around, waiting for the lights to go out so that at least he could be sure Farah was safely tucked up for the night.

His state-of-the-art alarm did what it said on the tin, but Isaac found it too restricting. There were a lot of burglaries in his part of town but the signage from the upmarket security company whose services he had engaged made his house a no-go area for any self-respecting thief, who would prefer to take his chances with properties a little less well protected.

Isaac had accidently set his system off a dozen times before he got tired of its restrictive nature. There was such a thing as being too well protected. That's where a good friend of Ray's had come in. Ray had experts in just about every sphere on speed dial. His friend had wired up the system in the basement so that it bypassed the main alarm. Isaac could let himself in and out that way without triggering the control centre but no one would know it, Ray's mate had repeatedly assured Isaac, unless an expert looked at the basement.

And since Isaac wasn't about to let anyone do so, he technically had nothing to worry about. He hadn't killed Dakin but had a pretty good idea who had. His problem was that grassing Hadleigh up with no actual proof would put a target directly in the middle of his own forehead, if one wasn't already firmly in place.

'Dig even deeper into Dakin's background, Ray. Go right back, see if you can find any connection to children.' Isaac hit his forehead with the heel of his hand. 'Damn! I wish now that I'd taken more interest in those pictures. I don't know if they were of the same child or a collage of his various victims. Not that I want to jump the gun and assume his guilt but there has to be something in his past that caused Hadleigh to latch on to him. And that same something got him killed, implying that it... well, implicates Hadleigh or one of his inner circle.'

'I'm on it, Isaac.'

'Good man. Make it a priority.'

'Everything I do for you is a priority.'

'That's why you're able to live in the lap of luxury, given your extortionate charges.'

'Hey, who said anything about living? I spend all my time in my man-cave, never seeing the light of day, solving your problems for you. Talking of which, laters.'

Isaac smiled as he hung up and tried to reapply his mind to the work that hadn't been holding it even before the untimely arrival of the police.

It now didn't stand a hope in hell.

15

———

Farah could see how much Daisy was enjoying the change of scenery, to say nothing of the opulence of the apartment they'd been loaned, and so tried to be happy for her sake. Her aunt looked better than she had in weeks and seemed to have more energy. There was absolutely nothing wrong with her overactive imagination either, which Farah knew had gone into overdrive, creating ever more implausible scenarios.

'That man has definitely gone above and beyond to help you,' she remarked, shortly after they had moved in on Sunday, at Isaac's insistence, and Daisy had exclaimed over the luxury.

Farah had wanted to point out that he had done it to protect Daisy but that would draw unnecessary attention to her immobility, which would be unkind. It was true for all that. Nothing and no one, no matter how persuasive, would have removed her from Lambourn if she'd only had her own welfare to consider. Farah did not believe in avoiding confrontation when the cause was just.

'This is just the way he lives, nothing special to him. I dare say his own place is even more lavish.'

'You haven't found out for yourself yet?' Daisy gave a mischievous lopsided smile.

'Behave yourself! He just wants to know who's pulling Dale's strings,' Farah said, plumping up the cushions on the chair that Daisy occupied, which afforded her an admittedly interesting view, and asking her if she would like some tea.

Daisy said that she would and Farah busied herself in the kitchen, staring out at the view from a different window. Crowds of colourfully clad tourists stomped along the walkways with their buckets and spades, returning to their lodgings after a day on the beach and taking a moment to admire the gleaming boats rocking gently on the moorings in the marina.

'Give me a muddy field full of horses any day of the week,' she muttered, refusing to be mollified by the luxurious standard of her temporary accommodation. The windows didn't rattle or let in draughts, there was no peeling wallpaper or mould, and the heating almost certainly worked. The plumbing wasn't dodgy and there was even hot water in abundance that didn't require a temperamental boiler to be coaxed into life in order to supply it. 'Holidays are overrated.'

'Doesn't it remind you of holidays with your uncle?' Daisy asked, nodding her thanks when Farah supplied her with tea and cake, her gaze fixed on the rapidly dwindling crowd on the beach.

'It does.' Farah squeezed Daisy's hand. 'It was the first thought that crossed my mind when I saw the place.'

'There's nothing wrong with a little nostalgia, darling,' Daisy said, her expression dreamy, her eyes moist.

The journey had tired Daisy, just as Farah had known that it would, but Isaac had put pressure on them in the most charming manner to move on Sunday rather than waiting until Monday morning, when they could have done so in a more relaxed fashion.

The man could teach the United Nations a thing or two about the power of positive negotiation techniques, she thought rebelliously.

Even so, he didn't completely own her and was unaware that she'd taken a private moment to contact a care provider in Brighton. She had arranged, at exorbitant cost, for a carer to come on Monday and look after Daisy for a twelve-hour period. That ought to be long enough to achieve what she had in mind.

There was somewhere else that Farah needed to be. Something playing on her mind that she hadn't shared with Isaac, mainly because she wasn't sure what to make of it. And because he would take that information, run with it himself and shut her out if she related the nature of suspicions that had only become... well, suspect after she'd learned of Michelle's true identity.

The carer arrived at ten on Monday morning and seemed both capable and empathetic. Daisy took an immediate liking to her and Farah left the two of them sitting on the terrace, watching the activity in the marina and chatting like old friends.

'I won't be late back,' she told Daisy, kissing her forehead.

Naturally Daisy had asked her where she was going and she'd implied that she was helping Isaac, which was sort of true. It was enough to pacify Daisy, who seemed to have taken on a new life as an old-fashioned matchmaker, and she waved Farah away, adjuring her to take all the time she needed and to enjoy herself.

Farah climbed into her borrowed car – as luxurious as her borrowed accommodation – and fired up the engine. It was a hundred miles to Lambourn but in this vehicle and most of it on motorway, Farah knew she'd do it in an hour and a half if there were no hold-ups. The drive would give her thinking time. She had no clear plan in her head, just suspicions that could be a product of her imagination.

Or not.

It was worth giving those suspicions a bit of a prod to see what fell loose. What was the worst that could happen, other than a wasted day?

She arrived in Lambourn before midday, bypassing the cottage that she shared with Daisy. It looked neglected, even though Farah had quit it less than twenty-four hours previously. She felt nostalgic for its shabby quirks and knew that she would exchange the luxury of the apartment for the unpredictability of a cottage that was completely out of tune with modern-day living in a heartbeat.

She parked the car in a quiet back street and walked to a small shop called, somewhat unimaginatively, Horse Canvas. The shop premises fronted a large workshop where a talented artist by the name of Colette Miller undertook horse portrait commissions for proud owners and jubilant trainers alike.

She also painted general horsescapes, which were sold in the shop, attended by a young female assistant. Farah peered through the window and could see that the assistant in question was busy selling a picture to a couple who were dressed in loud clothing that screamed American tourists. There was no sign of Colette, which implied she must be in her workshop.

'Great!'

Farah slipped into the alley beside the shop, aware that it led to the workshop itself. The holy of holies. Premises that were strictly private, invitation-only, and invitations Farah happened to know were rarely issued, only adding to Colette's reputation as a temperamental and reclusive artist. Her antisocial behaviour had earned the forty-something French woman an aura of mystique that probably bolstered both sales and her ego in equal doses.

It hadn't occurred to Farah to think of the woman's nationality in conjunction with Michelle before linking up with Isaac. Now she suspected everything and everyone – without just cause, in all probability. This was likely to be a wild goose chase but it made Farah feel as though she was being proactive. Of course two women of the same nationality would strike up a friendship. There was nothing unusual about that. Foreign nationals in any country tended to gravitate towards one another.

Farah knew that they were friends. What was less obvious to her was why they felt the need to keep that friendship quite so private. As far as Farah was aware, Colette had never attended any social functions at the yard, which was odd, given her love of horses and friendship with Michelle. That thought had got Farah's mind revving along in overdrive. She had noticed them once or twice, in quiet, out-of-the-way parts of the town where they obviously wanted to avoid being seen, heads together, talking in rapid French. On those occasions Farah had, for reasons she hadn't understood, felt uncomfortable and taken a different direction to avoid intruding.

But today she had every intention of intruding on Colette, recluse or not, to ask her about her relationship with Michelle. Farah could not have said why but she had become increasingly convinced that Michelle's secret friendship with Colette was pivotal to whatever was going down at Guy's yard.

Farah paused at the gate that led to the workshop. It was six-foot high and bore a notice proclaiming it to be private property and asking visitors to call at the shop. Farah ignored that request, took a deep breath and lifted the latch. To her relief, the gate wasn't locked and swung inwards on silent hinges. She closed it again behind her and allowed herself a moment to take stock of her surroundings.

She was in a small courtyard garden with access to the back of the shop. Thankfully no windows in either structure looked directly onto her location but she couldn't dither for fear of someone appearing out of the blue. She could see a storeroom with the door open and packing materials neatly lining the shelves. If the assistant made a sale to the Americans, there was every possibility that she would need packaging.

With that thought in mind, Farah crept towards the workshop, wondering why she didn't simply stride up to it with confidence. Ignoring the fact that she had... well, ignored the 'no trespassing' sign, that is. But something urged caution and she kept as much as possible out of the line of sight of the small windows to the side of the workshop, gluing herself to the wall. She gasped when she reached the corner, peered round it and saw full-length windows on the opposite side of the structure, providing maximum light that the majority of artists would die for, she imagined.

She kept her body pressed against the wall, thinking that perhaps she should have... well, thought her strategy through before barging in like the proverbial bull. If Michelle and Colette were somehow involved with whatever was happening at the yard then Colette was hardly going to admit it just because Farah asked her nicely. By coming here, Farah could well have shown her hand for no good reason.

'Stupid, Farah. Stupid!'

She bashed her already bashed forehead with the heel of her hand, aware that Isaac's unwillingness to involve her had provoked her into acting rashly. Ergo, it was all his fault and she really should scarper before she was caught snooping.

But since she was here...

Farah slipped round the corner and peered through the glass directly into the studio, which was devoid of human presence. A half-finished painting of a horse that Farah recognised sat on an easel, the skill of the artist in bringing the horse to life on canvas taking her breath away. She forced herself to look away from it and take in the rest of the space. There was a small kitchen area and some comfortable-looking couches arranged in a semi-circle around a small log-burning stove. Several half-finished canvases were leaned against walls and a spiral staircase led to what was presumably a sleeping loft.

Before Farah could decide what to make of the situation, a movement in the loft caught her eye. A naked woman strolled to the window and stared out at the garden. Farah flattened herself against the wall, confident that the woman wouldn't be able to see her from her vantage point, shocked to the core to recognise that woman as Michelle. She had barely recovered her breath before an equally naked Colette came up behind her and kissed her shoulder. Michelle smiled in a way that Farah had never seen her smile at Guy and turned to take Colette into her arms, kissing her with a passion that Farah could sense, reinforcing her position as uninvited voyeur.

She extracted her phone from her pocket and took a couple of snaps of the embracing pair, just because it seemed like the right thing to do. Their affair was none of her business – just so long as it wasn't the catalyst for the goings-on at the yard.

But she had a sneaking suspicion that it might well be.

Farah was so shocked that she moved away from the wall and placed her hands on the window glass to support her shaking legs. A loud clatter of an alarm caused her to jump out of her skin and quickly turn in the direction of the gate. But not so quickly that the panic in Michelle's voice didn't reach her through the open window.

'We have an intruder,' she said in English.

Farah didn't wait to be caught. Instead she turned on her heel and ran as fast as her aching body permitted, reasoning that neither woman would come after her naked and as long as they didn't have cameras dotted randomly about then they would never know it was her. Even so, she ignored the pain in her ribs, the pain everywhere, walking fast now until she got back to the car. She let herself into it and sat panting in the driver's seat, assessing what she had just seen, but not for long. She couldn't afford to be caught anywhere near that shop once the ladies came looking for their intruder. And she was pretty damned sure that they would come looking.

The question was, would they kill in order to protect their secret affair?

Farah didn't know and had no pressing desire to find out. She fired up the engine and drove on autopilot to her cottage. Preoccupied, only as she pulled the car onto the drive did she notice a car already parked at the kerb. She panicked, worried that someone had been sent to finish the job that they'd started when they failed to kill her the first time. Damn it, Isaac had been right!

A man rounded the side of the cottage and saw her. She didn't recognise him but he wore a smart suit and seemed unthreatening. *Did thugs dress in expensive suits nowadays?* She almost laughed hysterically at the turn her thoughts had taken, deciding to stand up to the man, rather than running. She had a small can of Mace in her pocket and she gave it a reassuring squeeze.

She would take her chances. What other choice was there?

'Miss Ash?' the man asked. 'Farah Ash?'

'Yes. Who are you?'

Another, younger man appeared in his wake, smirking when his gaze landed on Farah.

'I'm Inspector Rice of Brighton Major Crimes. This is DC Burke.'

Police! For a ridiculous moment, she thought her trespassing on Colette's private domain had been reported. Of course it hadn't, and wasn't likely to be, even if they knew it was Farah who had intruded, she sensed. Michelle wouldn't want anyone to know about her relationship with a particular member of her own sex. Besides, these officers had flashed their warrant cards, Farah had examined them and they had looked kosher.

'Oh. You're a long way from home,' she said. 'How can I help you?'

'Can we go inside?' the inspector asked.

It seemed like a reasonable request and so Farah extracted a key from her bag, forcing the door open over the flagstones in a gesture born of familiarity. 'This way,' she said, leading them into the sunroom. 'Now, what's this all about?'

She took exception to the manner in which the constable appeared to note down the registration number of Isaac's car. She wanted to object but wasn't sure if he'd done anything objection-able in the eyes of the law and so kept her mouth shut.

'You look flustered,' the inspector said, not unkindly. 'Perhaps we should all sit down.'

'I've never been interviewed by the police before.' Farah took a seat because her legs felt weak – a combination of what she had just observed closely followed by the introduction of two police officers – and waited for the inspector to sit across from her. 'It makes even an innocent person feel as though they ought to admit to some-thing, just to seem cooperative.'

'You've been in the wars, it seems,' he said, nodding towards her facial injuries.

'Drove my car into a tree,' she said, thinking it better not to admit the truth, not even to the police. Isaac had specifically warned her to keep what they knew about the tampering to herself. Mind you, he'd warned her not to go off investigating on her own either and she belatedly wondered if she should have listened to his advice.

She mentally chased that thought away. She had a mind of her own and had discovered a valuable clue as to Michelle's purpose, albeit by accident. But then, fortune favoured the brave, and all that. Not that she felt particularly brave at that precise moment, especially given that she was being subjected to the exacting scru-tiny of two policemen, the elder of whom was definitely not wet behind the ears.

'That's not your car, then?' the DC asked, nodding towards the Merc.

'It's on loan from a friend.'

'Generous friend,' the constable replied, smirking as though he had anticipated what Farah had been required to do in return for its loan. She wanted to slap that smirk off his face but made do with turning away from him and maintaining her dignity.

Not wishing to prolong the interview either, she strove to take charge.

'You still haven't told me what brings you all this way,' she reminded the inspector, pointedly ignoring his sidekick.

'Ah yes, about that.' The inspector paused. 'Are you acquainted with a former bookmaker by the name of Paul Dakin?'

'Dakin?' Farah widened her eyes, not having to feign surprise. She had naïvely hoped that he had come to talk to her about the shenanigans at the yard or better yet Hadleigh. What Dakin had to do with either situation, she was at a loss to explain. 'Yes, I was at his house on Sunday as a matter of fact. Why do you ask?'

'Did you go alone?'

'No, I was with a friend.'

'The same friend who lent you his car?' the constable asked, consulting his phone. 'A car that belongs to Isaac Fernandez,' he added, clearly having checked out the ownership.

'Yes, we were there together.'

'Funny, that,' the inspector remarked. 'When we asked him about it, he said he'd gone alone.'

'Did he?' Farah flexed a brow. 'I don't know why. Anyway, ask Dakin. He will tell you the truth.'

'We would but unfortunately he was brutally murdered last night,' the inspector said calmly.

'Murdered?' Farah sat forward too quickly and her ribs jabbed a painful protest. She felt the colour drain from her face as her head whirled with unpalatable possibilities. 'No, that can't be right. Who would want to…? He was fine when we left him.'

'What time was that?'

'About midday, I think. I'm not sure. We went for lunch straight from there so it would have been about then.'

'Why did you go to see him?' the inspector asked.

'To try and find out why he sold his trackside pitch. He told us that his son required expensive medical attention.'

The inspector nodded. 'Mr Fernandez has not discussed the murder with you?'

'No,' Farah replied, firming her jaw. 'It must have slipped his mind. Annoyingly, he seems to think that I require his protection.'

She could see that the inspector believed this was the first she had heard of it. Her reaction must have been too genuine to leave much room for doubt. Besides, she knew, although he could not, that she was a terrible liar – very unconvincing. If she had tried to fool him, he would have seen straight through her.

'I can't help wondering why he denied you were with him, given that you can alibi him,' the constable remarked.

Farah lifted a shoulder and winced when the gesture caused pain to rip through her ribcage. 'Does he need an alibi? Isaac had no reason to kill the man, and nor did I. Anyway, he probably didn't want to drag me into it.' Farah decided against mentioning the happenings at the yard. She was pretty sure that Isaac wouldn't have done so. Besides, she had no actual evidence to support her claims. 'As I say, he can be overprotective.'

'Did you notice anything in particular about that house?'

'Other than its shabbiness, you mean?' Farah nibbled the end of her index finger as she gave the matter some thought. 'No, I can't say that I… other than his pictorial shrine to his sick son, of course.'

'He doesn't have a son,' the constable told her, his smirk back in place.

'What? No, that's not right. Of course he does. Why would he make something like that up?'

'Do you have his mobile number?' the inspector asked.

'No, but he definitely had one. I saw it charging in the kitchen. Ask around amongst the other trackside bookies. I dare say one or two of them kept in touch. They compete with one another but are also close-knit, if that makes any sense. They look out for one another.'

'We'll do that.' The constable made a note in his book.

'What brought you to my door, given that Isaac didn't tell you I was with him?'

'Well, miss, your fingerprints,' the inspector said, looking a little sheepish.

'You don't have them... Hang on.' She frowned at both men. 'I gave them for elimination purposes after that break-in at the yard about a year ago.' She planted a fist on her hip indignantly. 'They were supposed to be destroyed.'

'So they should have been but they obviously got overlooked.'

'Well, I shall be making a complaint. This is an invasion of my privacy.'

'It wouldn't have been necessary if your friend, Mr Fernandez, had told us the truth,' the constable pointed out nastily. 'It might be worth keeping that fact in mind.'

Farah had had quite enough of his bullying. 'And it might be worth your leaving my house, both of you,' she said, standing and pointing to the door. 'It seems you were brought here by illegal means. I am absolutely sure that it was illegal for you to act upon the discovery of my fingerprints, given that you should no longer be in possession of them.'

The inspector smiled at her. 'We're only trying to establish the truth, Miss Ash,' he said, extracting a card from his wallet and handing it to her. 'Call me at any time if you think of anything that might help our investigation.'

As soon as the policemen had left the cottage and driven away, Farah grabbed her mobile and called Isaac. He answered on the first ring.

'You okay?' he asked, worry in his voice.

Seething with anger, Farah didn't stop to temper her words. 'When were you going to tell me about Dakin's murder?' she asked hotly.

'What? How did you... It hasn't hit the media yet.'

'Answer the question, Isaac.'

'Where are you?'

'Typical diversion tactics,' she said crossly. 'Answering a question with another question. But since you insist upon knowing, I popped back to Lambourn to collect a few bits that got left behind because you insisted on rushing us. I got doorstepped by a detective inspector and his sidekick.' He huffed indignantly. 'What's going on?'

'You popped over a hundred miles when I told you to order anything you need online?' There was disbelief in Isaac's voice. 'We need to talk.'

'Now he's getting it!'

'Come back to Brighton. Is Daisy okay?'

'No, I left her alone with a can opener.' Farah threw her free hand in the air, even though Isaac couldn't see the gesture. 'Yes, of course she's being taken care of! What do you take me for?'

'Get back here then and come to my office. We need to clear the air.'

Since Farah couldn't agree more, she cut the connection without actually voicing her agreement, pocketed her phone and headed for the Merc.

16

Isaac couldn't settle, convinced that Farah would be driven off the road again, or worse, before she got back to Brighton. The damned headstrong woman had gone against his most specific instructions and landed herself in danger. She'd also inadvertently proven to Rice that he'd lied to him. That couldn't be good. He paced up and down, wondering how Rice had got on to her so quickly. Wondering what she had really been doing back in Lambourn. Seriously considering putting her across his knee and teaching her the meaning of obedience.

He smiled to himself when the turn his thoughts had taken belatedly registered. She would tell him in no uncertain terms that her behaviour was nothing to do with him, and she'd be right, but for the fact that they had agreed to work together. In which case he ought to have told her about Dakin's murder, he accepted. And he would have done so but had wanted to give her a few more days to recover from her accident before adding to her stress.

A series of phone calls from the States kept him occupied for the next hour or so and he had only just hung up from the final one when Kristen buzzed to tell him that a woman who didn't have an appointment insisted upon seeing him. Isaac had forgotten to warn Kristen that Farah would be calling and knew his gatekeeper, more tenacious than the fiercest Rottweiler, would have attempted to turn her away. No one, but no one without an appointment got past her. He was equally sure, though, that Farah would have stood her ground.

'Let battle commence,' he muttered as he opened his office door and saw the two women engaged in a glaring match.

'Farah,' he said, conscious of Kristen's jaw dropping open in the periphery of his vision. Farah was dressed very casually and still displaying her war wounds, in direct contrast to Kristen's catwalk appearance and perfect grooming. He knew that his PA would be having trouble wondering why Isaac would possibly give up any of his ordinarily micro-managed time for such a person. 'Do come in.'

'Thank you, Isaac,' she said, sending Kristen a pointed look as she walked through the door that Isaac held open for her.

'No interruptions,' Isaac said to Kristen before closing the door on her still-astonished face.

'Is she for real?' Farah asked indignantly. 'She looked at me like I was something she'd scraped off the sole of her Manolo Blahnik shoe.' She glanced down at her scruffy jeans and allowed herself a brief grin, probably making the same comparison that he just had and finding her own appearance wanting. Isaac could not have agreed less. He much preferred her fresh-faced look and natural beauty, the bumps and bruises on her forehead notwithstanding, to Kristen's cosmetic perfection. 'You need to get a more empathetic receptionist. Her attitude will cost you valuable clients.'

Isaac smiled at the thought of Kristen's reaction if she could hear herself being described as a receptionist. She actually had a first from UCL in economics and was definitely not just a pretty face. But he never mixed business with pleasure and nothing that Kristen could dream up was ever likely to change his mind.

'Sit down, Farah. You look done in. Tell me what's happening. Why did you really go back to Lambourn?' He waved a hand as he lowered himself into the chair across from hers. 'And don't insult my intelligence by pretending that you'd left something vital behind.'

'I had,' she insisted. 'My sanity.'

'Ah, well, there is that, I suppose. What other explanation could there be for your irrational behaviour? Anyway,' he added on a sigh, doing his best to quell his annoyance at her stupidity, 'tell me first how Rice got on to you. Did he have that objectionable DC with him?'

'Ah, so you didn't like him either. Good!'

Isaac listened to her account, scowling when she mentioned her fingerprints still being on record. 'Well, if you told them anything incriminating, it will be inadmissible. I'm pretty sure about that because they discovered your identity by illegal means, but I will run it past my lawyers.'

'How could I have said anything incriminating when I didn't do anything wrong?' She pointed a finger at him accusingly. 'You're the one who screwed up by pretending to have been there alone.'

'I was trying to keep you safe!'

'I don't need your protection, Isaac,' she shouted back at him. 'How many more times do I have to spell it out?'

'Okay, let's put Rice to one side for now.' Isaac took a deep breath, striving to hold on to his temper and not point out all the very valid reasons why she most emphatically did need his protection – not least of which was one dead ex-bookie. He seldom let his sometimes volatile temper get the better of him but this annoying lady appeared capable of rousing him to the heights of anger without putting any effort into it. 'We left Dakin alive and well. I don't think there will be any CCTV on his road but there is on the main drag approaching it. They'll look at that and at least be able to confirm that no vehicles registered to me went anywhere near the place after we left.'

'It was Hadleigh, wasn't it?' Farah said into the deliberate silence that Isaac allowed to stretch between them.

'Almost certainly. Dakin had probably been told to report in if anyone came asking questions. I don't suppose he thought it would cost him his life.'

'Is it true what the inspector said about Dakin not having a son?' she asked.

Isaac nodded. 'Yep. Ray confirmed it.'

'Then all those pictures?' She scowled. 'Who were they?'

'Ray's looking to see if any allegations have ever been levelled against him having an unnatural interest in young boys,' Isaac replied, firming his jaw.

'Hmm. The same thought had occurred to me. He gave me the creeps and I can well imagine him being into something that awful.' She glanced up at Isaac. 'But why keep pictures of his victims, if that's what they were? And why look at me in the way that he did if he prefers children?'

'I've been wondering about that myself.'

Farah shuddered, unable to believe that any adult would willingly inflict such a terrible torture on innocent children. Well aware that it happened all the time.

'And it occurs to me that perhaps someone close to Hadleigh had a hand in the paedophilia.'

'One of his loutish sons perhaps?' Farah nodded emphatically, as though answering her own question. 'From what you've told me about them, I wouldn't put it past them. It could well be what they held over Dakin that forced him to sell out. But they didn't know he'd kept evidence in the form of pictures and perhaps other stuff that could link Hadleigh Junior to the crimes. Not until Dakin rang Hadleigh to inform him of our visit. Hadleigh, or more likely someone trusted and closely connected to him, called round, saw the pictures and that sealed Dakin's fate.'

Isaac admired her clarity of thought. 'It would also explain why the place was turned over. Hadleigh's cohort had to find whatever else he was holding that could incriminate Hadleigh's precious offspring.' Isaac sighed and stretched his arms above his head. 'It's the only explanation that makes any sense.'

'I suppose.'

'Did Rice ask where you're living?'

'No. I think he just assumed that I was still at the cottage and I didn't disabuse him of that notion. Why? Don't you trust him?'

'I don't trust anyone but I'm as sure as I can be that Rice plays with a straight bat. Not so sure about that DC, though.'

'I agree.' Farah shuddered. 'I thought he was creepy too.'

'Now then, what really took you to Lambourn?' Isaac asked, skewering her with a look that ought to have made it clear he wouldn't accept half-truths or excuses.

To her credit, she launched straight into a story about Michelle Levant's friendship with a French artist based in Lambourn. Highly sceptical at first, Isaac changed his tune pretty quickly when she told him what she'd observed.

'Well, well,' he said, sitting back as he absorbed that information. '*Cherchez la femme.* I must admit that I hadn't considered her desires lay in that quarter. I might have done so,' he added, fixing Farah with a significant look, 'had I known of Colette's existence and Michelle's clandestine friendship with her.'

'See how it feels to be kept in the dark like a mushroom,' she shot back at him.

'I wonder if Hadleigh knows which way the wind blows insofar as his daughter's sexuality is concerned. I ask only because he's a fully fledged, badge-carrying homophobe.'

'Why would we enlighten him?'

'We won't, not unless we can prove what she's up to and that Hadleigh has a hand in it. But it's a moot point anyway since we don't have any evidence.'

A smug smile caused the corners of Farah's mouth to elevate as she extracted her mobile from her bag, brought up the camera app and handed the phone to Isaac. 'Does this work as evidence?' she asked sweetly.

'Holy shit!' Isaac blinked several times, just to be sure that his eyes weren't playing tricks on him. 'You got pictures,' he said, stating the obvious.

'Well, I didn't go there for the sake of my health.'

'You kept cool enough to think of pictures.' Isaac couldn't keep the admiration out of his tone as he flipped through them, settling back on the original one, which gave a clear view of Michelle's face, albeit with eyes closed. The other woman's face was turned away from the camera but there could be no mistaking her gender. There was no mistaking either the passion in Michelle's expression, or the fact that she was naked and being held in the arms of an equally naked woman. 'Well done! Now this changes everything and I'd say it will work perfectly, if we decide to involve Hadleigh,' he said. 'But are you sure you weren't seen?'

'If they have cameras, which is highly likely, then I'm screwed. But still, they'll have to find me to do anything about it.'

'Which means we have to cut them off at the knees, find out what this is really about before they do.'

'How?'

'Well, there's the question I don't have an answer to. Yet. But I know one thing: Michelle is a nasty, grasping individual who knows how to bear a grudge and will trample over anyone to get what she wants.'

'She and Guy are supposed to be trying for a family. It's what Guy wants above anything but you can bet that Michelle is on the pill, or whatever, since a child clearly doesn't fit into her agenda. Guy told me once that she's resisting IVF. Why would she do that?' Farah looked endearingly confused. 'Surely if she wanted a baby as badly as Guy does, which is presumably what she's told him, then she'd be willing to try anything?'

'You're asking the wrong person. Babies aren't my field of expertise but I do know that women go to extraordinary lengths to have a family.'

'Exactly! But at least we now have a good idea why she hasn't taken that route. She's stringing Guy along for some reason, pretending to feel the way that he does, probably because she needs him for now.' Farah glanced at the picture still displayed on her screen. 'Otherwise, she'd have left him already and gone to live with the woman she obviously adores.'

'I tend to agree.' Isaac nodded. 'If she really wanted a child then there's nothing stopping her. Same-sex couples have kids nowadays.'

'Yes, but they use a donor. If Michelle had Guy's child and then left him, he'd fight tooth and nail for custody.'

Having made her point, Farah yawned and wilted in her chair.

'Are you okay?' Isaac asked, genuinely concerned. 'Silly question, of course you're not. You've just driven over two hundred miles with bruised ribs, nearly got caught trespassing and then got doorstepped by the police. It would be enough to knock the wind out of anyone.'

Tears trickled down her bruised face, which was the last thing that Isaac had expected to see and it totally floored him. Feisty, argumentative, stubborn, hot-headed – he could cope with Farah in all of those moods, after a fashion, but when she showed her vulnerability he was at a loss to know how to deal with it. So, he did what came naturally to him and took charge.

He took her hand and gently pulled her to her feet. 'Come on,' he said.

'Where are we going?' she asked, blinking up at him as though struggling to remember where she was, who he was. God forbid that she was still concussed. You heard of such things. Isaac's blood ran cold at the thought of her driving all that way with a concussion. If he had even suspected that she'd take matters into her own hands then he never would have offered her his car.

How could he not have known that she wouldn't try something reckless? She was most definitely not the passive type.

'Up to my apartment.'

She rolled her eyes. 'Your chat-up line could use some work.'

Isaac shook his head. 'When did you last eat?'

'What are you, my mother?'

When Isaac said nothing and let the silence work for him, she grudgingly admitted that she'd skipped lunch. It was his turn to roll his eyes. No wonder she was almost collapsing with fatigue.

'You can either walk up the stairs or I'll carry you. Your choice.'

She huffed indignantly. 'Who put you in charge?'

'You did when you ran off with some cockamamie plan in your head. I am not going to try and seduce you, Farah, but I am going to order in some food. Don't fight me on this.' She nodded obediently, which Isaac found highly suspicious. Even in her wrung-out state, she wasn't usually so compliant. 'Come on!'

He took her hand and walked her out through Kristen's office. The lights were out, her desk tidied away for the night, just as Isaac had known it would be. He walked slowly beside her as she climbed the stairs. She seemed interested in the artwork on the walls, or there again her interest could be feigned – an excuse to take the stairs slowly without losing face. She brightened a little when she entered his square sitting room, with its full-length windows and original iron fireplace, corniced ceiling and arrangement of carefully sourced, comfortable yet authentic furniture.

'This is... nice,' she said, making the admission grudgingly.

'Not what you expected.' He flipped through his phone. 'Now, what do you like? Indian suit you?'

Farah told him that it worked fine, the spicier the better. He took her at her word and ordered *dhansak*. Farah sank into a chair that gave her a view over the gardens and the sea beyond and appeared lost in thought.

'Would you like a drink?'

The sound of his voice caused her to jump violently, telling Isaac just how shaken up she still was by her day's experiences.

'A glass of wine would be good,' she said.

He poured one for her and opened a beer for himself before taking the chair across from hers, thinking just how at home she looked in his private domain. He didn't bring many of his dates up here for fear of giving them the wrong impression but those who had graced his living room hadn't seemed to appreciate the trouble he'd taken to modernise the space without sacrificing its antiquity. Farah, he knew without having to be told, was absorbing the ambiance and finding it as soothing as he did.

'We need to decide,' he said, leaning his elbows on his splayed thighs and holding his beer bottle between the fingers of one hand, 'what to do with those pictures. Could you send them to my phone, please?'

She pressed a few buttons. 'Done.'

Isaac's phone pinged to alert him to the incoming message. He checked to ensure that they had come through before speaking again.

'What can you tell me about Colette Miller?' he asked.

'She's been in Lambourn for about ten years and made quite a name for herself as *the* horse portraitist of choice.'

'She didn't arrive at about the same time as Michelle, then?'

'No.' Farah took a sip of her wine and simultaneously shook her head. 'I've never heard her name mentioned by Michelle either. Not that I have much to do with her but even so, recluse or not, if they had an innocent friendship, which would be natural given that they both grew up in France...' She paused, her expression speculative. 'Why did she never break her reclusive tendencies and visit Michelle, at least on open days when she could have smooched with rich owners like yourself and drummed up more business?'

'We know the answer to that question now but not why she chooses to be a recluse.'

'Perhaps she doesn't like people very much. I can relate to that. I much prefer the company of horses. You know where you stand with them. Most of the time,' she added after a brief pause and with a wry smile.

Isaac extracted his own phone from his pocket and googled the woman's name. 'I see what you mean about being a private person,' he said, looking at her website, which was heavy on art and very light on personal information. 'I can't find any interviews with her either. Most artists bite off the hands of journalists for the sake of the publicity.'

Farah gave a careless flip of one wrist. 'It's a different way to keep punters' interest, I suppose. Or then again, perhaps she doesn't need any more work. She is in great demand.'

'Yes, but there's more to it than that; I'm absolutely sure of it.'

Isaac called Ray and told him he had another job for him, one that was top priority.

'What do you suppose he will find out?' Farah asked, having listened to Isaac asking his investigator to dig deep into Colette's background.

'A connection to Michelle.' He put his empty bottle aside and rubbed his jaw. 'It's too much of a coincidence to suppose that they both finished up in the same small village by chance.'

'It's only non-coincidental if they knew one another previously. France is a big country.'

'True, but there's a real connection between those women that makes their presence here feel contrived. We know that Michelle likes to play the long game. She plans meticulously, is as ruthless as her father and has the patience of Job.'

'And me asking questions of Dale has forced her hand.'

'And almost got you killed,' Isaac thought it prudent to remind her.

'As if I could forget,' she replied sullenly, subconsciously reaching up to touch the bump on her forehead.

The doorbell rang, heralding the arrival of their food. Isaac ran down the stairs to collect it. When he returned he found Farah in the same chair he'd left her in, looking pensive.

'Come on, lazybones,' he chided. 'We'll eat in the kitchen and carry on this conversation there.'

She untangled the legs that she had curled beneath her backside and padded barefoot into the kitchen, where Isaac placed the food in its containers directly onto the island.

'Help yourself,' he said, indicating the stool across from his and putting a warmed plate in front of her. He filled her wine glass and then his own, thinking it was kind of domesticated to have a woman eating in his kitchen with him. *And* it didn't scare the shit out of him. Being a commitment-phobe, that gave him food for thought.

'This is good,' she said, tearing off a piece of naan bread, dipping it into her sauce and then popping it into her mouth. 'I didn't realise that I was hungry.'

'Daisy will be all right for a while longer, I take it.'

She glanced at her watch. 'It's not seven yet. I have a carer until ten.'

'Christ, what did you expect to do for all that time?'

She lifted one shoulder, but cautiously. Sudden movement clearly still hurt her. 'Dunno. Just wanted to be prepared for anything.'

'Fair enough.'

They ate for a while without feeling the need for conversation. The silence wasn't awkward and anyway, Isaac was enjoying both the view and the fact that Farah seemed comfortable enough not to worry about making small talk.

'Thanks, that was lovely.' Farah pushed her empty plate aside and sighed with contentment. Well, he hoped it was contentment.

'Glad you enjoyed it.'

'What are you planning to do with those pictures?' she asked, when they moved back into the living room.

'Depends what Ray comes back with.' Isaac paused to assemble his thoughts into some sort of coherent order. 'This is all speculation, but I think something happened to Michelle when she was growing up in France that caused the resentment she now feels towards me. As I say, I think she's been planning her revenge for a long time but I don't think Colette and she have been an item for the past ten years. Well, we know they probably haven't because Colette came to this country a good five years before Michelle graced our shores with her questionable presence.'

'You think Colette might have been some sort of mentor and that her having established herself in Lambourn was the reason why Michelle got Hadleigh to set Guy up in the town.'

'I do.' Isaac nodded grimly. 'The connection between them is horses but I hope that Colette isn't involved with whatever's going down at the yard.'

'Because you think we should confront her?'

Isaac waggled a hand from side to side in a considering fashion. 'It would be a risk, but depending upon what Ray finds out, a calculated one. We have to start somewhere and my instincts tell me that Colette might be the weak link that gets us to the truth.'

'How good are your instincts?'

'Well, not wishing to boast, but all this came out of nothing more than a fierce determination to prove myself to a sceptical world.' He waved a hand in an expansive arc. 'Men who wouldn't cross the road to piss on me if I was on fire now practically beg me to take them on as clients. That means something.'

'I'm sure it does,' she said, nodding. 'So, we'd best give your man time to do his digging. There's nothing we can do until he reports back to you. But,' she added, wagging a finger at him, 'if *you* decide to confront her then I want in on it. You are not doing this alone. I deserve to be there and have earned the right.'

'Agreed.'

'Agreed?' She eyed him suspiciously. 'What, no arguments? No assuming you know best? Heavens, Isaac, are you sure you're feeling well?'

He chuckled. 'Hey, when someone else is right then I'm not so insecure that I can't admit it.'

She huffed. 'There is absolutely nothing insecure about you.'

He slowly shook his head. 'Oh, Farah,' he said softly. 'How little you know about me.'

'What do you...' She yawned expansively behind her hand. 'Never mind. I should get going.'

Isaac could see that she was struggling to stay awake. The food, on top of two glasses of wine and a hectic day, to say nothing of delayed reaction to her accident, were combining and taking their toll.

'Come on,' he said, standing. 'You're in no fit state to drive. I'll call a cab for you.'

She stood at the same time as him, stumbled and only his quick reaction prevented her from crashing into his coffee table.

'Steady!' He grasped her upper arms, horrified to see fresh tears tumbling down her cheeks. 'Hey, what is it?'

She simply rested her head on his shoulder and sobbed her heart out. Isaac held her gently, conscious of her injuries, at a loss to know what else to do. He soothed her back with rhythmic sweeps of his hands, waiting for the tide to abate, and kissed the top of her tousled head.

'God, I'm sorry!' she said, finally lifting a tear-stained face to his. 'I don't know what's wrong with me.'

'No apology necessary. You've been through a lot. It's delayed reaction, I expect.'

But there was nothing delayed about Isaac's physical reaction to the feel of her body pressed against his. It was torture because he knew he couldn't make a move on her. She was tired, suffering and vulnerable. Farah, though, had other ideas. Her despondent expression gave way to a sensual look as she wrapped her arms round his neck and kissed him, hard and with purpose.

'What was that for?' he asked when the kiss stopped as abruptly as it had started. 'Not that I'm complaining.'

'I don't want to go home,' she said in a sultry tone. 'Not yet.'

17

Farah was horrified the moment the words slipped past her lips. She hadn't meant to say them out loud. Nor had she intended to kiss Isaac. She didn't make a habit out of kissing men. Truth to tell, she seldom even felt tempted. But on this occasion her impulses, to say nothing of his reaction, had caused a spark to ignite deep within her core. She felt invincible because she knew that Isaac was attracted to her. The evidence had been pretty hard to ignore.

'Farah, you're—'

'If you dare to tell me I'm suffering from shock and don't know my own mind then Dakin won't be the only one suffering from the results of blunt force trauma, and we both know that didn't end too well for him.'

'Come and lie with me,' Isaac said, holding out a hand to her almost as though she was a recalcitrant child in need of mollycoddling. But the expression in his dark eyes implied that he looked upon her as anything other than a child, or an inconvenience.

She sensed his conscience warring with his instincts and knew that the lying down bit was a compromise. He probably thought she would fall asleep. Perhaps she would pretend to and that would get her out of this awkward situation. She imagined that women who looked like Kristen propositioned him all the time so he'd find her easy to resist, despite the fact that his body had reacted to her.

Well, of course it had! He was a red-blooded male in his prime, wasn't he? It didn't mean anything but, hell, it had been so long since she'd had sex. She hadn't known that she missed it.

Now she couldn't seem to think of anything else.

She slipped her hand into his and walked with him to the top floor of his abode, willing to play along and hand the control back to him. His bedroom was massive, and stark, and furnished exactly as she would have done it, given free rein and an open cheque book. A large four-poster bed took up a fraction of the space and full-length windows with the curtains open gave a clearer view of the sea from this level. There were padded window seats beneath both of them and the cushions on one of them wore permanent indents. She could imagine him sitting there at night, staring at the view and perhaps reading one of his endless financial reports. In his position, she would do the same, but her reading material would be horsey fiction.

There was low lighting and a bedspread in lieu of the ubiquitous duvet. Farah hated duvets too but had never met anyone else who shared that view.

'It suits you,' she said, turning in a circle and examining the room from all angles.

'Glad you approve.'

Farah had recovered from her temporary insanity and felt awkward, embarrassed. What the hell was she doing here? She glanced up at Isaac, wondering what thoughts occupied him, but his expression gave nothing away as he watched her with unnerving stillness.

'Tell me what it is that I don't know about you that you think I should,' she invited, sitting on the edge of the bed, bouncing once or twice as though testing the mattress and then swinging her legs up. Barefoot still, she lay with her head on the pillows, staring up at a tasteful chandelier. He could join her or not; she no longer cared.

The opposite side of the mattress dipped beneath his weight as he stretched out beside her, fully clothed but for his shoes. He snaked out an arm in invitation and it seemed like the most natural thing in the world to rest the side of her face on his broad shoulder.

So she did.

Overthinking the situation would achieve nothing. She was a mature adult who knew her own mind – most of the time – and wasn't afraid to go after what she wanted. This wasn't the dark ages. Women could have the hots for a good-looking man without having to worry about their precious reputations.

Women in this day and age could be anything they wanted to be.

'There's something, isn't there?' she said, pressing him, determined to find out what it was about Hadleigh precisely that had Isaac so wound up. Sensing his antagonism towards the man. 'What did he do to you?'

'Hadleigh?'

'That's who we're talking about, isn't it? I get that your resentment of him predates the recent knowledge that he fathered your half-sister so come on, give. It might be relevant to our investigation but you're too close to realise it. I, on the other hand, am Switzerland.'

'Switzerland?' He sent her an amused look.

'Yes, you know, Isaac. That landlocked country that always manages to remain neutral in any conflict.'

'I know where Switzerland is.'

'Well then.'

Isaac fell quiet for several long minutes, the only sound the beating of his heart close to where Farah's head rested on his chest.

She wouldn't say anything more. The ball was in his court and if he wanted to keep his secrets, she was damned if she'd continue to probe.

'I grew up knowing nothing other than a criminal world,' he eventually said. 'A world where the police were the enemy and no one who wanted to live to see their old age ever grassed anyone up. My father was always on the make, and in Hadleigh's pocket. He boasted at home about how he'd be the big man one day, how much Hadleigh relied on him.' She sensed the disdain beneath Isaac's words. 'But not so much that he resisted the urge to screw my mother.'

'Learning about that now must come as a hell of a shock,' Farah said, sympathy in her tone.

'Nah, I knew. He'd come round to our flat when the old man was out running errands that Hadleigh had set him. That way, he knew the coast was clear. They seemed to forget that I was there.'

'But... hang on.' Farah leaned up on one elbow, ignoring the protest from her ribs as she looked down at Isaac's handsome face, currently twisted into an expression that implied physical pain but was probably a reflection of a more deep-rooted agony he seldom talked about. 'Michelle is five years older than you. Are you telling me that the affair went on after she returned from France, having given her child up for adoption, and Hadleigh really didn't have a clue? That your father didn't realise it hadn't stopped?'

'Yep, he knew all right. So did I.' Isaac stared up at the ceiling, lost in the past. 'I was only two or three but I remember Hadleigh's visits clearly. He used to pat me on the head and bring me sweets, so I looked forward to that. My actual father barely knew I was born, until I was old enough to be useful. Anyway, Hadleigh would make a fuss of me, then I was told to stay in my room and I was too young to know any different, but looking back...'

'Surely your father suspected?'

'I'm sure he did and he must have felt conflicted. He adored my mother but took his frustration out on her through violence, perhaps because he couldn't put a stop to what she was doing. Not if he wanted to stay tight with Hadleigh. Bizarre as this might sound, he still looked up to him and wanted to impress him. Hadleigh was the undisputed king in the East End at the time and by turning a blind eye to Mum's infidelity, he was assured of a position in his hierarchy.'

'Blimey!'

'"Blimey" barely covers it. It was the way that it was. The old man got frustrated and took it out on Mum with his fists. He never touched her face but wanted Hadleigh to see the bruises. Bruises that he would only get to see if she was naked and he couldn't confront the old man about. Pa wanted to climb the ladder in Hadleigh's organisation more, it seems, than he wanted to keep his wife for himself but he still had to make an obscure point. Keep me on the payroll or say goodbye to your bit on the side.'

'And your mother?'

'We never talked about it but she knew that I knew.' Isaac allowed a reflective pause. 'Well, I say we never talked about it but she did apologise to me a few days before she died.'

'For subjecting you to that.'

'No.' A bitter smile touched Isaac's lips. 'For loving two men and bringing my father's anger down on me.'

'He hit you?'

Isaac shrugged. 'It was common enough in the place where I grew up. Men were still the unquestionable heads of their families, entitled to do as they pleased to instil discipline. A swift backhander was no big deal. I reckon he was frustrated because his progress with Hadleigh depended upon my mother spreading her legs for his boss. It would make anyone see red.'

'He could have done something else?'

Isaac gave a harsh laugh. 'He didn't know anything else, other than strong-arming and intimidation. Not much call for those skills down the job centre. Besides, he had no history of employment – nothing to recommend him to any legitimate employer.'

'Where is he now?'

'I have no idea. Back in Spain, I imagine. He hit my mother once too often, seeming to forget that I'd grown taller and stronger than him. He punched her in the stomach in front of me and I saw red. I beat seven shades of shit out of him. Mum had to pull me off, otherwise I might well have killed the bastard. Anyway, I told him to get out and leave us be, or he'd get more of the same. Like all bullies, he knew when he'd met his match and I haven't heard from him since.'

'But Hadleigh didn't leave you alone.'

The shoulder that Farah was using as a pillow lifted in a shrug. 'He seemed to think I might be his son.'

'But you're not.'

'I'm not. I had a DNA test before the old man scarpered. I'm his all right. Besides, I'm a dead ringer for him. Even so, Hadleigh didn't care. He said he looked upon me as a son and wanted me to join his organisation. He had great plans for a man whom he could trust who had two brain cells to rub together – or so he insisted. I told him to fuck off but he seemed to think I'd be back with my tail between my legs, begging to come in from the cold. When that didn't happen and I started my business, he tried to back it financially. I refused, so he tried to get people not openly connected to him to put their money into my start-up.'

'He wanted to control you?'

Isaac gave a derisive sneer. 'He wants to control everyone and everything that he thinks can be useful to him. He had his grubby fingers into every dodgy pie in the East End back in the day. Prostitution, the protection racket and, of course, drugs. He was the king. Untouchable and clever, or so he thought. Now, I hear the Albanians have forced him out but that won't stop him from having something ongoing on the dodgy side of legal, which is where Michelle probably comes in. He's a wealthy man but finds going straight boring as hell, so pitting his wits against the law is how he gets his jollies.'

'He must be delighted to have found in Michelle what he hoped to find in you. A ruthless kindred spirit.' Farah paused. 'But I'm still not convinced that he didn't know about her.' She reached up and touched his face. 'Poor you. Still, you've done well to distance yourself from that life and achieve what you have of your own volition.'

'That sounded dangerously like a compliment,' he said, chuckling. 'I thought I was a self-entitled owner with more money than sense.'

'Not my words but... if the cap fits.'

'Witch!'

He leaned over and kissed her, slowly and passionately. Every nerve ending in Farah's body came alive and desire pooled in the pit of her stomach as she responded to him.

'I wish...' he said, looking down at her and shaking his head, his eyes dark with passion.

'What do you wish?' She slid the tip of her tongue along her bottom lip. 'Tell me.'

'I wish that I could...' His mobile chirped into life and a soft curse slipped past his lips. 'Saved by the bell,' she thought she heard him mutter. 'I need to take this,' he added in a more normal voice. 'It's Ray.' He pressed the green button. 'Yeah, Ray. What have you got for me? Whatever it is, it was quick.'

'Put it on speaker,' Farah insisted. 'I want to hear what he has to say without you giving me a sanitised version.'

'You said it was urgent.' Ray's voice echoed round the room. 'Anyway, Colette Miller is an interesting person. I called a connection of mine in Paris and it didn't take him long to dig the dirt. I don't suppose you're aware that she worked as a PA for Blanchett.'

Isaac shared a look with Farah, whose pulse had quickened. Here was their connection. 'Michelle's adoptive father?' he asked, seeking clarification.

'Nope, her adoptive mother.'

'Holy fuck!' Isaac breathed, clearly attempting to compute that information. 'What was the mother's business?'

'Fashion design.'

'Ah,' Farah said. 'Colette's artistic flair would have made her an asset in that world.'

'You're not alone?' Ray asked.

'I have Farah Ash with me. Farah, say hello to Ray.'

'Hello, Ray.'

'Hi, Farah. Sorry about your accident. Hope you're recovering.'

'I'm getting there, thanks.'

'Good to know.'

'Was the fashion business a success?' Isaac asked, already guessing the answer.

'At first but she got overconfident and overreached herself. And that is where the father lost his money. He ploughed it into her failing empire. Fashion is all about guessing the next big trend and staying ahead of the game, apparently.'

'But the woman guessed wrong.'

'Precisely, and the business went down the toilet.'

'So Colette must have known Michelle.'

'I've seen pictures of a young Michelle modelling her adoptive mother's stuff. They knew one another all right.'

'Has Colette ever been married?' Isaac asked. 'I know her taste is for her own sex nowadays but what about in her past?'

'Can't find that she has ever been married, or had kids, so it's reasonable to assume that she's a lifelong lesbian.'

'Fair enough,' Isaac replied, 'but that makes me wonder how she enticed Michelle to become her lover.'

'What makes you think that Michelle has ever been attracted to men?' Farah asked. 'My guess is that she uses them for her own ends.'

'Very likely,' Isaac agreed.

'I've gone back through her emails. I can't find any contact between Colette and Michelle when Colette first came to England, unless she has another account that I can't find and, frankly, I'd be insulted if she's managed to hide it from me.'

'When did they start talking?' Farah asked.

'About a year before Michelle came here and set up home with Guy. Reading between the lines, they appear to have bumped into one another in Lambourn by chance when Michelle was over on a visit with Guy, who was her fiancé at the time.'

'If Colette has always been a recluse then what are the chances?' Farah asked.

'My thoughts exactly,' Ray said, sounding pleased with Farah's reasoning. 'The same question occurred to me and, for the record, Colette had started to make a name for herself by that time and was seldom seen in public. However, they met when she held a rare exhibition of her work in support of a charity close to her heart.' Ray allowed a pause. 'A charity that supports the victims of domestic violence.'

'Ain't that telling,' Isaac muttered.

'Not sure what it tells us, though,' Farah replied, assuming that Isaac's mind was focused on the domestic violence that he grew up surrounded by.

'Right,' Ray agreed. 'Anyway, that's all I have for you to date but I thought you'd be interested.'

'Is the adoptive mother still alive?' Farah asked.

'She has Alzheimer's and is in a care facility, paid for by the state. The family home is long gone and it seems Michelle has no interest in paying for her care and making her final years more comfortable.'

'So much for gratitude,' Farah said disdainfully.

Isaac thanked Ray, asked him to keep digging into Colette's past and all the other assignments he'd given him, and cut the call.

'Well,' Farah said. 'What do you make of that?'

'What I make of it is that I'm now convinced we need to risk approaching Colette.'

'I agree. Something weird happened in that family and I'm betting that Colette knows what it is. I also think that Michelle deliberately came to Lambourn so that she could be close to a woman she admires... maybe even already desired. Anyway, she came to Lambourn and their affair started then. Quite why she hasn't left Guy and set up with Colette, who, if those camera shots only paint half a picture, she's insanely in love with, is less obvious to me.'

'I think Michelle's perceived neglect by both of her families is the answer to that one. She has a twisted mind and an overinflated sense of entitlement, is convinced she's been treated badly, and can't settle until she has her revenge.'

'She sees how well you've done for yourself and has decided that being abandoned, given up to an obviously wealthy family in France, somehow held her back.'

'I agree.' An emphatic nod accompanied Isaac's words.

'So when shall we see Colette and anyway, if she's so reclusive, what makes you think she will see us?' Isaac tapped his phone, indicating the explosive pictures captured on it. 'If you can get cover for Daisy again tomorrow, I'll pick you up at about eleven and we'll drive down together.'

'I can. She likes the woman who's looking after her today and I know she's free tomorrow if needed. It came up in conversation,' Farah said defensively in response to Isaac's raised-eyebrow look.

'Come on then. I'll put you into a cab,' he said, taking her hand and levering her gently but effortlessly from the bed. 'And,' he added in a seductive drawl, indicating the bed with his eyes and a modicum of regret, 'we'll pick up where we left off at a more suitable time.'

18

Isaac dealt with the morning's markets with fast efficiency, for once not totally focused on their movements overnight but instead preoccupied with thoughts of the previous evening with Farah. What the hell had he been thinking when he'd taken her up to his room? Had he completely lost his marbles? Temporary insanity or a strong case of masochism were the only explanations he'd been able to come up with.

In his own defence, he had genuinely hoped that she would sleep. It was evident that she needed to but why he thought she would manage to with him looming over her like some sort of predatory protector bought him down firmly on the side of a masochistic defence. He would congratulate himself upon curtailing his natural desires but for the fact that had she not been injured, and exhausted, he would almost certainly have tried it on. There was just something about her, something that set her apart and when he was anywhere near her, he sometimes had trouble remembering what day of the week it was.

'Geez!' He ran a hand distractedly through his hair as he tried to make sense of a sudden surge in electronic Japanese stocks.

Patrick and Kristen watched him leave just before eleven with identical expressions of surprise, and curiosity. It was almost unheard of for him to play truant. If he had engagements, Kristen always knew exactly where he would be. Today he had decided to keep his movements to himself and he could see that his PA wasn't at all happy to be left in the dark.

He arrived at the apartment to find Farah looking more rested than she had the night before. At least one of them had managed to sleep, it would appear. She greeted him with reserved familiarity and made little contribution to the conversation he then conducted with Daisy, who appeared to be on excellent form.

'How are you today?' he asked Farah when they were in his Lotus, speeding towards the motorway.

'Apprehensive but eager to get some answers.'

'Right back at you,' he replied, sending her a sideways smile.

They spent most of the journey in silence after that. Farah appeared preoccupied and so he left her to her cogitations. His phone rang several times. It was always Kristen with problems she wouldn't ordinarily trouble him with and his responses became increasingly brusque, making it clear that he didn't appreciate her less-than-subtle interference.

'What now?' Farah roused herself from a semi-doze when they reached the outskirts of Lambourn.

'I'm all for the direct approach,' Isaac replied, grinning at her. 'You're welcome to stay in the car if you'd prefer.'

'Not a chance! Why would I come all this way just to sit the fun part out?'

'Point taken. But I had to try.'

'Sorry to snap at you,' she said contritely. 'Seems all this cloak and dagger stuff is getting to me.'

Isaac found a parking space in a side road and they walked the short distance to Horse Canvas in tense silence. He was pleased to see that she got in and out of his low car more agilely today, no wincing required, but she was on edge, anxious, and he knew that any efforts on his part to try to protect her finer feelings would be thrown back in his face. Some women, he decided, were too stubborn for their own good. It was a surprise revelation since he'd never come across one before. Farah had been right to suggest that his dates tended to hang on his every word and clung to him like leeches. Being challenged at every turn was, he decided, a novel and not unwelcome experience and certainly kept him on his toes.

'Ready?' he asked, pushing the door to the shop open. An old-fashioned bell tinkled as Farah walked through it ahead of him.

The young assistant approached them, asking if she could help them find what they were looking for.

'I'm sure you can,' Isaac replied, turning on the charm. 'We'd like to speak with Colette Miller please.'

The assistant smiled and simultaneously shook her head. 'That's not possible, I'm afraid. I'm sure you're aware that Colette seldom engages with customers direct; that's my job and I'm sure I can help you.'

'That, I very much doubt,' Isaac replied. 'Be so kind as to give her this.' He produced an envelope from inside his jacket and handed it to the woman.

'What's this?'

'As you can see, it's strictly private and confidential.' He pointed to the stamps on the outside of the envelope to support his assertion. 'If she doesn't wish to see us after examining the contents then we shall know what to do and will leave you in peace.'

The assistant looked dubious, her gaze flitting between Isaac and the envelope. Isaac treated her to his most winning smile, at which point the woman's cheeks flooded with colour, but it seemed to do the trick.

'Wait here,' she said.

'What would you have done if she'd asked for your name?' Farah demanded to know. 'If Colette had advance warning of our identities then the first thing she would have done would be to call Michelle.'

'I was counting on her assistant being too flummoxed to enquire.'

'More like bamboozled by your charm,' Farah said in a disgruntled tone.

'Hey, don't shoot the messenger.' He sent her a puerile grin. 'It worked, didn't it?'

'If she sees us.'

'She can't afford not to, provided she opens the envelope, and I suspect that curiosity will get the better of her and she won't be able to help herself. That envelope, in case you hadn't figured it out, contains a printout of one of the pictures you took.'

'I had worked that much out for myself, surprising though it might seem to you. Even so, it doesn't seem fair to expose Collette's private life to the entire world when as far as we are aware, she's done nothing wrong.'

'As far as we know.' Isaac repeated Farah's words. 'That's why we need to talk to her and this is the only way I could think of to make it happen.'

Farah tapped her fingers impatiently on her forearm. 'What's taking so long?'

Before Isaac could point out that it hadn't been more than a couple of minutes, the assistant returned. 'Colette will see you,' she said, sounding rather shocked. 'Go through the back door,' she added, pointing to the direction from which she had just emerged, 'and follow the path.'

Isaac thanked her and placed his hand in the small of Farah's back to guide her in the appropriate direction. He could sense her nervousness, probably assuming that Michelle had ordered her to be driven off the road and that Colette was a party to attempted murder. He wanted to reassure her but the walk was a short one, leaving little time. Besides, he couldn't be sure yet that Farah had got it wrong.

Isaac let out a low whistle as they rounded the side of the studio and were confronted by the full-length windows that Farah had described. She had just forgotten to mention what a fantastic, unimpeded view they provided of the prehistoric Seven Barrows, a well-known site of scientific interest. He had read all about the bronze age cemetery but never found the time to visit – another reminder of the manic hours he worked that left little opportunity for other interests.

Perhaps it was time to reassess his priorities, he thought, glancing at Farah.

'Nice,' he said, aware of the woman standing just inside the glass, wearing a smock smeared with paint, watching their approach. As far as Isaac could ascertain, she was alone. There certainly hadn't been time for her to call Michelle, or for Michelle to arrive even if she had.

'Ah, so you're my trespassers,' she said, opening a door and ushering them into her private domain. 'I wondered when we would have the pleasure.'

'I'm Isaac Fernandez and this is Farah—'

'I know who you both are.' She seemed remarkably unperturbed by their arrival and politely ushered them towards the arrangement of chairs in front of the log burner. 'What you want with me is less obvious.'

'Really?' Isaac raised a brow and gave the printout of the picture he'd given her, which now lay face up on a coffee table, a significant look. When Colette simply shrugged, Isaac made do with taking the space beside Farah on a sofa. Colette took a chair across from them.

'I won't offer you refreshment since you won't be staying long.'

The first signs of anger slipped past her guard. 'You've discovered my fondness for Michelle by nefarious means. I simply need to know why you've come to me with that evidence rather than going directly to Guy.'

'It will break his heart,' Farah said, almost to herself.

'Hearts do not break. That is a load of romantic clap-trap.'

Isaac was inclined to agree but loyalty to Farah prevented him from saying so. Colette's command of English was excellent, even if it was heavily accented, and he sensed a sharp intelligence lurking beneath her carefully schooled expression. She was an attractive woman with high cheekbones and near flawless skin. The backs of her hands gave her age away, though, as did a slight sagging of the jaw and a creped neck. Isaac figured she had to be pushing a well-preserved fifty.

'We aren't interested in your romantic attachments,' Isaac said.

It was Colette's turn to raise a meticulously plucked eyebrow as she directed her gaze to the incriminating picture staring up at them all. Isaac was convinced that she had deliberately left it out so that they couldn't avoid seeing it, almost as though making it clear that she neither regretted her affair nor felt any need to apologise or justify it. Very likely she did not. She seemed supremely confident in her own skin and Isaac admired that about her. But if he even suspected that she had helped Michelle with her vendetta in any way then this attractive Frenchwoman would soon discover just how ruthless he could be. He hadn't forgotten all the dirty tricks he'd been forced to absorb during his fractured childhood surrounded by hardened criminals and although he hadn't had any cause to fall back on them in the interim, if the circumstances called for retaliation...

'We need to understand why Michelle is so set on making trouble for me.' Isaac paused. 'And for Farah.'

Colette's responding smile owed little to humour. 'You are aware that you're related?'

'I am now but I only found out by accident a few days ago, after Farah's car was tampered with and she was nearly killed.' Isaac's voice hardened. 'What I don't understand is why Michelle didn't tell me herself when I took my horses to her husband's yard. To the best of my knowledge, I have never done anything to harm her.'

'I told her!' Colette threw her head back, closed her eyes and gave a long-suffering sigh. 'Are you aware who her father is?'

Isaac nodded but since Colette's eyes were still closed, he belatedly realised that she wouldn't have seen the gesture. 'I am,' he said curtly.

'Well then, it doesn't take a rocket scientist to work out that she's inherited a lot of her father's characteristics.'

'So that makes it all right to try and murder people,' Farah said hotly.

Colette opened her eyes, returned her head to its regular position and fixed Farah with a look of icy resolve. 'She told me that she had nothing to do with that and I believe her. We have few secrets and anyway, I always know when she's lying.'

Farah muttered something unintelligible beneath her breath. Isaac sent her a warning look and she fell silent. Isaac wanted to hear Colette's story, not antagonise her.

'Very well, I accept your word for it, even if I'm fairly sure Hadleigh was behind it. Whether Michelle or Dale enlightened him as to Farah's curiosity is, however, entirely another matter.'

'Dale?' Colette looked confused. 'He's the yard manager, isn't he? What's any of this to do with him?'

Isaac exchanged a look with Farah, who appeared to be as perplexed as he was by Colette's apparent ignorance. He sensed it was genuine. If it wasn't then she ought to be nominated for an

Oscar. She was a better actress than many of those who had received that coveted accolade.

'Tell us how you came to link up with Michelle,' Isaac said, leaning back in his seat and crossing his left foot over his opposite thigh. 'You knew one another in France, I think.'

'You've clearly done your homework.' Colette let out a long sigh. 'Yes, I worked for Flavia Blanchett in a design capacity for her fashion empire. Flavia. How to explain her.' She shook her head at the apparent impossibility. 'A very pretty name for a cruel and vindictive woman.'

'Cruel and vindictive how?' Farah asked.

'Was her fashion empire successful?' Isaac asked at the same time, curious to see if Colette's recollections coincided with Ray's discoveries. It would be as good a way as any to gauge the woman's truthfulness.

'It was successful only because her husband financed it. He adored Flavia and would have walked on water for her, but—'

'—But she was gay,' Isaac finished for her.

'How very perceptive of you.' Colette briefly bowed her head in acknowledgement. 'In case you are wondering, Flavia and I were never an item but she did employ me on the basis of my sexuality. I was trying to make a name for myself at the time and jumped at the opportunity, little knowing then just how demanding and spiteful she could be.'

'She overreached herself?' Isaac asked. 'Success went to her head and she expanded too quickly.'

'Right, and that's how her husband lost all his money. He poured what he had left into her business in the hope of retrieving what she'd once had in the fashion of gamblers the world over. Maurice would never accept that she had feet of clay.' She fell momentarily silent, lost in a previous time. 'They never shared a bed after their wedding night, you know.'

'I had a feeling that might have been the case,' Isaac said thoughtfully. 'Flavia wanted a child but didn't want to be pregnant, which would explain why she was ready to adopt my mother's unwanted baby.'

'Not quite. Flavia didn't want a baby in the house but it was the one point upon which Maurice refused to give in to her. He found out very quickly that she was a lesbian and made the best of things. Frenchmen don't attach the same stigma to affairs that you stuffy Brits do and he satisfied his needs in that way. His only stipulation in agreeing to stay in what had become an old-fashioned marriage of convenience between two friends was that they adopt a child. He desperately wanted one and made it clear that he would withhold funding from Flavia's business if she didn't go along with it.'

'You hear about women's maternal instincts but I guess men can have the equivalent of male broodiness,' Farah said pensively. 'Why did he hang himself? Was it the loss of his money that drove him over the edge?'

'*Non*.' Colette slowly shook her head, looking incredibly sad. 'He discovered how Flavia had been treating Michelle all those years and never forgave himself for not noticing what she'd been through. Mind you, Michelle never forgave him either, but nor did she enlighten him, well aware that Maurice wouldn't believe her unless she showed him the proof. She finally did, at my urging, the day before he died.'

'What proof?' Farah asked.

'The burns all over her body, the unexplained tumbles and broken bones. The hours being locked in a darkened cupboard or sent to bed hungry. Michelle withstood it all because she had her horses and lived for eventing. Well, it was gymkhanas at first and Flavia would withhold permission at the eleventh hour, after Michelle had spent hours grooming her pony and getting excited, simply because she could. As I say, cruel.'

Isaac and Farah shared a look. The donation to domestic violence charities made so much more sense now, Isaac thought.

'She really did that?' Isaac asked.

'She really did. I saw her deliberately burn the child's leg with a lighted cigarette because she'd tripped on the catwalk whilst modelling. But she only tripped because there was a ruck in the carpet. Anyway, that's when I lost it completely. I'd seen Flavia bully her employees and reduce them to tears. She didn't try it with me because she knew I wouldn't take it and because she needed my expertise. I gave notice and walked immediately but kept in touch with Michelle and encouraged her to tell Maurice what Flavia had done to her.' She sighed. 'Then I was invited to England to paint a portrait of a rich owner's horse. He had seen some of my artwork in a gallery in Paris, apparently, and was impressed.'

'And that's how you finished up in Lambourn?' Farah asked.

'More or less. I lost contact with Michelle until we met by accident here in town before she moved here.'

'You think it really was an accident?' Isaac asked.

Colette lifted one shoulder. 'I cannot honestly say. Perhaps not but I could see that she was unhappy with Guy and, let's not deceive ourselves, I also knew that she'd married him to get away from Flavia, who expected Michelle to support her once Maurice died. But Michelle had learned all there was to know about spite at the feet of a mistress of the art and had no intention of seeing Flavia ever again. As far as she's concerned, she can rot in hell, and who can blame her for that. Anyway, with Guy, Michelle saw an opportunity to pursue her interest in horses, even if she's missed the opportunity to become a professional eventer, which was always her dream.'

'But she's not with Guy at any price,' Farah said. 'She clearly doesn't want a child, much as her adoptive mother didn't.'

'The scars run deep. She grew up in a household where there

was tension between her adoptive parents and in which Flavia conducted affairs in front of Michelle. She knew Michelle would be too scared of the consequences to tattle on her but I also think – no, I know from speaking with her about it – that watching her adoptive mother with her various girlfriends excited Michelle. Even so, flaunting herself in front of Michelle in that manner, leaving a vulnerable teenager to think she was cheating on a man whom she didn't actually share a bed with, was a method of mental torture that she enjoyed almost more than the physical chastisements that she regularly dealt out.'

'Which is why she started looking into her birth mother's circumstances and somehow made the connection to Hadleigh. She saw how successful he was, probably without knowing that his wealth had come from criminal activity, and felt doubly let down. She could have been a part of a *real* family.' Isaac nodded, satisfied that he had reached the right conclusion. 'It makes so much more sense now but why she couldn't simply have come to me and talked about it...' He spread his hands, unable to adjust his thinking to that of a bitter woman.

'What means of revenge is she plotting against Isaac?' Farah asked.

'That I cannot say.' She held up a hand. 'It's the god's honest truth, I swear it. She knows I don't approve and that I'd try to talk her out of anything she's planning. Bearing grudges is both exhausting and pointless, or so I keep trying to make her see.'

'She and Hadleigh are up to something,' Isaac said into the ensuing silence. 'Something to do with horses. Can you shed any light?'

Colette shook her head, even before Isaac had finished asking his question. 'She knows that I don't approve of her association with Hadleigh either, even if he is her biological father and so his name is seldom mentioned between us. Michelle is headstrong and nothing I say will change her mind once she makes it up, so it is better not to court disagreements and spoil the limited amount of time we have together.'

'Michelle's part of the operation centres around buying and selling eventing horses,' Farah said slowly, 'and a lot of those horses come from the continent—'

'In Guy's horsebox,' Isaac finished for her, a lightbulb exploding inside his head. 'They're smuggling something in for Hadleigh. Most likely drugs.'

'It would explain why Force was pulled from that race when there was nothing wrong with him,' Farah added. 'He was our only runner that day and I overheard a disagreement between Guy and Michelle. She wanted the box to bring a horse over but Guy said it could wait until after the weekend. The racing was more important. Then Force went lame, according to Dale, whose word Guy wouldn't doubt, so the box became available.'

'The question is,' Isaac mused, 'where is Hadleigh selling his drugs? He was a big-time supplier in London and wouldn't lose face by lowering his sights to the suburbs. But the Albanians run the majority of his old patch...'

'Albanians, *oui*.' Colette looked highly agitated. 'I overheard Michelle on the phone here once. I think she was talking to Hadleigh.' She paused. 'She said something about his being clever enough to know who to form allegiances with.'

Isaac shared a look with Farah and then gave a slow nod of understanding. 'He hasn't given up at all. He's simply realised that it's in his best interests to get into bed with the opposition and let them take all the flack,' he said.

'*Mon dieu*, she has put herself in danger, *non*?' Colette clutched her cheeks between her hands. 'It should not have come to this. I should have made her talk to me but I took the path of... how do you say, less resistance.'

'What will you do about it?' Farah asked, addressing the question to Isaac.

'I am not sure yet,' he said. 'I need to think.'

'Do not tell her that you have spoken to me, I beg you.' Tears swamped Colette's eyes. 'She may not look it but she is fragile, not in her right mind perhaps. She needs care and understanding, not censure.'

'We will try to keep your name out of it,' Isaac replied, standing and indicating to Farah that it was time to leave. 'But that is all I'm prepared to promise. Thank you for seeing us. Come on, Farah, let's get out of here.'

19

Farah could see how conflicted Isaac seemed following Colette's revelations and wondered if his attitude had changed from antagonism towards his half-sister to sympathy. For her part, Farah had precious little sympathy to spare for such a self-centred prima donna. She'd had a tough time of it, but then so did a lot of other kids. The majority put their experiences behind them and got on with life without bearing massive grudges. They certainly didn't use the devotion of decent people like Guy for their own twisted purposes.

'I am sorry about Michelle's upbringing,' she said, once she and Isaac had returned to his car. 'Of course I am. There is absolutely no excuse for child abuse, but it doesn't sound as though you had any better time of it, even though I suspect you haven't told me the half of it.' She touched Isaac's thigh. 'Besides, none of what happened to her is your fault.'

'She's clearly unstable,' Isaac said as he fired up the engine and pulled away from the kerb. 'She grew up in a wealthy family and had her own pony, yet the things she saw, the abuse she suffered, must have warped her mind.'

'Perhaps,' Farah said diplomatically, deciding against arguing the point. 'Where are we going?'

'To your cottage. We need to talk about this out of sight of the locals. As it is my car has likely already been spotted. I should have brought the Merc.'

Farah nodded, smiling at his idea of a Mercedes being an understated car, and fell to mulling over everything that Colette had told them. She was fairly sure that the older Frenchwoman had been candid, mainly because she cared about Michelle but knew she was dangerously close to running out of control and had no idea how to rein her in. Colette's shocked reaction implied that she'd been kept in the dark by the woman she loved, who had told her only what she wanted her to know. Farah wondered if Colette would stick by Michelle or cut her losses. Michelle needed professional help and Colette was arguably the only person capable of persuading her to seek it. It would be a test of the depth of her feelings for Michelle to see which way she jumped.

Farah extracted a key from her bag and unlocked the warped door, leading the way to the sunroom that seemed empty without Daisy's cheerful presence in it.

'I've been thinking about the shenanigans at the yard,' she said, wandering back from the kitchen, having put the kettle on. 'And I reckon that Michelle intends to give Force performance-enhancement drugs, then use her tame bookie to spread the rumour of cheating. That would get the stewards' attention, especially if Force won his race.'

'When he would be routinely tested anyway.'

'True, but she can't be sure that he will win. Remember, he's going up a class, so the rumours would almost ensure random testing. And if he did win, it would look suspicious even before the rumours started.'

'Possibly,' Isaac agreed. 'It would be as good a way as any to tarnish my reputation within the sport, and beyond. No one will believe that I didn't know. And the bookies gossip like a bunch of girls. They always seem to have the inside scoop. Dakin said as much to us if you recall. But why get rid of him? I'm sure he'd have done Michelle's bidding in return for a cash inducement. You saw how quickly the notes I gave him disappeared into his pocket. Then, we're pretty sure he called Hadleigh to tell him we'd been asking questions, hoping presumably to further feather his nest, much good it did him.'

'You've answered your own question,' Farah pointed out. 'Dakin didn't know the meaning of loyalty. He'd have done anything to earn a fast buck. If the stewards had got wind of him starting rumours and came asking questions, he'd have lost his bottle and likely fessed up, painting himself as whiter than white. "*She made me do it!*"'

Farah returned to the kitchen, made mugs of instant coffee, rummaged in a cupboard for a packet of biscuits and carried the tray back into the sunroom.

'So, what next?' she asked, repeating her earlier question as she handed Isaac his coffee.

'Thanks. I have two choices: confront Hadleigh or confront Michelle. I'm not prepared to sit back and be made to look like a cheat, or worse.'

'If Hadleigh was so keen to help you set up in business, why would he now help Michelle to destroy you?'

'Because I didn't accept his offer of help.' Isaac grinned. 'And turned it down none too graciously. He will see that as being disrespectful, losing face, even if no one else knows about it. I know.' He flapped the hand not holding his coffee in response to Farah's quizzical look. 'It makes no sense, but also makes perfect sense, if you understand the character of a hard man like Hadleigh who wanted to use wealth accrued from criminal activities to turn himself into a modern-day messiah. Bear in mind that he carried on with my mother and at the same time rewarded my old man for his loyalty. It's all a game to him. Makes him feel invincible. Anyway, he's likely been waiting for an opportunity to even the score with me.'

'What's in it for you if you confront Hadleigh?' Farah asked.

Isaac raised a brow. 'A very good question. What I suppose you're really asking is do I care about his smuggling operation? Well yes, I hate drugs, I have seen plenty of evidence of their destructive qualities in my line of work. Young brokers have to be firing on all cylinders twenty-four seven. It's crippling and a ton of them turn to drugs to stay awake, to get high and walk the walk...' He flapped a hand. 'It never ends well.'

'But Hadleigh won't stop just because you know about the operation and confronting him could put you in danger.' She paused. 'You could tell DI Rice.'

'I could, and might actually do so. I don't abide by the *no grassing up* code, not being a criminal myself.' He flashed a self-deprecating smile. 'Well, some disappointed investors who ignored my advice might give you an argument on that one, but still.'

'You don't trust the police?'

'I trust the majority of them but you can be sure that Hadleigh and his Albanian partners have several on the payroll. Word would leak out to a bent copper and Hadleigh would be warned before all the hoops could be jumped through and a sting operation pulled together to catch them in the smuggling act, which is the only way they'd get charges to stick. Anyway, if I did that then my life expectation would be...' He made a cutting motion with the side of his hand against his throat.

'Right.'

'I can't right all the world's wrongs, darling, but I can and will look after my own interests and those of people who matter to me.' He fixed her with a significant look that caused her cheeks to warm.

'In other words, we're going to confront Michelle.' She put her empty mug aside but when she made to stand Isaac stayed her with a wave of his hand.

'*I'm* going to and there's no time like the present. But this is something I have to do alone. I hope you can understand that.'

Farah opened her mouth to argue but then settled for nodding. 'I suppose,' she said dubiously.

'I want you to stay here where you will be safe. But, and I don't mean to sound paranoid, please lock the doors. We can't be absolutely sure that Colette hasn't warned Michelle that we're on to her and then she will try to stop the rot.'

Farah gasped. 'She can't seriously imagine that she'll keep you quiet.'

'There's no second-guessing the mind of a deranged woman. Keep your mobile close and call me if you have any concerns. I can be back here in ten minutes.' He grinned. 'Five if I give my car its head.'

'Okay, go and make peace, or war, or whatever it is you have planned with your sister. I'll be fine here.' She covered her mouth with a hand to disguise a yawn. 'In fact, I might take a nap.'

'Good plan.' He stood, picked up his keys, bent to kiss the top of her head and was gone.

'Just like that,' Farah said, listening to the throaty roar of his car's engine as he reversed out of the drive. 'Anyone would think he couldn't wait to get away from me.'

She still hadn't decided what to make of the time she'd spent in his bedroom the night before, an interlude that he hadn't once referred to that day. She remembered vividly, because she'd been waiting for him to raise the subject, but it seemed he'd forgotten all about it. Either that, or it hadn't been sufficiently significant to be deemed worthy of a mention.

'So much for my enduring charm,' she said, wearily climbing the stairs to the familiarity of her own bedroom. It might be a quarter the size of Isaac's but it was hers; she loved every nick and scratch in the old furniture and wouldn't swap it for anything more salubrious, the vagaries of the unreliable roof notwithstanding.

She kicked off her shoes, lay fully clothed on the bed and decided to have a good old think about Isaac's antics. What exactly was it that he wanted from her? Did he want anything? He seemed to enjoy sparring with her, which had to be a novel experience for him. Was that all there was to his interest – that and a burning desire to stop Michelle in her tracks? Had he only brought her along today because she'd insisted upon it? Why had he loaned her and Daisy his apartment, and his car?

And what of her own feelings for the glamorous financier? She could so easily fall for him but what would be the point? She would finish up getting hurt, she knew, since they inhabited different worlds. Her growing obsession with the man was both infuriating and pointless. But still, the moment they had resolved the situation with Michelle things would go back to normal, he could continue raking in the cash and she would hardly see him. As soon as she was no longer constantly with him, common sense would prevail.

Wouldn't it?

Questions without answers rattled around inside her brain, threatening to bring on a headache. Another one. She'd never admit it but she'd been getting them regularly since her accident.

Since someone had attempted to kill her, she mentally amended.

She felt a certain degree of sympathy for Isaac. To find that he has a sister he knew nothing about who actively disliked him to the extent of wanting to ruin him must be traumatic. But, of course, men didn't show their feelings in that way. It wasn't considered to be... well, manly.

Her eyes fluttered to a close and she didn't attempt to fight the drowsiness when it claimed her. Isaac would be gone for a while and for once she had nothing else to do.

What felt like five minutes later, the sound of the kitchen door being opened and scraping across the flagstones woke her. Shit, she'd forgotten to lock it! She glanced at her watch and felt the tension leave her body. She'd been asleep for half an hour. More than long enough for Isaac to get to the yard and back.

'Up here!' she called.

She sat up and grabbed a brush, attempting to untangle the knots from her hair whilst simultaneously trying to convince herself that she didn't really care what she looked like. No sort of premonition warned her to expect the unexpected – not until her bedroom door opened and Michelle's face, rendered ugly by a vindictive scowl, filled the opening.

'You?' Farah dropped the brush and stared at Michelle, her heart pounding against her aching ribcage. 'What the hell are you doing here?'

'I've come to visit the sick and infirm,' Michelle replied, her reptilian smile more frightening than her scowl.

'How did you...' Farah was about to ask how she had known she'd be at the cottage. Her car wasn't outside. Then she recalled that Michelle didn't know she'd moved to Brighton and, of course, her car was history. 'I'm recovering, thanks,' she said, deciding to play along. 'A bit tired but that's to be expected, I'm told.'

Michelle strode into the room, dominating the small space with her vindictive presence. She was like a tightly coiled spring, Farah thought, ready to explode without warning. Had she always been that way or had recent developments heightened Farah's perceptions?

'Shall we go downstairs? It's a bit cramped in here.'

Farah swung her legs onto the floor but Michelle prevented her from standing by stamping down hard on her toes.

'Ouch!' Farah glared up and was terrified by Michelle's hard, merciless expression. 'Hell, what was that for?' she asked, trying hard not to show her fear.

'You and my little brother, sticking your pert little noses in where they have no place.'

'Sorry.' Farah reached down to massage her toes. 'I don't follow.'

Michelle clearly wasn't buying a denial that sounded lame, even to Farah's own ears. 'You and Hercule Poirot were seen in the village in that flashy car of his.' She grinned maliciously. 'If it were not for you then I'd have been able to—'

Her words abruptly cut off, as though anger had made her blurt out more than she'd intended. Farah's own anger was in danger of erupting, pushing away a healthy wedge of fear. She had no intention, she was fast discovering, of being a passive victim. She'd had quite enough of people trying to kill her, or telling her what to do.

She stood up anyway, ignoring the protest from her bruised toes, wondering what Michelle had almost blurted out.

'Did you think that Isaac might go the same way as your adoptive father did?' she suggested slowly, playing a hunch. 'That he'd be unable to live with the shame of being exposed as a cheat?'

Michelle looked momentarily vulnerable but then the vicious mask slipped firmly back in place. 'It was you!' She pointed an accusatory finger at Farah. 'I thought as much. You broke into Colette's grounds and that's where you've been again this morning. I expected Isaac to appear at the yard long before I saw his car sneaking up the back drive.' Farah wanted to point out that the car was built to be noticed, not to sneak, but it seemed trivial so she kept her mouth shut. 'That was a mistake. I wouldn't have known if he'd come in the traditional way but my private domain looks out over the back.'

That explained why she'd come here, aware that she'd catch Farah alone. It was equally clear that she hadn't spoken with Colette since Isaac and Farah had left her. 'If Isaac were to top himself, or appear to have done, you would qualify as his closest relation and stand to inherit the lot.'

'You're not as stupid as you look.' Michelle's expression had turned smug. She was proud of her manic plans and actually thought they would succeed.

'I still don't get why,' Farah said, frowning. 'Okay, you had a tough time of it. No child should have to go through what you endured, but why live in the past when nothing you do will ever change it?'

'She told you?' Michelle seemed pensive rather than angry by what she probably perceived as a betrayal.

'She's worried about your intentions because she loves you,' Farah said simply.

'I don't want her implicated,' she said, almost as though talking to herself. 'I didn't think she knew what I have planned.'

'Guy loves you too.'

She flapped a hand, as if his feelings didn't come into it. 'He's been useful, but annoyingly protective. I needed protection years ago. I've long since learned to take care of myself and not rely on anyone else.'

'You do realise that if your plan to ruin Isaac had succeeded, which of course it now can't, then Guy would have been finished too. Don't you even care?'

She shrugged. 'Not especially, no.'

'So, why here and why now? You can't kill us all. What would daddy dearest have to say if you brought unnecessary attention down on his lucrative little enterprise?'

Farah knew she'd said the wrong thing when Michelle's expression went through several shades of infuriated. Her gaze darted nervously from side to side, like a trapped animal looking for an escape. 'What do you know about that?'

'Enough to see you all rot in jail for the rest of your days,' Farah replied, annoyed when a tremor came into her voice. Michelle heard it, of course, and a slow, evil smile suffused her features.

'Head injuries are funny things,' she said conversationally. 'I hear you refused another precautionary scan. No one would be surprised if that turns out to have been a bad decision.'

'Don't be so ridiculous.' Farah sent her nemesis a scathing look. 'We're the same height and I'm at least as fit as you are, even debilitated. And I'm younger,' she added just for the hell of it. 'If you try to attack me there's no way I'll sit back and let you. So if you intend to kill me it'll get messy, there will be battle scars and no one will believe that I died from an old head injury.'

'Ha! You make the mistake of assuming I care.'

'But you do.' Farah softened her tone. 'You love Colette and want to make a future with her. You could, as well. Her business is thriving. Why do you need to take what Isaac has? Why do you need to get involved with smuggling drugs either, for that matter?' Farah shuddered as the pounding behind her temple got harder to bear. 'Is it for the excitement?'

Michelle took Farah completely by surprise when she leaped forward with the grace of a panther and knocked Farah back into her bed, winding her. The limited space worked against Farah, as did her headache, and she was slow – too slow – to respond. She tried to bring her knee up but a woman's groin wasn't her weakest spot and her efforts made little difference.

Michelle was heavier than she looked and pinned Farah down, causing agony to ricochet through her when she struggled to escape. Her ribs gave her hell, bringing tears to her eyes and blinding her vision. She couldn't prevent herself from crying out, wondering what the hell had made her goad the woman into action. She knew that she was unbalanced. She should have tried to reason with her, to keep her talking in the hope that Isaac would return soon, having failed to run Michelle to ground.

That possibility gave her hope and with one massive lurch of her hips she caught Michelle unawares and threw her off. On an adrenalin rush, the pain in her ribs and toes barely registered and she sprang to her feet. But Michelle was up too and they faced one another from opposite sides of the bed, both of them hampered by the limited space in which to either fight or take flight. Annoyingly, Michelle was on the side closer to the door. Farah wasn't above running from a fight that she'd likely never win but Michelle would prevent her from getting to the stairs. Either that or she'd give her a hefty shove in the back and send her tumbling down them.

'Give up now,' Michelle said with an evil smile, prancing slowly round the end of the bed to invade Farah's space.

* * *

When Isaac arrived at the yard, he found Dale and Guy in deep discussion over the state of a horse's back. Something about a trapped sacroiliac nerve, which meant absolutely nothing to Isaac. Dale glanced at him, a veil descended over his eyes and he quickly looked away again, uncomfortable and a tad nervous. So he damned well should be. Dale was up to his grubby neck in nefarious activities that would come back to bite the man who had placed so much trust in him on the arse.

And Dale knew that Isaac knew it.

'Can't stay away nowadays, I see,' Guy said, shaking Isaac's hand, genuinely pleased to see him and not appearing to notice the tension between Isaac and Dale. 'Come to see your pampered nags?'

'Just passing,' Isaac said. 'Actually, I have a gift for Michelle in the car.'

'Really? Trying to tempt my wife over to the dark side with cheap trinkets?' There was levity in Guy's tone but worry in his expression.

'I wouldn't dare!' Isaac assured the trainer.

'And won't get the chance. She's just gone out.' Guy grinned. 'Probably to avoid your questionable advances since I had no idea she intended to go anywhere today.' He frowned. 'Odd that she didn't tell me where she was off to but she can be impulsive sometimes and I'm never entirely sure what's on her agenda.' He shrugged nervously, seeming to think that he owed Isaac an explanation for his wife's erratic behaviour. *You don't know the half of it.* 'Can't clip a free bird's wings, eh?'

'Why do you think I'm still single?' Isaac quipped.

'Over here, guv'nor.'

Guy looked annoyed when one of the stable lads beckoned. He apologised and excused himself, leaving Dale and Isaac alone. Dale sent Isaac an assessing look and cleared his throat, but before he could speak, Isaac got in first.

'I think it's time you told me what's going on.' Isaac dropped all pretence at civility and fixed the yard's foreman with a high-intensity glare. 'And you can start by telling me where Michelle has gone running off to.'

Dale met Isaac's gaze. Finally. His eyes were bloodshot and the bags beneath them would contravene the trades descriptions act. 'I will, but I'll tell you on the way.' His eyes snapped into focus and there was a sudden urgency in his tone. 'We need to get a move on. I think she might have gone after Farah.'

'Fuck!' Isaac muttered, running towards his car with Dale close on his heels. 'Get in!'

Dale did so and Isaac tore out of the space as though his tail was on fire, sending gravel shooting skywards and spooking the youngsters in the closest paddock.

'Talk to me,' Isaac said, all his concentration on the narrow road as he tore along at a reckless speed. 'You have one chance to redeem yourself.'

'Look, I didn't mean for any of this to happen. You have to believe me.'

'I don't have to do anything. You maimed a child, for fuck's sake. Why didn't you own up to your misdeeds like a man and get help for your alcoholism?'

'I... I wanted to. I'd hit rock bottom and knew it. But then, all of a sudden, the case against me was dismissed. I got a ban but no mention was made of the injured child. I couldn't believe it, had no idea why but—'

'—But didn't use it as an opportunity to quit the booze.' Isaac took a corner too fast and corrected a skid by the skin of his teeth, narrowly missing a collision with a post box. The possibility of himself killing someone by driving so recklessly brought him to his senses and he slowed to a more moderate speed.

'I tried, for a while. Like I say, I didn't have a clue why the child's name wasn't brought into it. I just assumed there was insufficient evidence. Perhaps the child had darted into the road and I hadn't been in the wrong.' He swiped his forearm across his mouth. 'Knew I had been, of course, but addicts are good at deceiving themselves.'

'Did you know Hadleigh before your miraculous escape from justice?'

Isaac, still concentrating on the road, sensed Dale's surprise. 'You know who...'

'It's not naïve stable girls you're attempting to dupe now.'

'Yeah, well, someone representing him approached me. Said I owed the people who'd bailed me out of trouble and the time had come to pay them back. This guy said they weren't the sort of people you could say no to, and given the influence they'd used to get me out of a serious charge, I kinda got the picture. Then I met the boss man.'

Isaac ground his jaw. 'How long did it take you to realise that Michelle was up to her conniving neck in things?'

'I ain't as daft as I look. You know what the scam is?'

'Importing drugs through a converted horsebox.'

'Right. I wasn't told that but like I say, I'm not completely thick. The imports were done whenever Michelle was bringing a horse over from France, or Germany, or wherever. I had to arrange for false panels to be put in the box. You wouldn't know they were there unless you get in the box with a measuring rod. Then I had to make sure the box was available on the days it was needed. That was easy enough because the racing calendar is arranged well in advance and—'

'—And Michelle had a reason to work around the racing schedule.' Isaac stopped to let a string of horses cross in front of him, tapping his fingers impatiently on the wheel. 'How long did it take you to realise she was involved?'

'I got curious at first when I saw her several times disappearing into the workshop of that French woman artist.' Dale paused. 'And then when I saw her in Newbury with Hadleigh. Everything fell into place, I realised that Guy was being conned by the woman who walks on water as far as he's concerned. Since I've been pulled into their grubby scheme, there was sod all I could do to warn Guy without dropping myself in it.' Dale sat a little taller in his seat. 'But

I'm off the booze, more or less, I've had enough of seeing the people I care about being manipulated and am ready to fight back.'

Either that, Isaac thought cynically, or he realised that the house of cards was about to come crashing down and he'd decided to switch sides.

20

Farah instinctively backed up as Michelle, her manic gaze focused on Farah's face, stepped towards her. She lunged without warning, grabbing Farah's arm. Farah cried out as she was jerked forward, Michelle's strong grip was that of a woman who'd spent years controlling spirited horses. Spots danced in front of her eyes as she fought the pain in her ribs and everywhere else and wriggled in an effort to get free.

'This will be the ultimate form of revenge,' Michelle muttered. 'Better than anything else I had planned for him. He will live the rest of his life blaming himself for the loss of his little tart.'

'His...'

Farah spluttered and stopped trying to talk. She needed to preserve what little air she still had whilst she figured out how to save herself. She was damned if she would let this unbalanced woman snuff her life out in a manic attempt to exact revenge for imagined wrongs done to her by a decent man. But her options were limited.

Make that non-existent.

She felt drowsy and the fight drained out of her. *Tired*, she thought, *so tired.* It would be so easy simply to let go. To have it all over with. She moved to her right, a situation that aggravated her ribs more than if she moved in the opposite direction. It hardly seemed important now. The pain would soon be over.

She was back against the wall now and her calves collided with her tall riding boots. She tried not to smile when she recalled the long whip housed in the left boot and reached her free arm behind her. Her finger made contact with the weapon but it would be hard to withdraw it without giving Michelle advanced warning.

She resolved that problem by again bringing her knee up, this time depositing it in Michelle's stomach. The woman swore in French and was momentarily distracted. She didn't release Farah's arm but that hardly mattered. A second or two was all she'd needed to remove the whip and slash it down across the side of Michelle's face with all the force she could muster. It wasn't a great deal but enough to draw blood and a surprised oath from Michelle. This time she did let go of Farah's arm and reached up to touch her face. Her fingers came away covered in blood.

'You bitch!' She reached forward, grabbed the whip from Farah's hand and for a terrifying moment, Farah thought she intended to use it on her. Instead she threw it aside and Farah heard it clatter as it hit the wooden floor and landed beneath the bed. 'You marked me.'

Farah almost laughed aloud. Michelle wanted to kill Farah but didn't expect her to fight back? *Get real, lady!*

Ignoring the blood trickling down her face and onto Farah's T-shirt, Michelle again leaped forward and her weight caused Farah to tumble back onto her bed. Landing on her right side, she again felt a sharp pain as something dug into her thigh. It was a different sort of pain that made her eyes fly wide. One that she hadn't expected. One that was less agonising than the protest put up by her ribs but one that felt as though it was trying to tell her something.

Something important.

Stunned by a combination of pain and fatigue, it took longer than it should have for Farah's increasingly hazy thoughts to fly towards the contents of her pockets. What the hell did she have...

Of course! Her can of Mace. The Mace that she had considered using on the police when they'd unexpectedly doorstepped her.

Euphoria surged through her, only to wither and die. Knowing it was there was one thing, reaching it entirely another. Michelle's weight was pinning her down. Farah was too weak to put up more resistance; her time was running out.

'Why?' she gasped, thinking that if she could keep Michelle talking she might actually release her hold just a little. She'd read somewhere that obsessed people who thought they had been ill-treated gloried in opportunities to justify themselves. She only needed the pressure of Michelle's body weight as she straddled Farah and pinned her down to ease and for Michelle to be distracted by the injustice that was purely a product of her warped mind.

'Why? You want to know why?' She made it sound as though the answer ought to be obvious. Farah nodded cautiously, jealously guarding the air now filtering into her struggling lungs.

Michelle's voice droned on but Farah blocked it out as she wiggled onto her side, making access to her pocket a little easier. She glanced at Michelle, who seemed to be away with the fairies. Although she was still pinning Farah down, she wasn't actually looking at her and clearly hadn't decided what to do next. Other than to kill her, of course, and since she was so unpredictable, there was no saying when she might decide to act on that decision.

It was now or never.

She thrust her hand into her pocket and with a determination born of desperation reached for the can of Mace. Michelle's voice abruptly stopped, presumably because she realised that she'd lost her audience.

'Here, I thought you wanted to... Arghh! You bitch!'

The weight of Michelle's body fell away when Farah thumbed off the cap of the Mace can and sent a shower directly into Michelle's eyes. At the same time the door burst open and Isaac stood there, flanked by Dale.

'Fucking hell!' Isaac breathed, taking in the scene.

Farah looked at him, smiled and passed out.

* * *

'Keep hold of her,' Isaac said, jerking a thumb towards Michelle, who was madly scraping at her eyes and turning the air blue with her language. 'Get some soapy water,' he added, seeing blood on both women as well as the Mace can that had rolled onto the floor and drawing his own conclusions.

Dale nodded and went off to do as Isaac had suggested. Michelle slumped on the floor, the cut to the side of her face bleeding as she muttered to herself and continued to rub her eyes. Isaac knew she wasn't going anywhere. Not that he cared if she did right now; she wouldn't get far. His priority was Farah.

'Hey,' he said, noticing her stirring. He sat on the bed beside her and took her hand. 'You okay? I'll call an ambulance. You're covered in blood.'

'Hers, not mine,' she said, her voice weak. 'I thought... thought she would kill me. Couldn't breathe. Had to think of something.'

'I am so damned proud of you, even if you didn't lock the doors like I asked,' he said, taking her in his arms and holding her carefully, astonished by her strength of will. Furious because he'd almost been too late. It could all have ended so differently.

'It's okay,' he said softly. 'It's all over now, darling.'

'She... she thought that killing me would... would...'

'Would be the ultimate form of revenge,' Isaac finished for her. 'She was damned right about that, too.'

Isaac knew it for a certainty the moment he thought he'd lost her that he'd fallen in love with Farah. When he'd arrived a few moments ago and thought he was too late, his heart had felt like a lead weight beating inside his chest. Love was an emotion he'd avoided like the plague for fear of where it might lead. The examples of marital love that he'd seen growing up would be enough to turn anyone off the idea, he'd long ago decided. But it seemed that when Cupid's arrow struck, when something felt so positively right, there was absolutely nothing to fear and everything to look forward to.

Dale returned with the soapy water. 'Stop thrashing about, woman,' he chided when Michelle tried to push him away. 'I'm trying to help you, god knows why.'

'Need an ambulance,' she muttered. 'The bitch has blinded me.'

'I wonder why,' Isaac replied, his voice reverberating with subdued menace.

'Most of it missed her eyes,' Dale said in a disinterested tone. 'She's made it worse by rubbing them. She won't be quite so good-looking for a while, though, especially with that cut.'

Farah insisted upon sitting up. Of course she did! Isaac didn't argue with her. As far as he was concerned, she'd earned the right to do whatever the hell she liked.

'Steady,' he said, holding her arm and leading her to a chair in the corner of the room.

She sank slowly into it and Isaac perched on its arm. He watched dispassionately as Dale finished swabbing Michelle's face. The woman rallied and sent Isaac a look of pure vitriol.

'Mind telling me what this is all about, before I call the police?'

Isaac asked, fixing his half-sister with a basilisk glower. Michelle flinched and hugged her arms around her waist. It must have been obvious to her and everyone else in the room that Isaac's was not a request. This would be Michelle's one chance to justify the unjustifiable.

'Ha!' The hatred behind the look she sent Isaac's way would have floored most men. But Isaac was too angry with her to allow it to affect him. 'You were our mother's precious little darling who could do no wrong, whilst I—'

'Where the hell did you get that crazy notion from?' Isaac asked, bewildered.

'You weren't given away, so it's obvious. And Hadleigh says you didn't need his financial help to get your business going, so *our* mother must have helped you with her nest egg.'

Isaac shook his head. 'I didn't take Hadleigh's help because frankly the man is amoral. I dislike him and everything he stands for. I dislike even more the way he ruined my family, simply because he could, taking what he wanted with no thought for the consequences. As to nest eggs, our mother barely had a penny to her name. What Hadleigh gave her she spent on clothes and beauty treatments, trying desperately to defy the march of time and hold on to her looks. I supported her for years.'

'In return for the idyllic upbringing.'

'You really are deluded.' Isaac spoke slightly less venomously. 'Colette has told us how much you suffered at the hands of your adoptive mother and I'm sorry about that but it wasn't exactly a bed of roses for me either.'

'Boo-hoo!' Michelle said sarcastically.

Isaac said nothing. Instead he slowly stood, pulled up his shirt and showed Michelle his lower back. She and Farah both gasped when they saw the welts across it.

'My father's belt buckle when he got pissed and angry,' Isaac said calmly. 'And as for our mother, she was anorexic. Always para-noid about putting on weight, which would mean no one loved her. That she would lose Hadleigh.'

'She did,' Michelle said with conviction. 'She ended it when she went to France to have me.'

'Is that what he told you?'

'Like some I could name, he doesn't lie.'

Isaac shook his head. 'I'm not going to waste my breath trying to convince you otherwise. Their affair drove my father to his violent outbursts because Hadleigh didn't make any effort to disguise the fact that he was screwing her senseless. So the old man took out his frustration on me, and my mother. I also had to learn look after myself or else starve and my mother barely knew I was alive. Looking back, I can see that she was obsessed with Hadleigh, and avoiding my father's fists, and not much else mattered to her. And so no, Michelle, it wasn't a bed of roses for me either. I knew phys-ical chastisements and parental neglect but I put it behind me and got on with my life.'

'Whereas she took up with Colette and planned to kill you, Isaac, so that she could claim to be your closest relation.' Farah shook her head. 'So I'll repeat the earlier question that you avoided answering. Why not simply leave Guy if you don't love him and live with Colette? She earns enough to support you both and to permit you to return to three-day eventing, if that's what you want to do.'

'That's what I'd like to know.'

They all turned to see Guy standing in the open doorway, his expression set in stone. Isaac had been so invested in reliving a past he never spoke about that he hadn't heard him arrive and didn't think anyone else had either.

'What... Guy, I—'

'I sensed something was off, has been for a while,' Guy said, 'and must confess that I thought you must be having it off with

Isaac when he came to the yard, brazenly asking after you. Anyway, I followed you here when I saw you leave, Isaac.'

'I'm sorry you had to hear her confession,' Isaac said, meaning it.

Guy sent his wife, still crouched on the floor, a scathing glance and looked close to tears. But there was also a determination in his expression that told Isaac he would recover from his disappointment without letting it destroy him.

Dale swallowed. 'Guy, I want to explain—'

'Don't tell him a fucking thing!' Michelle screamed at Dale, her features rendered ugly by a combination of Mace, the whip cut and anger.

But Dale, to his credit, did. He told them everything about the smuggling, about how he'd been drawn into it. About how Jonah, the head lad, was up to his eyes in it. Guy nodded and looked sad, but not especially surprised.

'I knew there was something odd going on and all the indicators made it seem as though Michelle was involved. I just didn't want to believe it,' he said.

'You poor, naïve man,' Michelle said venomously, struggling to her feet. 'I guess I'll go and pack my stuff. I wish I could say that it's been fun but...'

'You are not going anywhere until Guy decides whether he wants to press charges. And Farah, for that matter.'

'He won't.' Michelle sent him a challenging look. 'Not if he doesn't want to bring the wrath of my father down on his head and ruin the reputation of his yard. Same goes for Farah.'

Guy and Farah exchanged a look and Isaac wasn't surprised when Farah shook her head.

'Just get out,' Guy said, taking his turn to shake his head. 'Don't go back to the yard. I'll have your things sent on to Colette's.'

'You sure about this?' Isaac asked after Michelle had struggled down the stairs, still cursing and complaining.

'Yeah, as sure as I can be. Her father financed the yard. I'll have to find a way to buy him out.'

'You're looking at it,' Isaac replied without hesitation.

Guy blinked. 'You sure?'

'Sounds as though you have a good thing going. Would be a shame to see it fold. Besides, I have history with Hadleigh and I will not permit his silent partnership in your business to hold you back.'

Guy offered Isaac his hand. 'Thanks, I appreciate it. But I guess you'll want to take a look at the figures before you commit.'

'Don't worry, I'll extract my pound of flesh.'

'I'd best pack up too,' Dale said, looking disturbed yet resigned.

'Nah, not unless you want to. You will have to stay off the sauce, though, Dale. You've let it get out of control and it changes you.'

'That's generous, given what I've—'

'It's not an entirely altruistic gesture. You are a damned good manager and got led off the straight and narrow by some pretty dangerous people. I sure as hell didn't know what was happening beneath my own nose, so—'

'Farah will need to be promoted to fill Jonah's shoes,' Isaac pointed out, taking Farah's hand and kissing the back of it. 'You can be sure that he'll scurry off into the night like a rat once he realises the game's up.' Isaac grinned. 'I've always wanted to say that, about the game being up, I mean.'

Farah rolled her eyes, a sure sign that she was recovering from her ordeal. Still holding her hand, Isaac pulled her gently to her feet.

'Sure you don't need to be checked over?' he asked.

'No.' Her voice was croaky. 'But I do need some water, please.'

Two weeks after her ordeal at Michelle's hands, Farah was back at work and enjoying her new role as head 'lad', second in overall command only to Dale. As good as his word, Dale had remained sober and was alert, full of energy and at the top of his game again. He knew he'd been lucky to escape prosecution and was out to prove himself. He had also not stopped apologising to Farah for the depths he'd fallen to and the way in which he'd treated her.

'I couldn't live with myself,' he told her, 'not after you were nearly killed, which was all my fault. I thought I was protecting you when you got suspicious by sacking you. Ha, I should have known that would only drive you on to find out the truth! I should have manned up and told Hadleigh to go fuck himself once it all started running out of control. I'd already decided to come clean and fuck the consequences when your Isaac came charging in like an avenging devil, throwing his weight around, demanding answers.' Dale chuckled. 'I thought he was gonna floor me, which is less than I deserved.'

'Well, first off he's not mine. I've barely seen him these past weeks but I know he had unfinished business with Hadleigh.'

'He'll be back. That man has the good sense to have the hots for you.'

Well, Farah thought, *he's got a funny way of showing it.*

As though summoned by the hostile nature of her thoughts, Isaac appeared at the yard later that afternoon. Farah ignored the fact that her heart lifted and she pretended disinterest when he approached her as she was in the process of grooming Federal Force ready for his appearance at Goodwood the following day.

'Hey,' Isaac said, leaning a shoulder against the door of Force's box and watching her work. 'How are you?'

'Better,' she said, because it was true.

'No nightmares?'

There were. She woke in a cold sweat, gasping for breath, feeling a massive weight pressing down on her chest but she wasn't about to admit it, even though she sensed that Isaac already knew. 'Not really,' she said, patting Force's quarters to move him over.

'Come and walk with me if you're finished here.'

'Well, I'm not, finished that is, but since you're the boss, I guess I'll have to do as I'm told or risk being sacked. Again.'

'So gracious,' he replied, chuckling.

'How was Hadleigh?' she asked. 'I assume you've seen him and come to some sort of agreement. Well, I know you have because Guy told me you've agreed terms to take over his investment in the yard.' The accusation that he hadn't told her himself went unspoken.

'How is Guy?'

'Surprisingly upbeat. I think the pretence of... well, pretending that everything was hunky-dory between him and Michelle had started to wear him down. He pretended because he desperately wanted it to be that way but I suspect that aspects of her vindictive character had come through.' She glanced up at Isaac's profile, wishing she knew what he was thinking. Wishing she knew why he'd come and asked her to walk with him. Did he have to have a reason? He was her boss. 'She needs help, in Guy's view, not imprisonment but that's partly self-preservation. He knows if the truth comes out then he will be finished. No one will believe that he didn't know what was going on beneath his nose and, if he really didn't, then he's not much of a trainer.'

'But you're not wanting to prosecute...'

Farah shrugged. 'She needs psychiatric help, not prison. Besides, we both know how vindictive she can be, and she would have bad-mouthed Guy and spoiled everything he's achieved here. He doesn't deserve that.'

'I agree.'

'All the time she has her freedom, she will keep quiet. Colette will make sure of that.'

'Very generous.' Isaac smiled at her. 'Hadleigh and I had a heart-to-heart last week and cleared up a few misconceptions.'

'I guessed as much.'

'He thought I'd disrespected him by not accepting his offer of fiscal help when I was starting out. I made it clear to him that his affair with my mother had ruined my childhood, deprived me of a father and made me determined to make my own way without the help of the criminal fraternity I'd been raised surrounded by.' He paused. 'In a way, I guess he did me a favour, otherwise it could so easily have been different. If the old man had stayed around and if I'd grown attached to him, my involvement would have been a foregone conclusion and that's really not who I am.'

'Did Hadleigh know what Michelle intended to do to you? Are we right to suppose that she wanted you dead?'

'I think Hadleigh suspected as much and the prospect wasn't keeping him awake at night, but he'd never admit it. He did wax on about my mother being the love of his life and how he'd hoped that I might be his son, which is why he'd offered his help. I disavowed him of that notion... again. Anyway, he's decided to scarper until the dust settles. His Albanian partners won't be best pleased when they discover that their lucrative means of bringing drugs into this country has been scuppered and Hadleigh has the good sense to be afraid of them.'

'You think they will kill him?'

Isaac waggled a hand from side to side. 'I think they will take over his London patch altogether and cut him out, which will be a severe blow to his pride and punishment of sorts because he'll lose face. But I really don't care either way.'

'What did they have on Dakin?'

'I asked him about that. He was circumspect, but reading between the lines, I think he did like young boys.' He paused. 'And so does Hadleigh's son, Henry. Dakin and Henry's paths crossed in that vile sphere and it was Henry who suggested to his old man that Dakin was disillusioned and would likely sell up. Of course, Hadleigh didn't know about Henry's other activities involving Dakin at the time, or that Dakin had kept pictures of the various kids they'd traumatised, as well as a diary. Dakin made the mistake of calling Hadleigh, telling him about our visit, which is when self-preservation kicked in and Henry told his father what Dakin had on him.'

'Which is what Hadleigh had to find and destroy.'

'Right. As I say, Hadleigh didn't admit much and I've had to fill in the gaps, but I'm pretty sure I'm right. The murder won't ever be solved, I don't suppose, but I can't find the energy to care.'

'Nor me.' Farah had run out of questions and didn't know what else to say.

'I'm thinking of building a house on that plot,' Isaac said, pointing to a large patch of ground to the side of the barns.

'Oh.' She blinked. 'Why?'

'It would be nice for Daisy, don't you think?'

'Daisy? What's this to do with...'

'That cottage of yours is a health hazard, to say nothing of harbouring nightmarish thoughts for you following your ordeal. I don't think another winter spent in it will be good for either of you.'

'You can't build us a house, Isaac,' she said, laughing. 'You've already done more than enough.'

'I was thinking of building it for me. I work too much and intend to pull back and have a more hands-on approach to my investment here.'

'But... but you love what you do.'

'True, but I can do it from anywhere. I'm a control freak but have good people in place whom I can rely on once I train myself to let go of the reins. I don't need to be breathing down their necks all the time. Besides, meeting you and living through what happened here has made me realise that there's more to life than work.'

'Well, yes, but are you absolutely sure you're not having a knee-jerk reaction?'

'How to convince you?' He stopped walking and took her in his arms. 'We have unfinished business and I dislike not finishing anything I start.'

Farah swallowed, aware of her heart palpitating and her mouth turning dry. Did he really mean what she thought he did? 'You want us to cohabit?' she asked, swallowing nervously.

'Only if the idea appeals. I don't want you to do it out of some misguided sense of owing me. You don't owe me a damned thing. The planners won't let me get carried away but there should be room for four bedrooms, which will give us plenty of space so we don't trip over one another.'

'Or two plus a very large master suite,' she said, looking up at him with newfound confidence. Her heartrate had tripled and happiness oozed from her pores. This was really happening. The man who invaded her dreams on a nightly basis had actually just offered to build a house for them all to live in. She smiled up at him because smiling seemed like the most natural reaction in the world. And because she couldn't seem to help herself. If almost getting killed by a crazy woman with a massive grudge led to this sort of happiness, she'd go through it all again without a second thought.

'Now that's a very sensible suggestion,' he replied, matching her smile with a glamorous one of his own as his arms tightened around her. 'I like the way you think.'

'Just so that you know,' she felt obliged to say, 'I don't do red carpets and I'm not sure if I even own any high heels.'

Isaac chuckled. 'You'll do just the way you are,' he replied, bending his head to kiss her.

ACKNOWLEDGMENTS

My thanks to all the wonderful Boldwood team and, in particular, to my talented editor, Emily Ruston.

MORE FROM EVIE HUNTER

We hope you enjoyed reading *The Chase*. If you did, please leave a review.

If you'd like to gift a copy, this book is also available as an ebook, digital audio download and audiobook CD.

Sign up to Evie Hunter's mailing list for news, competitions and updates on future books.

https://bit.ly/EvieHunterNewsletter

The Fall, another nail-biting revenge thriller from Evie Hunter, is available to order now.

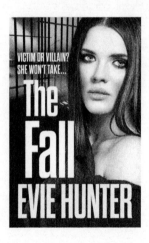

ABOUT THE AUTHOR

Evie Hunter has written a great many successful regency romances as Wendy Soliman and is now redirecting her talents to produce dark gritty thrillers for Boldwood. For the past twenty years she has lived the life of a nomad, roaming the world on interesting forms of transport, but has now settled back in the UK.

Follow Evie on social media:

 twitter.com/wendyswriter

facebook.com/wendy.soliman.author

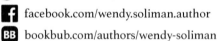 bookbub.com/authors/wendy-soliman

ABOUT BOLDWOOD BOOKS

Boldwood Books is a fiction publishing company seeking out the best stories from around the world.

Find out more at www.boldwoodbooks.com

Sign up to the Book and Tonic newsletter for news, offers and competitions from Boldwood Books!

http://www.bit.ly/bookandtonic

We'd love to hear from you, follow us on social media:

 facebook.com/BookandTonic

 twitter.com/BoldwoodBooks

 instagram.com/BookandTonic

Printed in Great Britain
by Amazon